Climbing the rest of th... ..., Jimoen set his hook, hung the naphtha bag, and after pumping his fist in celebration, leaped from the gate.

At least that was the plan.

Instead of dropping, though, the young fool just hung there. Somehow, he had managed to hook not only the leather sack, but also his cloak. He flailed his arms and kicked his feet, trying desperately to break free, but to no avail. Seeing this, several of the French archers leaned out over the wall again, and tried to finish him.

As Will and Allan fired at the bowmen, Robin dashed toward the castle. Halfway there, he scooped up a discarded shield, practically without breaking stride. When he reached the base of the gate, he shouted Jimoen's name and tossed the shield up to the lad.

Jimoen caught it, and put it over his head, barely in time to block a bolt that would have pierced his skull.

Robin began to climb, hearing cheers behind him.

"Look what they do for the Lionheart!" he heard the king call out.

The French archers were still firing, but as he drew closer to Jimoen, Robin caught the scent of something far worse than arrows and bolts. Boiling oil. The French were preparing to pour it over them. He reached the young soldier and after a moment's struggle managed to unhook him. They dropped to the ground and rolled away just as the oil splashed down the castle walls. Grabbing hold of the shield, Robin and Jimoen sprinted back to safety, bolts and arrows pelting the ground and the shield. More cheers greeted them when at last they ducked behind the barn door.

OTHER TOR BOOKS BY DAVID B. COE

ROBIN HOOD

A novelization by
David B. Coe

Based on the screenplay by Brian Helgeland
and the story by Brian Helgeland
and Ethan Reiff & Cyrus Voris

TOR®

A TOM DOHERTY ASSOCIATES BOOK
NEW YORK

This is a work of fiction. All the characters, organizations, and events portrayed in this novel are either products of the author's imagination or are used fictitiously.

ROBIN HOOD

Edited by James Frenkel

A Tor Book
Published by Tom Doherty Associates, LLC
175 Fifth Avenue
New York, NY 10010

www.tor-forge.com

Tor® is a registered trademark of Tom Doherty Associates, LLC.

ISBN 978-0-7653-6627-6

First Edition: May 2010

Printed in the United States of America

0 9 8 7 6 5 4 3 2 1

For Nancy, Alex, and Erin—my merry band

Many thanks to Tom Doherty, Liz Gorinsky, Steven Padnick, Seth Lerner, and all the great people at Tor Books, especially Linda Feldman who put in effort above and beyond the call of duty to make sure production on this book was successfully completed; Cindy Chang and Julie Margules at NBC Universal, for answering my queries and getting me still images from the movie; my terrific agent, Lucienne Diver; my editor, Jim Frenkel, for making this happen; and to Nancy, Alex, and Erin, for putting up with me while I worked at breakneck speed to get this done.

CHAPTER

❦

ONE

From within the brooding shadows of Broceliande Forest, Robin Longstride could see the pale colors of dawn touching the morning sky; glimpses of pearl and pink and pale yellow sifted through branches and leaves. A wren sang from the shelter of a nearby thicket and a woodpecker drummed in the distance. A fox slinked through the underbrush, pausing to regard Robin and his companions with luminous eyes before slipping away into the darkness. A peaceful morning, the air still and cool. If not for the subtle scent of a hundred cooking fires lingering in the wood, and the faint murmur of a thousand voices not too far off, it would have been easy for Robin to forget that he was at war.

He had been up with the first hint of morning light, as had the two men walking with him, Will Scarlet and Allan A'Dayle: a hunt to begin their day. And a successful one it had been. They were carrying back to their camp coneys and quail, a brace of pheasants, and two plump grouse that Allan had managed to kill. They couldn't know what the coming battle would bring, but at least they would start their day with a good meal.

Robin had grown fond of his two companions through their travels together. Will, with his fiery orange hair and beard, and a spirit to match; Allan, bearded and long-haired, less flamboyant in appearance than Will, more reserved and considered in manner. They were younger than Robin by several years, and both were prone to the foibles of youth. Will's exuberance occasionally landed him in fixes that a more seasoned soldier might avoid, and more often than not Allan blindly followed his friend into trouble. But they were brave and loyal, and good in a scrape. A man could hardly ask for more in his comrades.

As they drew nearer to the encampment of the English army, the forest around them thinned and brightened. They passed through a small camp of Moors and Gypsies. It was common for such bands to follow armies on the Continent, hoping to make some coin catering to the various appetites of fighting men. Though a few of the dark-skinned men looked up at Robin, Will, and Allan as they made their way through the camp, none of them offered much by way of greeting.

But a Gypsy girl sidled up to Robin, her hips swaying, dark eyes peering up seductively through long lashes.

"I tell your fortune?" she asked him sweetly. "Read your palm?"

Robin grinned but didn't break stride. "I've been in this army ten years. I've a fair idea what's going on."

"You have a quest," the woman said.

"Indeed I do: Breakfast."

He continued past the girl, as did Allan. Will, however, eyed her with obvious interest.

"Tell me about our future, you and I," he said. "Does it rhyme with luck?"

She took his hand, stared at his palm a moment, and then gasped. Robin and Allan stopped to listen.

She looked up at him, her eyes wide. "You will always find love . . . by your own hands."

Robin and Allan burst out laughing and continued on. Will hurried after them. His face was still bright pink when he caught up.

The three men reached the edge of the forest and entered the enormous camp of King Richard Coeur de Lion's army. Beyond the army loomed the French castle to which they had been laying siege for the past seven days. The banners of the French lord still flew above the battlements, but the stone walls of the fortress were blackened and her gates scarred though still intact.

As the three men wound through the army camp, Robin began to distribute some of their kill from the morning's hunt. He gave a quail to one man who'd shared a meal with him a few nights before, and offered a rabbit to a fletcher, receiving a stack of arrows in return. Some of the meat he gave for no apparent reason, sharing a good word and a laugh with the surprised recipient. After ten years he had learned that there were two things an archer in the king's army should never have in short supply: arrows, and the good will of his fellow soldiers.

By the time he, Will, and Allan had reached the embers of their campfire they had just enough game left to feed themselves. Before they could even get their meat on spits, though, they were joined by young Jimoen, a foot soldier they had befriended during their return from the Holy Land. He was gangly and pale, and he regarded them now with an apology in his eyes.

"Archers are called to ranks."

Allan stared ruefully at his breakfast. "Bloody typical."

Robin merely shrugged and set the meat aside. "It's alright boys. Hide it well. We'll have it for supper instead."

He reached for his armor, he began to suit up for battle.

MARION OF LOXLEY should have been asleep, dreaming of her husband's return from Richard's Crusade. The time she and Robert of Loxley had shared as husband and wife had been all too brief, though the memory of their wedding night was still enough, after all these years, to bring a smile to her lips and heat to her cheeks. To relive that bliss, even if in a mere dream, would have been a balm for her uneasy heart.

Instead she tossed and turned, listening to the sounds of the night: the sweet tones of a nightjar, the resonant hoot of a nearby owl, the howl of a wolf, the soft rustle of countless leaves as a gentle wind stirred the boughs of Sherwood Forest beyond the walls of Peper Harrow, the Loxley home.

She lived with her husband's father, Sir Walter Loxley, a great man in his day, now reduced by age and blindness to awaiting the return of his son from war. She wondered if he was awake as well, if it was some whisper of fate, some purposeful foreboding that kept her from sleep. She considered going to check on the old man. Deciding against it, she rose and crossed to the narrow window that looked out from her bedchamber toward the Loxley fields and the wood beyond.

Doing so, she beheld something puzzling. It began as a flicker of shadow at the edge of Sherwood Forest, and then a second. Soon there were nearly a dozen of them: animals, moving with purpose and stealth across the fields toward the town of Nottingham. She spied a badger, a boar, and a fox, a wolf, a sheep, and a bear; as unnatural a company of creatures as she could imagine. Comprehension came to her just as the alarm bell in the town watchtower began to toll.

"They're coming!" the sentinel called, his voice echoing from the village.

Marion rushed to her door and out into the corridor. She could hear some in Nottingham raising the alarm, while others shouted angrily at the raiders in their fields. Just as she reached Sir Walter's chamber she met up with Gaffer Tom, who had worked here at the Loxley house since well before Marion's marriage to Robert. Pausing at Walter's door, she heard the old man within. He was mumbling to himself and moving about. Marion pushed the door open.

Sir Walter Loxley might have been blind, but as soon as she and Tom entered, Walter turned toward them unerringly, his sword in hand. He was still tall and lean, despite his years, and the fearsome look on his face would have given pause to any intruder.

"Don't be foolish, Walter!" Marion told him. "You can do nothing for them." It broke her heart to speak to him so. He deserved better, as did all of Nottingham.

Walter appeared to sag a bit at her words.

"Keep him in here," Marion told Tom quietly. "Bar the door."

She hurried away. Walter could do nothing, but she had some skill with a bow, and she was angry enough to kill.

"I'm still master of this house!" Walter called after her.

Marion continued on to the armory, where she retrieved a bow and hastily wrapped a creosote cloth around the head of an arrow.

Reaching the gates of Peper Harrow, she could see enough of what was happening below in the town to confirm her worst fears. The "animals" were running rampant through the lanes of Nottingham, some carrying chickens, others with pigs slung across their backs, and still others laden with the hard-earned foodstuffs of the townspeople. She raised her bow, the arrow already nocked, and drew it back smoothly, just as her father had taught her long ago. With great care, she touched the cloth to a candle, igniting it, and then she loosed the flaming dart into the night.

It arced over the walls of Peper Harrow and descended like a flare, illuminating the hoar-covered field and the edge of Sherwood. The raiders were in retreat, carrying away Nottingham's food stores.

"I see you, you bastards!" Marion called to them, "I see you!"

The "animals" were running now, disappearing back into the shadows of the forest. She wanted desperately to chase them down, but she had responsibilities here. With a sigh, she left the gate and made her way to Peper Harrow's barn. Tom was there, ruddy-cheeked and solid, holding a lantern and looking forlorn. The grain bin was empty.

"They've taken the seed grain," he said.

She stared at the empty bin, her chest aching. "I can see that, Thomas. I can see."

She turned away, knowing she needed to tell Walter that they had nothing left to plant, and that a hard life had just gotten harder.

CHAPTER

TWO

Philip the Second, King of France, known to some as Philip Augustus, sat beside his campaign table on the banks of the Seine, the expansive grounds of the palace at Fontainebleau at his back. A servant held a platter of oysters, while the king alternately pored over a military map that covered his table and opened the shells with the skill of a surgeon. Occasionally he looked up to gaze out over the river. Philip was a handsome man, in the way of the French. Godfrey thought there was something slightly soft about his looks, something that bespoke the decadence of his land and his people. But Godfrey was also wise enough to understand that it was the king's libertine nature, his utter lack of scruples, that made him the perfect ally.

Godfrey watched the man, his eyes drawn repeatedly to the brilliant glittering ruby on the hilt of the king's ornate dagger, which Philip used in place of a more traditional oyster knife.

The king opened yet another shell, held it to his lips, and tipped back his head, so that the treasure within slid into his mouth and down his throat. Smiling with satisfaction, he glanced at Godfrey and gestured at the grand plate of oysters, clearly intending for the Englishman to help himself.

Godfrey smiled thinly, but remained as he was, eyeing the king.

"You and John," Philip said, reaching for another shell, "you go back a long way together."

"To the same breast."

The king's hand hesitated over the plate. "I trust you are referring to your wet nurse."

"And we have remained close ever since," Godfrey said.

The king appeared as satisfied by this as by his meal. "Good, because England under your friend John is a country with no fighting spirit. I can take London with an army of cooks. But King Richard is on his way home. Under Richard . . ." He shrugged, gesturing with the dagger. Godfrey's gaze was drawn once more to the ruby. "England would be a different animal altogether."

Philip took another oyster from the plate and jabbed at it with his blade. This time, the point slipped, slicing into his hand, which began to bleed profusely.

"*Merde!*" the king said. "Even dying animals can be obstinate." He opened the shell with a second twist of the dagger and offered the oyster along with a generous helping of his own blood to Godfrey. Godfrey eyed the king for just an instant before taking the proffered shell, tipping his head back and swallowing the bloodied oyster.

"Richard will return home through the Forest of Broceliande," Philip said, watching Godfrey in turn. "We know the exact place." He swept aside several empty oyster shells with one hand and with the other pointed to a spot on the map. "He always travels ahead of his army, with only a few trusted knights around him."

By way of answer, Godfrey took another shell, opened it deftly, and drank down first a half-shell of seawater and then the oyster.

"With him gone," the king concluded, "there will never be a better moment to invade."

"*A votre service, mon seigneur,*" Godfrey said, inclining his head slightly. At your service, my liege.

"*Non. C'est moi qui suis a votre service.*" No, it is I who am at your service.

ELEANOR OF AQUITAINE walked with purpose through the cold corridors of London's White Tower, her footsteps echoing off the stone walls and arched ceiling, her hands clenched in fists at her side. By any measure, she had lived a full and fruitful life. She had married and loved two kings, though her love for Louis had been short-lived, a folly of youth. She had given birth to two more, and had already seen one of them buried, which had been harder by far than losing her second husband. Indeed, of her ten children—two by Louis and eight by Henry—only four had survived to this day. For nearly sixteen years, she had lived as a prisoner, moved from fortress to fortress by order of her husband, Henry, who had accused her, with good reason, of plotting with her sons to rob him of the crown.

She had gone on a crusade, survived naval battles in the Mediterranean, and been called a traitor and an incestuous whore and worse. Even now, old enough to feel winter's lingering chill in her bones, she was still Duchess of Aquitaine and Countess of Poitiers.

And yet, for all she had accomplished, for all the challenges she had met and overcome, for all the tragedies that had marked the long arc of her life, no one —*no one*—had ever vexed her as much as her youngest child. That John, prince regent of the realm, was dissolute, irresponsible, and untrustworthy, not even his mother could deny. Though several years past his thirtieth birthday, John was still more child than man, at least in temperament. But these were faults that she had seen in his father, and, though Eleanor was loath to admit it, in his brother, the king, as well. Perhaps not to the same degree, but certainly Richard could be as debauched and irresponsible as any man of the court. What was it about men in power that rendered them utterly sapless when confronted by a flask of Benedictine wine and the comely girl serving it?

What troubled her most about John wasn't so much his weakness of character as his utter lack of kingly qualities. He lacked his father's subtlety and wit, he wasn't charming or gracious like his brother Henry, and he had shown no sign of possessing even a fraction of Richard's courage. Treachery, malice, pride— these he had in abundance. But Eleanor feared for England if ever John should ascend to the throne. At least as he was now. Perhaps it was motherly weakness, but she still entertained some hope of changing him, of helping him grow into the promise that flowed in his blood. She would have to act quickly, though. She had learned all too well that none of her issue could live forever, not even her Lionheart.

Turning a corner onto the hallway of John's bedchambers, Eleanor saw his wife, Princess Isabel of Gloucester, stooped before John's door. Isabel was a nice enough girl, but she was no more fit to be queen consort than John was to be king. Eleanor supposed the girl was pretty, though none would have called her beautiful, but she was vapid. And one had only to see her now, outside her husband's bedchamber, listening at the man's keyhole, to know how weak she was.

Eleanor cleared her throat as she approached, not wishing to give the girl too much of a start.

Isabel straightened and turned, all in one swift, whirling motion. Seeing Eleanor, she staggered back several steps, clearly intimidated.

"Your Majesty!" the girl said breathlessly.

"Your Royal Highness," Eleanor answered, unable to keep the disdain from her voice. "An English princess shut out of her husband's bedroom by a piece of French pastry. Aren't you ashamed?"

The girl raised her chin, showing more spirit than Eleanor had expected. "The shame is surely his."

"If you think so, go in and tell him." The words were hard, but Eleanor said them with somewhat more sympathy than she had been inclined to offer moments before. "Mewling at his keyhole is neither one thing nor the other."

She brushed the girl aside and opened John's door.

Immediately, Eleanor heard giggles and she turned

toward her son's bed. The cover was stretched over the length of the bed, clearly concealing two bodies. She could see two pairs of hands gripping the cover at the head of the bed, and now, in unison, they flipped the cover upward so that it billowed over them before descending again. More giggles followed this, and the hands flipped the cover a second time.

Eleanor had had enough. She strode to the bed, gripped the cover and tore it back, revealing John and a very pretty girl who, despite her good looks, appeared to be barely more than a child. Eleanor knew her to be called Isabella. She was heir to the countship of Angouleme in France, and she was also the great granddaughter of France's King Louis the Sixth, who happened to have been the father of Eleanor's first husband.

The girl stared up at Eleanor, her eyes wide, her mouth opened in a small "O."

"Ma'mselle," Eleanor said. "You will excuse us. My son has need of my advice."

"No, I don't!" John said. He tipped his head toward the French girl. "Ask *her*!" He threw the cover back over Isabella's head. "Have you no decency?" he went on, glaring defiantly at Eleanor. "I happen to be in a condition no mother should see her son in."

Isabella pushed the cover off her head and pouted reproachfully at John. *"Hélas, c'est finis!"* Alas, it is over!

John looked at her, clearly wounded. "Yes, but it's my *mother*!"

"Enough!" Eleanor snapped, making both John and Isabella jump. "On second thought," Eleanor told the French girl, "you had better hear what I have to say. But I will not have you in my presence." She grabbed the cover and threw it over the girl yet again. She turned her attention back to John. "My purpose in your bedroom is to save the realm from the consequences of an unsuitable . . . amusement."

"Unsuitable?" John said. "Her uncle is the bloody King of France!"

Again, Isabella popped her head out from under the cover. *"C'est vrai!"* It's true! *"Mon oncle* is the—"

Eleanor glared at her. "Get down!"

The girl dove back under the cover.

"Her uncle wants her back," Eleanor told her son. "Philip wants an excuse to cross the channel with an army, and you are giving him that excuse. Take up your lawful wife and save England."

"My lawful wife is as barren as a brick," John said, raising his voice, no doubt knowing that the poor girl was in the corridor. Eleanor thought she heard a small whimper from beyond the bedroom door.

"Is that the wife you truly want for me?" John asked. "You, who honored your husband with eight children so that even now, when death has taken the rest, you have a king and the runt of the litter to call you mother?"

Eleanor felt her own cheeks burn. It was one thing to think of her son as the runt; it was quite another to hear him speak so of himself.

"Better none than bastards," she said, gathering herself. "And better the bastard of a servant girl than bed the niece of England's jealous enemy."

"Bed her and wed her, Mother. I've asked the Pope's man to arrange an annulment."

This was met with another soft sob from the corridor.

But John had Eleanor's attention. Perhaps there was more to the man than she credited. "Do you think the Pope will favor England's royal runt over the King of France?"

John actually grinned at her. "He might see his way for the son of Eleanor of Aquitaine."

The girl practically leaped out from beneath the covers, revealing a body that was not quite so child-like as her face. "And for King John of England!" she said. "Richard Coeur-de-Lion is forty years if not more, and no babies. I am a queen in the making."

John's grin broadened and he looked up at Eleanor again, seeming to realize that he had gained the advantage. "You see? She is my Eleanor."

Isabella, blushing furiously, had covered herself. But she met Eleanor's gaze steadily. "Your Majesty," she said, an apology of a sort.

Eleanor regarded her anew. It seemed there was more to this one, too. It would be easy to cast aside the weak girl in the corridor. But this one had spirit. *"Princesse,"* Eleanor said at last, drawing a small smile from Isabella, and from John.

THE CAMP OF Richard's crusading army awoke slowly, like some great slumbering beast, belching smoke from cooking fires and the field kitchen. Grooms began to tend to the horses; footmen ran back and forth between store carts and campfires. Pickets cast a wary eye toward the besieged French castle.

Robert Loxley tried to stretch the night from his war-weary bones as he waited outside King Richard's pavilion, watching for any sign that someone stirred within. A squire arrived with a folding table, opened it, and set it upon the ground beside Robert. Loxley handed the man his map, which the squire spread over the table. Robert looked toward the king's tent once more, frowning. Surely the king had to be awake by now.

But still Loxley waited.

THEY CALLED HIM Coeur de Lion. The Lionheart. The Saracens had referred to him as Malek al-Inkitar, the King of the English. At one time or another he had been Duke of Normandy and of Aquitaine and of Gascony, Lord of Ireland and Cyprus, Count of Anjou, Maine, and Nantes. His mother had called him Richard.

What would she call him now?

The sounds of the soldiers outside his pavilion reached him as if from a great distance and he tried to wake himself up. But slumber filled him, like the wine he had drunk the night before; both sleep and drink drained slowly from his head and his belly.

His valet entered the pavilion. The lad should have tapped on the outside first, should have waited for Richard's leave to enter. But they both knew that Richard hadn't been up long enough to do much more than grunt. The boy placed a tray on the camp table beside Richard's bed. Opening one eye, Richard saw that it held a pitcher and beaker. Water. Yes, the lad was right. Water would help with the ashes in his mouth and the pounding of his head. While Richard forced himself up to a sitting position, the boy poured water into the cup and held it out to him. The king took it in a shaking hand and raised it to his lips. He drank deeply, his eyes closed. When he'd had his fill he nodded and the boy took the beaker from him.

Taking a breath, Richard stood, swayed a bit, then steadied himself. He stripped off his stale, wine-stained shirt, his breeches, his underclothes, until he stood naked in the cold air and the dim light. The valet placed a basin in front of him, and Richard leaned over it while the boy poured a pitcher of fire-warmed water over his head, his torso, his limbs. Richard rubbed at his skin, trying to bring life back into his bones. He was too young to feel so worn, so weary. Once, not long ago, he had been a sight to behold. A king in body and aspect as well as in title. Now his body ached. His hair, which once had fallen to his shoulders in golden waves, now hung limp and dank. His face was a ruin of what it once had been, ravaged by the years and the miles and more battles than he cared to count.

The Lionheart, indeed.

His valet handed him a towel and Richard dried himself ruthlessly, as if he might scour the years from his skin. Next the boy brought him his clothes: clean undergarments, clean breeches, a tunic emblazoned with the red and gold crest of his family. Then his boots, his chain mail, his belt and sword. With each article of clothing, with each piece of his armor, he felt the night receding; he felt more himself. When, at last, the boy handed him the crown, and Richard placed it on his head, he was able to muster a smile and a wink for the lad. The valet smiled back at him and bowed.

Richard looked toward the pavilion door. Sunlight

seeped in around the edges of the opening, and Richard steeled himself. It was going to be bright and loud. He looked the part now, but he would have preferred to sleep another hour or two.

What he really wanted was a cup of wine.

THREE

The sun had risen into a clear, bright morning sky, and the entirety of the English army had gathered outside Richard's pavilion. Foot soldiers, archers, knights; all of them arrayed in their companies, all of them staring at the king's tent, expectant, silent. Banners had been raised. Pennants flew in the morning breeze. Trumpeters stood ready, their horns gleaming. Just off to the side, Richard's white charger stood beside his groom, the creature resplendent in the royal colors.

Robert Loxley had mounted his horse, and waited with the other knights for the king to emerge from the tent. His armor, like that of the men sitting their horses on either side of him, had been polished to a high shine, and the red and gold insignia on his surcoat seemed to glow in the sunlight.

When at last the canvas at the pavilion entrance was swept aside and Richard stepped out into the morning, Loxley nodded to the trumpeters, who began immediately to blow their fanfare. The men let out a mighty roar, raising their weapons and pounding their shields.

The king, who had squinted at the brightness of the sun, winced now, squeezing his eyes shut and screwing up his face in pain. Loxley nearly laughed to see his liege so hungover. But he heard something in the cheering of Richard's warriors change, and the sound sobered him. It was one thing for him to know how much Richard had imbibed the night before. It was quite another for his men to realize it.

"For the love of Christ, Loxley!" Richard roared over the "Hurrah! Hurrah! Hurrah!" of the men. "Would you stop them doing that! My head's going like the bells of hell!"

Loxley nodded to the groom, who led Richard's charger over to the king. Seeing this, the men quieted down. Robert also beckoned to the nearest knight and instructed him to take the other knights and prepare the king's forces to renew their assault on the French fortress. In short order Loxley and Richard were as alone as two men could be in the midst of the English army.

Richard eyed the castle, squinting again. His breath still smelled of wine. "Is that it?" he asked, indicating the castle with a nod. "It looked bigger last night."

"One more castle to sack, Sire, and home to England."

The king's expression remained sour. "From crusading to debt collecting, Loxley! We have taken cities and put thousands to the sword in Palestine, and I end up robbing a Frenchman so that I can return home with something to show for years of campaigning."

He swung himself onto his mount. "Let's hope he is as rich as rumor has it."

The white charger reared, pawing the air, prancing gracefully. Loxley saw men pointing, awe on their faces, and he had no doubt that from a distance, in that moment, the king looked as regal as he had in years. But none of the men were close enough to see Richard wince again at the pounding of his head, or to hear him growl at the horse, "Don't do that, you whore!"

The Lionheart spurred his horse to a canter, and Robert Loxley rode after him, following his liege to battle once more.

WHILE HUNDREDS OF their fellow soldiers watched from beyond crossbow range, cheering and shouting encouragement, Robin, Will, and Allan, and dozens of their fellow archers crept toward the castle, joined by several men carrying leather sacks filled with flammable naphtha. They moved in small companies, each group of men carrying a barn door over their heads, as if they were tortoises bearing a giant shell. It was slow going, and Robin's back and legs ached with the effort of carrying the damn thing. But before long they would be within range of the French bowmen on the castle walls, and he would be thankful for the cover.

Ahead of his group, a battering ram rumbled up the slope toward the castle's portcullis. Overlapping shields covered the ram like dragon scales, protecting the men within as they pushed it forward, the muscles in their arms and necks bulging with the effort. The soldier leading them, a man known simply as Little John, was as powerfully built as any man

Robin had seen in his travels. His arms were as thick as oak limbs, his shoulders as broad as the wings of an eagle. He had the look of a brute and was as strong as any three men in the king's army. Robin had seen him on the battlefield, and so knew that John was a fearsome warrior. He had also sat across from him at a gambler's table and shared more than a little whiskey with him. John was a good sort, but usually had little success at games of chance. Just the kind of man Robin liked.

He saw Little John look up at the castle now, as if gauging the progress he and his company had made with the ram.

"Whoa!" John called. "Close enough!"

The ram slowed, then halted. The men within straightened and tried to catch their breath. All except John, who barely looked winded.

As Robin's company walked past, still under the protection of the barn door, Little John caught Robin's eye.

"Hoy, archer!"

Will and Allan looked over at the man.

"Stay alive!" John said. "I'll see you tonight!"

Robin grinned. "Make sure you bring your money, little man."

Will gestured obscenely at the man, drawing a smile from Little John.

Moments later, the first crossbow bolt embedded itself in the door with a loud *thwack*. Within a few seconds bolts and arrows were raining down on them. Cheers and war cries went up from the French and were answered by the English soldiers behind Robin and his men. King Richard rode forward on his magnificent white charger, seemingly heedless of the volleys coming from the enemy fortress. He hefted a spear, snagged an English flag on its point, and spurred his horse to a gallop toward the castle gate.

Robin nearly shouted a warning, wondering what the hell the king could be thinking. But he kept his mouth shut and watched, expecting at any moment to see Richard felled by one of the enemies' darts. But no. Perhaps the king was touched by God after all. He rode to the castle doors, threw his spear so that it stuck in the wood, and wheeled his mount back to safety.

"By God, I'm myself again!" he shouted, drawing new cheers from his men. "We'll put these French to bed with shovels! Charge! For England!"

Robin and his company hurried forward, as did the other companies of archers. Bolts and arrows still hammered into the barn doors; so many that Robin guessed they must now look more like hedgehogs than turtles. The darts that missed the wood dug into the earth, each bolt and arrow whistling like a giant bug so that the air seemed to be alive with them. The company was close to the fortress now. Robin could see that some of his men were beginning to look fearful, including Will and Allan, and young Jimoen.

"Don't worry about them," Robin said with breezy confidence. "If you ignore them, they won't sting." They were close enough. "Hup!" Robin shouted.

All four companies of archers halted and tilted up their doors, one end set hard in the ground while the other was lifted and held at an angle, so that the men were still shielded from the French.

Still the bolts carved through the air and struck at the wood. One burst through just in front of Will's face, missing him by a hair's breadth. Scarlet's eyes widened and his face paled. But he managed to flash a weak smile Robin's way.

The first of the men carrying the sacks of naphtha came forward, crouching behind the barn door and watching as Robin, Will, and Allan nocked arrows to their bows. Robin looked down at the bag carrier, who slung the sack over his shoulder and secured it in place before looking back up at Robin.

"Stay calm," he told the man. "It's them inside who are having the bad day. Ready lads? Together. Hup!"

The man with the leather sack dashed out from behind the door. At the same time, Robin, Will, and Allan stepped out from the sides, their bows drawn, looking to keep the man covered, and loosing their arrows at the first sign of a threat. Down the line, the same thing happened. Naphtha carriers ran out from behind the other three barn doors as well, all of them covered by archers who fired up at the crossbowmen on the castle ramparts.

Robin's first arrow hit a Frenchman who grunted once, twisted in agony and as he began to fall, discharged his bow into the soldier next to him, who also went down. At the same time, the first of the naphtha runners reached the castle gate and immediately began to scramble up like a monkey, using the metal bracing on the gate for hand- and footholds. In no time he had reached the top, nearly twenty feet off the ground.

As Robin nocked another arrow, two French soldiers with crossbows leaned out over the parapets, trying to get an angle on the naphtha runner. Before they could fire, Will and Allan loosed their arrows, striking both of the enemy.

The naphtha runner pulled an iron hook in the shape of an "S" from his belt, anchored it to the bracing of the gate and hung the naphtha sack on it. Another French bowman leaned out just above him, and the runner dropped to the ground below, landing deftly and charging back toward the English lines and the safety of the barn door. As this first man returned, a second runner, a leather sack slung over his shoulder, stepped out from behind the door.

"Go, lad!" Robin said, slapping this second man on the back. And the man was off.

Robin fired at another crossbowman, his arrow striking true. Will and Allan fired as well.

The second runner reached the gate, climbed to the top and hung his sack, just as the first man had done. As he started back, a third man stepped out from behind the door. He had only gone a few steps, though, when he stumbled and sprawled to the ground, spilling much of the liquid he carried. He tried to stand, but was struck by a bolt from the castle. As he struggled to his feet once again, a flaming arrow arced high from the castle walls and started dropping toward him.

Robin and the others urged him forward, marking the missile's descent. But Robin could tell the man wouldn't make it. An instant later, the flaming arrow hit the sack he carried. A flash of bright orange flame, a concussive *whoosh*, and the man was incinerated. There wasn't even time for Robin to shield his eyes. He flinched, but then merely stood there and watched the poor soldier burn. A stunned silence settled momentarily over the English lines. Cheers rose from the castle.

But Richard's men rallied quickly. The king waved his sword, crying, "Blood up! Blood up for France! By God, would you ruffians die in your beds!"

Jimoen was the last of the naphtha runners waiting

at Robin's barn door. He looked frightened as he adjusted the sack he carried. But he looked up at Robin and returned the archer's nod. Taking a deep breath, he scrambled out from behind the door and started toward the gate, while Robin, Will, and Allan loosed arrow after arrow.

Robin saw another runner go down with a French arrow in his back, but quickly turned his attention back to Jimoen. The young soldier was at the gate already and halfway up to the top. A French bowman leaned out to get a shot at him, and Jimoen flattened himself against the gate. The enemy's bolt appeared to skim Jimoen's back, but it did no serious damage. And in the next instant, the French soldier toppled off the castle wall, Will's arrow in his chest.

Climbing the rest of the way to the top, Jimoen set his hook, hung the naphtha bag, and after pumping his fist in celebration, leaped from the gate.

At least, that was the plan.

Instead of dropping, though, the young fool just hung there. Somehow, he had managed to hook not only the leather sack, but also his cloak. He flailed his arms and kicked his feet, trying desperately to break free, but to no avail. Seeing this, several of the French archers leaned out over the wall again and tried to finish him.

As Will and Allan fired at the bowmen, Robin dashed toward the castle. Halfway there, he scooped up a discarded shield, practically without breaking stride. When he reached the base of the gate, he shouted Jimoen's name and tossed the shield up to the lad.

Jimoen caught it, and put it over his head, barely in time to block a bolt that would have pierced his skull.

Robin began to climb, hearing cheers behind him.

"Look what they do for the Lionheart!" he heard the king call out.

The French archers were still firing, but as he drew closer to Jimoen, Robin caught the scent of something far worse than arrows and bolts. Boiling oil. The French were preparing to pour it over them. He reached the young soldier and after a moment's struggle managed to unhook him. They dropped to the ground and rolled away just as the oil splashed down the castle walls. Grabbing hold of the shield, Robin and Jimoen sprinted back to safety, bolts and arrows pelting the ground and the shield. More cheers greeted them when at last they ducked behind the barn door.

Jimoen sunk to the ground, gasping for breath. Robin grinned at Will and Allan, who smiled back at him.

They didn't have much time to rest, though. Somewhere in the distance someone barked an order. Robin and the other archers nocked arrows to their bows once more. This time, however, the arrows had been set afire. As one, the bowmen stepped out from behind the barn doors and fired at the hanging sacks of naphtha. A hundred flaming missiles carved across the sky and struck the bags. Naphtha began to wash down the doors, tendrils of flame spreading across the wood and licking at the bags, until suddenly all the bags exploded at once. In seconds, the blaze had engulfed the doors and was blackening the castle stone like dragon's breath.

CHAPTER

FOUR

As night fell, dark, acrid smoke from the fires burning on the besieged castle drifted across the camp of the English army, mingling with the smells of cooking fires. King Richard's soldiers were in high spirits, even as they made preparations for the renewal of battle in the morning. Foot soldiers oiled and sharpened blades, bright sparks leaping from steel and stone. Archers restrung their bows, testing and adjusting the tension. Fletchers made new arrows. But all the while men talked and laughed. Some sang war songs.

Robin, as was his wont, had taken to gaming.

Will Scarlet was by the fire, stirring a pot of stew and eyeing Robin and his companions nervously. Allan sat nearby, tuning his lute. And Robin sat before a low makeshift table, facing a cluster of gamblers. The man sitting directly across from him had placed a meager bunch of carrots on the table next to Robin's onions. The man's eyes were fixed on Robin's hands, as Robin moved three shells around, sliding a hidden pea from shell to shell. He had started slowly, as he always did—if he started too fast, his quarry would object and he would wind up with nothing. But by now his hands were moving so quickly that the man's eyes had begun to glaze.

Allan tinkered with his lute, but he was watching Robin's hands, too, smiling appreciatively. After a few moments, Robin stopped moving the shells and sat back, looking expectantly at the man before him.

The soldier hesitated, then chose the shell on the right. Robin flipped it over revealing . . . nothing.

The soldier groaned. Some of the other gamblers laughed; others shook their heads. "Next!" Robin called, as another soldier took the place of the man who'd lost.

Robin grinned at this new man, showed him the pea, and began to move the shells. Slowly, to start . . .

ROBERT LOXLEY SAT with the king outside his pavilion, a map of Northern France and Southern England spread before them, wine glasses at hand. Loxley studied the map for some time, leaning close so as to see better in the candlelight. He glanced up at the king repeatedly, wishing that Richard would show as much interest as he in their planning. But the king seemed far more concerned with his next cup of wine than with the French or the return trip to England.

At last, Robert pointed to a spot on the French coast just to the east of Calais, where the Strait of Dover was most narrow, and where a crossing would offer them easy access to the Thames.

"With a fair wind we'll be in London three days after our business here is finished," he said.

Richard said nothing. He barely even glanced at the map. Instead, his eyes were drawn once more to the distant flames on the castle. A small group of archers and foot soldiers remained by the castle walls, harassing the French, denying them any opportunity to extinguish the flames or attempt a clandestine assault on the camp.

Eventually, realizing that no response from the king was forthcoming, Loxley rolled up the map. Richard poured himself a glass of wine, drained it, poured himself another. He sat back, sipping this time.

"You will return to Nottingham?" he asked Loxley.

"Yes, Sire. I have a wife who waits for me."

Richard raised an eyebrow. "After ten years? You're sure of yourself."

Robert had to smile. "Of her," he said. He thought of Marion often. It had been so long since he had seen her, held her, and their time together had been so brief. Yet the memory of her still burned as bright as the king's siege fires.

The king studied his wine glass. "I have a mother who won't die, and a brother who wishes me dead. The first thing I'm going to do is lock them up."

Loxley found himself in the odd position of feeling sorry for his king. It made him uncomfortable. "Your Majesty," he said gently, "your people will rejoice at your return home."

Richard took another long drink, nearly draining his cup once again. "That's what I'd like. To be remembered as I was. But my army knows better. The Lionheart is mangy."

"Every man in this army idolizes you, Your Majesty," Robert said. Even as he spoke the words, however, he wondered if this was still true. It had been once; that much he knew. There had been a time when every man in the English army would have followed Richard the Lionheart to hell and back if the king had but asked it of them. But these years of crusading had taken a toll on all of them.

Richard turned to look at him. "For God's sake, Robert, don't mollycoddle me. Let's find some ruffians . . . drink . . . laugh . . . and see if we can find an honest man."

This was hardly the night Loxley had envisioned. He wanted to eat and rest. He wanted to end this siege and go home to Marion. But how could a knight refuse such a suggestion from his king?

"Yes!" Robert said with as much enthusiasm as he could muster. "Let's do that!"

Richard nodded decisively, stood and stepped from the tent, leaving Loxley with no choice but to follow. They threw cloaks over their shoulders, raised the hoods over their heads, and thus began to move among the men, unrecognized, so that they could enjoy the company of Richard's soldiers without intimidating them.

ANOTHER GAMBLER HAD just sat down opposite Robin at the table, when Little John emerged from the darkness, lifted the man out of the seat, and took his place.

The first soldier eyed John angrily, but seemed to think better of complaining. Robin could hardly blame him. In the flickering light and shadows of the campfire and nearby torches, John looked even larger than he did during the day. Robin wouldn't have thought that possible.

"Back again, little man," Will said. "Did you bring your purse?"

Little John nodded. "Aye, I brought enough, Wee Orange."

Will drew himself up to his full height. "My name is Will Scarlet."

"Is that so?" John said, his eyebrows going up. "You're more orange with a touch of pink to me." He turned back to Robin. "Enough chatter. Are we going to play?"

The big man placed a large stack of coins on the table. Murmurs ran through the crowd of onlookers.

Allan had been playing his lute quietly, but he stopped now, staring at John's money. "That bet's too big, Robin."

Robin kept his gaze fixed on Little John. "Now do you understand that if you bet and lose, your money is mine?"

"I'm a very lucky man, Robin Longstride," John said pointedly. "Always have been. Lucky and sharp."

"Luck's got nothing to do with this game, Little Man," Robin said, lowering his voice and leaning in toward the table. "It's the science of memory and a quick hand."

Little John leaned in, as well, so that he and Robin were nearly nose-to-nose. "I've got a quick eye, archer, and I'll be watching you." He glowered at Robin, a warning in his eyes.

Robin leaned back and tipped his head in acknowledgment. He showed John the pea, covered it, and began to move the shells, slowly at first, almost hypnotically. Gradually he sped up, shifting the shells from side to center to side, passing the pea from one shell to the next, until his hands were nearly a blur.

At last he stopped and looked up at John.

"You have three choices," Robin said. "Left, right, middle."

"I think I'll take a fourth choice." Another murmur rose from the men around them, this time more ominous. Robin felt a cold fury building in his chest, but he merely glared at the man, saying nothing.

John glared back at him. "There is no pea. That's my choice."

John reached out a mighty hand and turned over the shell in the middle. He glanced at the crowd, a knowing grin on his lips. But the men around him laughed and pointed. His grin fading, John looked back at the table. There, where the middle shell had been, was the pea.

Behind John, the other gamblers all seemed to exhale at once. Then they began to chatter among themselves. "Knew it was the center one." "Liar!" "I thought the giant was right for sure."

John stared at the pea for several seconds, his mouth opening and closing, as if he couldn't think of what to say. He licked his lips, his gaze flicking up to Robin's face before shifting to that pile of coins he had placed on the table. Robin had the feeling that it represented all the money Little John had. Not that he would allow the Scot to welsh on their bet.

John's hand shot out toward the coins. Robin caught him by the wrist with his left hand and threw a punch with the right, catching John full on the bridge of the nose. John's head snapped back, but then he grinned, grabbed Robin by the collar and pulled him across the table, spilling the shells, the pea, and the money.

Instead of resisting, Robin grabbed the big man's shoulders and pushed hard off the table with his feet, overbalancing John so that they both tumbled to the ground. The men around them formed a wide circle, cheering, shouting, egging both of them on. Robin and John rolled around in the dirt for several moments, John trying to grab hold of Robin's neck, Robin peppering him with punches to the gut and face. Robin was the quicker of the two, and at first he thought that might be enough. That was probably his biggest mistake. He managed to get himself on top of John briefly, and he grabbed the man's neck and threw another punch.

John caught Robin's fist in one of his mammoth paws and began to grind the bones in Robin's hand. He wrapped his other hand around Robin's throat and squeezed, rolling them over so that he had Robin pinned to the ground. With his free hand, Robin clawed at the fingers that were strangling him, but it did him no good. Straining for air now, frantic, he looked around for help.

Seeing none, Robin flailed at Little John, battering him with his free hand. John released Robin's fist and tried to block the blows. And in doing so, he also loosened his grip on Robin's throat.

Robin punched John in the jaw, in the nose, in one eye and then the other. John rolled off, clutching his face and Robin dove back onto him, throwing more punches. The first couple got through, but John blocked the rest, grabbed Robin's wrists in his vise-like fingers and head-butted Robin's brow.

Dazed, Robin toppled over onto the ground. John slowly climbed to his feet and kicked Robin hard in the ribs. Robin flew several feet and landed in a crumpled mass. John followed and kicked him a second time and then a third. Walking to where Robin lay sprawled in the dirt, John bent over, lifted Robin, and threw him into the crowd of soldiers who were still shouting. Several of the men exchanged coins, some wager fulfilled.

Robin tried to get up, but couldn't, at least not until he felt himself hoisted to his feet by both arms. Will and Allan.

"You're ahead, Robin," Scarlet told him.

Allan nodded encouragement. "Very impressive."

And they shoved him back into the circle. Robin stumbled, but caught himself and used his momentum to tackle John, slamming into his midsection, wrapping his arms around him, and driving the big man to the ground. Robin managed to land another punch or two, but John connected with one of his own, and Robin flopped onto his back. John got up, lifted Robin again, and threw him a second time. His arms pinwheeling, Robin flew toward a pair of cloaked, hooded men standing slightly apart from the others. Robin glimpsed their surprised faces, had time to realize that they looked familiar, and then hit. All three of them went down in a heap. Will and Allan rushed to Robin's side to help him up again, but by now Robin's mind was racing. He knew those two faces!

But it wasn't until he saw one of the men scramble to his feet and heard him bellow, "Kneel you insolent bastards! Kneel before your king!" that he realized how much trouble they were in. All of them.

The rest of the soldiers shuffled back, still on their knees, separating themselves from Robin, John, Will, and Allan.

"No, no, Loxley," the king said beneficently. "These men are soldiers at play." He grinned and looked

around at his men. Always Richard had been the
fighting man's king, a leader who basked in the good
will of his soldiers. Loxley might have been furious
at the lapse in discipline, but Robin could see that
the king had enjoyed what he saw of the fight. He
chanced a look at Little John and saw that the big
man was already watching him. They nodded to one
another. John even managed a small smile.

"They are sinners after my own heart," the king
went on. "Who started the fight? Come on, own up."

John's face fell, his smile giving way to a look of
terror.

Robin looked up at the king. "I did, Sire. I threw
the first punch." He felt Little John gaping at him, but
he didn't look away from Richard.

"Ah," the king said, looking at Robin with an
appraising eye. "An honest man. And who were you
fighting?"

"My own impatience, Sire," Robin told him.

"Ha!" Richard nodded, clearly pleased with Robin's
answer. "We have common ground, you and I."

"He was fighting me, Your Majesty," John said. "I
mistook him for a lesser man and he was showing me
different."

The king regarded the man, nodding again, slowly
this time. He glanced back at Loxley, as if to say, You
see what good can come of a little fun?

"An enemy that pays you respect," the king said,
turning back to Robin. "Stand, the pair of you."

Robin and Little John climbed to their feet. When
Richard saw how big John was, his mouth fell open.

"What in God's name possessed you to take on
this?" the king asked Robin, unable to take his eyes
off of John. "You must be brave, as well as honest."

He looked back at Loxley again, his eyebrows up.

Facing Robin once more, he narrowed his eyes. "Are you brave enough to tell your king something he doesn't want to hear? What is your opinion on my crusade? Will God be pleased with my sacrifice?"

Loxley, who was standing behind the king, stared hard at Robin and gave a small shake of his head, clearly warning him not to engage in this game. But Robin didn't need the knight to tell him that Richard's mood had taken a swift and dangerous turn. He had heard whispers of the darkness that had crept into Richard's heart in recent months, but this was the first he himself had seen of it.

Robin hesitated. No one else made a sound. Even the wind seemed to have died away. The only noise came from the castle, where the fires still burned and men still loosed their arrows fighting Richard's war. Robin knew better than to think that there was a right answer to the king's question. The truth might well earn him a rope around his neck; a lie would ring false to all who listened. And lying to one's liege was also a hanging offense. Better, at the last, to be true to himself.

"No," Robin said. "He won't."

Loxley shook his head again. Richard's eyes glittered lethally in the firelight.

"Why would you say that?" the king asked, his voice like a blade.

"The massacre at Acra, Sire," Robin said, his voice barely more than a whisper.

"Speak up!" Richard roared.

Robin looked at him, remembering that day in the Holy Land: the cries of frightened women and children echoing through the streets of the city, the dust hanging in the air, the hard flat light cast by a scorching sun.

When he spoke again it was in a stronger voice. "When you had us herd two and a half thousand Muslim men, women, and children together and stand over them. The young woman who knelt before me, hands bound, looked up at me, and in her eyes there wasn't fear, there wasn't anger. There was only pity. For she knew that when the order came and our glinting blades would descend on their necks, in that moment we would all be Godless. All of us, Godless."

Robin still stared at the king, and Richard stared back. Around them, quietly, many of the men muttered in agreement, perhaps remembering the faces of those they killed, perhaps feeling once more the same guilt that plagued Robin each night as he lay down to sleep. Richard glanced around, marking the response of the others. A black veil seemed to have fallen over his eyes, as if he had retreated into his own memories of that day and whatever emotions they carried with them.

"Honest, brave, and naïve," the king said, his voice so low Robin wasn't sure that any of the others heard. "There is your Englishman, right there." He shook himself slightly, as if rousing himself from a dream. He regarded Robin coldly, looked briefly at the others. "Snap all four of them in the stocks," he ordered, his voice now crisp. "I will decide their fate in due course." He paused, then started to say more. But that distant look had come into his eyes again.

Without another word he stepped out of the firelight. The crowd of soldiers parted to let the king through, and then, slowly, the men began to disperse.

CHAPTER

⌒══⌒

FIVE

Wham! The impact of the battering ram against the blackened gate of the French castle reverberated across the English camp. Part of the ram's roof was burning, and arrows and bolts jutted from it at all angles. But the ram looked a far sight better than did the castle doors. With each blow, the gate shuddered, splinters and black dust flew from the charred wood. It wouldn't be long before the gate gave way. Counting their rhythm the men heaved the ram back once more and hammered at the gate yet again. *Wham!*

Several of the burned timbers cracked and several French soldiers within the castle rushed forward to block the opening and keep Richard's men from swarming into the fortress.

Robin would have cheered along with the rest of the English army, but though the stocks offered a fine view of the siege, they also took some of the fun out of it. Along with Allan, Will, and Little John, Robin had been locked in the stocks since well before dawn. His muscles had long since started to cramp, and his head still hurt from where John had hit him.

"Well done, Robin," Allan said, his voice dripping with sarcasm.

"You showed him," Will chimed in.

They had been saying things like this throughout the morning, and Robin had little hope that they would stop anytime soon. He merely glared at them.

King Richard rode toward the shattered French gate, his sword in hand, drawing another cheer from his men. The king advanced on the gate and his soldiers followed.

"The whipping will be the worst of it," Will said, sounding forlorn.

Robin rolled his eyes. He had heard this already, too.

Allan shook his head gloomily. "The branding iron. That'll be the worst."

"Unless they hang us," John said.

"This will be the worst of it, and this will be the end of it," Robin told them. "As soon as I get out of here, I'm gone. I don't owe God or any other man here another minute of service."

He strained against the stocks, gritting his teeth. But the blocks held him fast.

GERARD DIDN'T LIKE being up on the battlements, with the English dogs below firing their crossbows and long bows. He wasn't a soldier, and had never wanted to be. Until the Coeur de Lion came with his army and his fires and his battering rams, he had never been anywhere near a war, and he would have been perfectly happy to live out the rest of his life that way. He was a cook; he belonged in the kitchens.

But with the gates giving way, and the soldiers—all of them—needed on the castle walls to keep the attackers at bay, he had no choice. The men needed to be fed, and he was of far more use to his lord with a ladle than with a blade.

So he followed the two boys carrying the vat of what could only most generously be called "stew," and he spooned it into bowls or helmets so that the men could fill their bellies.

As he moved among the soldiers, he felt his fears giving way to something else, something unexpected. Perhaps there was more soldier in him than he had thought.

After serving a few more of the men, he stepped to the outer edge of the battlement and looked down upon the fighting. Almost as soon as he did, an arrow soared past him, whistling like some bird from hell.

Gerard jumped back, more startled than frightened. And instead of cowering in fear, he felt himself growing angry. A soldier had fallen nearby, and the cook reached down and lifted the dead man's crossbow. It already had a bolt in place, and the bowstring was already drawn back. All it needed was someone to pull the trigger.

Gerard stepped to the parapet again and, looking down, picked out his target. More soldier in him, indeed. Taking careful aim, he fired.

To his amazement, the bolt found its mark. He turned to the nearest of the soldiers, giddy with surprised and pride. *"J'ai tué le roi!"* he said. *"J'ai tué le roi!"* I killed the king!

* * *

ONE LAST BLOW from the battering ram, and the
burning doors finally gave way, sagging in the middle
and then collapsing entirely. A huge billow of black
smoke rose into the air, and gleaming sparks of yellow swam upward through the cloud. Robert Loxley
heard the men behind them cheer, and he saw a smile
light Richard's face.

The king turned to look at Loxley, triumphant,
the cares and the years and the festering guilt dropping away momentarily to make Richard look young
again. For just an instant he was the Lionheart once
more: dashing and confident; indomitable. The king
drew his sword and raised it over his head. More
cheers echoed from behind. The battering ram rolled
forward, clearing the way for the king and his army.

"For England!" Richard cried, his voice ringing like a church bell as he steered his white mount
toward the breach in the gates.

And then, seemingly from nowhere, the crossbow
bolt struck. At first Loxley didn't understand what
had happened. As quickly as the king had started forward he halted again. Something dark appeared on
the back of his neck. That's what Robert could see:
something jutting from his neck. Crimson. Blood
dripping from the tip, and spreading from the wound
down the king's back.

Loxley rode forward, wanting to call the king's
name, but unable to make a sound. Pulling even with
Richard, he saw the tail of the bolt sticking out of the
front of the king's throat. His Majesty sat utterly still,
his back straight, his chin tucked, as if he was trying
to get a better look at the shaft of the dart.

Then Richard started to fall, unsettling his charger

so that the creature reared awkwardly. Both horse and rider toppled over, the animal rolling over the man.

The horse scrabbled back up, its eyes wide and wild, its head thrashing from side to side. And then it was off, galloping back away from the castle.

Loxley leaped off his horse and sprinted to where the king had fallen. His heart ached, as though it too had been pierced by a bolt. He called frantically to the nearest English soldiers, and with their help, pulled the king back beyond the reach of the French archers.

Richard's hands were up around his neck, and Loxley tried to move them away, gently first, then more firmly when the king resisted. Seeing the wound, Loxley suppressed a sob. Blood pumped from around the bolt with each beat of the Lion's heart. And with each beat, the flow grew weaker. It was all Robert could do to keep from bawling like a child.

He raised the king's hands again, allowing Richard to cover the wound once more.

"I need a physician here!" Loxley cried, his voice hoarse, his throat raw.

"Why, Loxley?" Richard asked, the words barely carrying. He smiled weakly. Then he whispered "Wine."

A soldier hurried forward with a wine skin. He put it to the king's lips and poured. Most of the wine poured over Richard's chin, but a bit of it found its way into his mouth. The king swallowed. Then his eyes glazed, his breath stilled, and the flow of blood from his wound ceased. Richard, King of England, was dead.

Loxley bent his head and whispered a prayer.

All around them, men continued to fight and die. English soldiers surged toward the growing breach in the castle gate. French defenders battled desperately to hold them back. No one seemed to have noticed that England's king had fallen.

Robert raised his head and looked up into the face of a young English soldier. The lad was staring down at the king. Someone had noticed after all. He looked to be barely more than a child. When had these soldiers become so terribly young? He tore his gaze away from Richard's face and looked at Loxley, a question in his pale eyes.

Loxley nodded.

"The king is dead," the lad whispered. And then more loudly, so that others could hear, "The king is dead!"

ROBIN AND THE others could see the battle unfolding from the stocks. They heard the great roar from the English army when the gates fell, and they watched as men swarmed the castle. Despite being held in the blocks, Robin was glad. As bad as things stood right now, they would have been far worse had the siege failed.

He was surprised when he saw Jimoen running back toward them, and even more so when he saw how pale the lad looked. Were those tears in his eyes?

"The king is dead!" the young man said, halting in front of them, out of breath and clearly frightened.

Robin felt as if he had been kicked in the gut. Richard had become less than he was; all that happened in Acra and on the long journey back from Palestine had diminished him. But still, he was their king, the leader of every English soldier on this field.

Robin looked at Will, Allan, and Little John, and saw his shock mirrored in their faces. They were all looking at him, waiting to see what he would do.

"Then knock the peg out, Jimoen," he said, facing the lad again. "We make our own fate now."

Jimoen unlocked the the stocks, starting with Robin's. One by one, he freed the others. The fighting continued by the castle walls on the hill above them. There had been no pronouncement about Richard; there had been no pause in the battle.

"I'll come with you," Little John said, retrieving his stave and pack.

Scarlet shook his head. "No, you're not. We don't take strays."

"Hold on, Will," Robin said, raising a hand to the welt on his forehead. "The more the merrier. The road could be dangerous. He might be useful."

Will scowled. "A useful Scotsman? Not possible."

"More probable than a useful Welshman," Allan said, grinning.

"You are welcome to join us," Robin told Little John. "You'll have to put up with these two though."

"Thanks," John said with a smile. "No problem. The wee orange one is quite amusing."

"Where are we going?" Jimoen asked.

Robin shouldered his pack. "To the coast. To a boat. Before five thousand desperate soldiers descend and the price for passage across the channel multiplies a hundredfold."

The others began to gather their things, but Will hesitated, glancing back toward the castle and the rest of the English army.

"What about our wages?" he asked. "They haven't paid us in a month."

Robin laughed bitterly. "You think it was tough getting wages when he was alive, try getting paid by a dead king. Collect your gear as quick as you can."

They made for the forest, and had no trouble leaving. The pickets had moved forward to join the fighting, leaving no one to guard the stocks or the edge of the camp. Soon they had stepped into the shadows of Broceliande and were heading toward the coast. Robin took the lead, and Little John walked at the rear, glancing back occasionally to make sure they weren't followed.

For the first hour or more, Robin pushed them hard, eschewing rests and setting a brisk pace. He didn't think anyone would come after them, but he wasn't taking any chances. At last though, as the sun reached its zenith over the trees, and the still air in the wood grew warm, Robin called for a stop by a small, sparkling stream.

Will, Allan, and Jimoen immediately removed their packs and began to rearrange their belongings. John walked down to the stream and splashed some water on his face. Robin took off his armor and fit it into his pack among his other things. When the others were ready, Robin shouldered his pack once more.

"Right," he said. "Let's get moving."

CHAPTER

SIX

Marion rode slowly through Sherwood Forest, steering her bay among the trees. She wore a brown bodice over her riding dress, but still the air was starting to grow cool, and she was eager to return to Peper Harrow and a warm fire. She'd had a successful hunt; the brace of pheasants hanging from her saddle would easily feed Walter and her, and Old Tom besides.

If she made it home. Suddenly she had the feeling that she was being watched, hunted. She slowed the bay and began to reach for her bow, which hung beside the pheasants.

Before she could nock an arrow, though, a figure dropped down from a tree, landing just in front of her. She started and gasped. But her fear was short-lived. The creature before her appeared at first glance to be a wild animal of some sort. It wore fur, and landed deftly on the path. But while it held a sharpened wooden lance that it pointed at her heart, it didn't look to be very threatening. Or very big, for that matter.

Marion heard a footfall behind her. Glancing over her shoulder she saw that a second . . . animal-thing had stepped onto the road behind her.

"Forfeit what ye have!" the first animal demanded. "Victuals, coin, clothing, or your life!"

She would have laughed had she not been so annoyed. Rather than give the creature anything, she reached out, grabbed the lance, and yanked it out of the creature's hands. The animal, who clearly hadn't expected this, scampered back away from her. And as it did, its animal mask slipped down, revealing a young boy. After a moment, Marion realized that she recognized him.

"Thomas Cooper! Is that you?"

Chagrined, the boy swallowed and gave a reluctant nod. She remembered that the boy's father had marched to war years ago, and his mother died soon after. There had been others like him, war orphans all. They hadn't been seen in ages.

"For two years you've been gone," she said.

He nodded again, and as he did, he broke into a hacking cough.

Looking at him more closely, Marion saw that his skin had a grayish cast to it. He had rings under his eyes and his face had a pinched look. She wondered when he'd last had a proper meal.

Eyeing the second boy, Marion realized that she recognized him, too. A moment later he fell into a coughing fit of his own. Was this where all the town's boys had gone? Were they creatures of the wood now, barely alive and scrounging for food? If so, they were fortunate to have survived this long. From the looks of them, they wouldn't make it through another season.

ROBERT LOXLEY RODE northward through the wood, with King Richard's riderless white charger galloping beside him. He had twelve knights with him, flanking him in twin columns, the hooves of their mounts rumbling like thunder on the forest floor. The king's horse carried a pannier that contained Richard's crown. The Lionheart would not be making the journey home to England, but his helm would. It had fallen to Loxley to inform the queen consort that her son was dead.

As they rounded a bend in the road, Loxley heard a sharp sound. Several. Axe blows. Before he could rein his mount to a halt or shout a warning to his men, two enormous tree trunks, as wide around as the battering ram that shattered the castle gates, fell onto the road in front of them.

One of his lead riders was crushed. The two men riding at the rear of the columns were knocked flying off their horses and sprawled onto the forest floor, their chests smashed in. Loxley managed to rein his mount to a halt, as did the other knights. He looked about frantically, taking in what had happened, looking for the likeliest escape route. But before he could so much as bark an order to his men, a dozen archers emerged from behind trees and began to loose their arrows.

As if from nowhere, riders bore down on them, lances leveled.

Loxley reached for his sword, even as he ducked under another volley of arrows. He barely managed to get his weapon free before a lance took him in the gut, knocking him off his horse and to the ground.

His sword landed beside him, its point sticking in the earth.

All around him his knights fell, pierced by arrows or run through with lances. Several more attackers rushed forward with pikes to finish the fallen. A few of Loxley's men raised hands weakly to ward off the killing blows. Others didn't move at all. Six more horsemen appeared on the road, galloping in from the far end, opposite the direction from which Loxley had come. Most of them wore what appeared to be French cavalry uniforms. But it was the man in front who drew Loxley's eye. He wore chain mail and over it a black tabard that bore a brightly colored insignia Loxley had never seen before. He might well have been a French nobleman.

His head was shaved, his eyes deep set, so that they appeared shadowed and dark. He was lean and lithe, and he rode with skill. When he halted and dismounted a few feet short of the first tree trunk, he did so with a swordman's grace. He regarded the scene coolly. The man who had ridden in beside him didn't appear to be a common soldier, either. He looked over the dead and dying while wearing a faint smile.

"Trouvez-le!" the leader called to the other men. Find him!

The attackers began to examine each of the dead, flipping over those who had fallen face down and pulling off helmets to get better looks at their faces. The leader stepped over the dead, pausing occasionally to use the flat of his sword to turn a dead face so that he might see its features more clearly.

"Richard? Richard, où êtes-vous?" Richard, where are you?

Loxley groaned, drawing the man's gaze. The

stranger sauntered over to where the knight lay. The lance was still in Loxley's gut, and now the leader leaned on it. Agony. Loxley felt as though his body was being ripped in half.

"Où est Richard Coeur-de-Lion?" the man asked in a silky voice. Where is Richard the Lionheart?

Still holding the end of the lance, the man walked a slow circle around Loxley, twisting the weapon in the knight's stomach. Loxley howled in pain, writhing against the wood.

"Tell me, sir," the man said, his English perfect, devoid of any accent. "Where is the king?"

"Dead," Loxley rasped. "This morning. A crossbow bolt."

The leader looked over at the man who had ridden in with him, his surprise obvious. The leader of the attackers gave the lance one last vicious turn, ripping another scream of torment from Loxley.

"I don't believe you," the man said.

Loxley could barely raise his hand to point. "There is Richard's crown—on his horse. We bring it to London, with the news."

The man looked at the white charger. Releasing the lance, he stepped to one of the dead knights and looked down at him. With his sword, he moved the man's arm, which bore a black band for the fallen king.

He looked up at his companion and laughed.

"We are on a fool's errand. To assassinate a king who is already dead." He turned to his pikemen. "Bring me the crown."

Two of the French soldiers started toward Richard's white horse. But as they drew near, the creature stamped, reared, wheeled and bolted, leaping over the downed log.

"Get the crown!" the man shouted to his men. "Kill the horse if you have to!"

Several of his men remounted their horses and gave chase.

AT FIRST, AFTER stealing away from the English army, Robin insisted that their small company keep off any established roads or paths. With Richard dead and the siege probably over by now, it wouldn't be long before others from the king's army were crossing through Broceliande Forest to the coast. Robin hoped to avoid all of them. Staying away from the lanes lengthened their journey a little, and slowed them down, but he had been away from England for too long. He wasn't going to risk the stocks again.

Having put a day's walk between themselves and the rest of their countrymen, Robin gave in and allowed them to follow a lane through the forest. Still, he remained watchful, and he set a brisk pace. The others complained. Robin merely walked, and despite their grousing, they kept up with him. Robin and Jimoen walked in front, followed by Will and Allan. Little John, lumbering and huffing like a bear, brought up the rear.

Near midday, as they followed the road through a lonely stretch of wood, a large white horse came dashing around a bend ahead of them. Jimoen jumped back out of the way, but Robin planted himself in the horse's path and raised his arms to stop the beast. It halted just in front of him, although it still looked spooked, its eyes rolling wildly in their sockets, foam at the corners of its mouth.

Slowly, Robin reached for the horse's bridle and took hold of it.

At the same time, two riders came barreling around the bend. One of them swung a rope bolas, clearly intended for the horse. But upon seeing Robin and Jimoen, they didn't hesitate. They bore down on Robin and the lad. The man with the bolas grinned.

Robin pulled his bow free and nocked an arrow. But he didn't have time to loose it before the lead rider threw his bolas hard, directly at Jimoen. The two balled weights wrapped themselves around the lad's throat and jerked him off his feet.

The other rider was almost on Robin now, but Robin managed to fire his arrow before the man reached him. He hit the man just below the chin, just above his chest armor. The rider fell, the point of Robin's arrow jutting from the back of his helmet, the point stained red.

The first rider had wheeled and, having tied the end of the bolas rope to his saddle, was dragging Jimoen roughly over the road back the way he had come.

By now, Will and Allan had their bows ready, and Robin had nocked another arrow. They all fired at the same time, and all three arrows struck true. The rider fell, but the horse kept running, still dragging Jimoen. An instant later, both the horse and the lad disappeared around the bend.

CHAPTER

❦

SEVEN

Robert could feel his life bleeding away. More than anything he wanted to kill these men who had slaughtered his soldiers and left him here with this bloody lance in his belly, pinned to the earth like a bug. But he was helpless, weak, dying. The men around him were ignoring him, as if he were already dead.

The leader was staring down the road, clearly waiting for some sign that his riders had captured Richard's charger. His associate called orders to the other soldiers.

"Prenez de que vous voulez." Take what you will.

Like vultures, the men descended on the bodies of the knights lying around Loxley. They rifled through packs and saddlebags, stripped armor and clothing off the bodies, cut purses from around the knights' necks, pulled rings from stiffening fingers. All the while they shouted to one another in French and laughed raucously. If Loxley could have called down the wrath of God on every one of them he would have done so gladly.

Instead, he looked up at the leader, who was ignoring the scavengers.

"Are you English?" Loxley asked, struggling to make himself heard.

The bald man grinned cruelly and squatted down beside Loxley. "When it serves me," he said. Loxley said nothing, but spat in his tormentor's face. The man's face contorted with rage, and Loxley thought for certain that he'd deal him a killing blow then and there. But at that moment, the horse of one of the man's riders came charging around the bend, hooves thundering, riderless. A man was being dragged behind the beast, bloodied almost beyond recognition, clearly dead.

The noble and his associate looked at each other, both showing fear for the first time.

Four more men came around the bend on foot. English soldiers! If Loxley had the strength he would have cheered. Three of the men had their bows drawn and they loosed their arrows, nocked new ones, and fired again, all without breaking stride. Several of the French cavalry fell.

One of the men—Loxley recognized him from the camp—fired two arrows in quick succession at the soldiers now standing with the leader. Both men went down, arrows in their throats between the top of the armor and their chins. Either shot would have been remarkable; together they defied logic.

The French soldiers who remained alive ran off the road into the trees. Several fell with arrows in their head and neck. Those who didn't ran into another man

Loxley recognized: the giant who had been fighting the archer just the night before. He carried a stave, which he used to deadly effect, blocking sword strokes, cracking skulls and ribs, the wood a bright blur in the forest shadows.

Within moments, the leader and his associate were the only attackers left standing.

"Suivez-moi!" the leader called. Follow me!

Both men leaped onto their horses and sped away down the road.

The archer stopped in the middle of the lane, drew an arrow from his quiver, nocked it and, taking careful aim, let it fly. Loxley knew immediately that the man had found his mark. At the last moment, though, the leader turned to look back over his shoulder. Rather than taking him in the back of the neck, the arrow hit him in the face. He screamed, nearly toppled off his horse. Then he righted himself, grasping his mount around the neck and riding on. A moment later, he and his companion were gone.

ROBIN WATCHED THE two riders vanish around a far bend in the road. Then he turned to survey the carnage they'd left behind.

Allan and Little John walked among the dead soldiers. Coins, bottles, jewelry, and other trinkets were scattered all around. At least they had kept the French from their ghoulish harvest.

"They're all dead," Little John said.

Robin wasn't surprised. "Keep an eye out for the living. They may return."

Will Scarlet walked up slowly, leading King Richard's charger.

"Robin look."

Will opened the pannier hanging from the saddle and pulled out the king's war helmet. Gold gleamed in the sunlight that trickled through the branches overhead. In all likelihood that helm was worth more than all the coin any of them would see in their lifetimes.

"Imagine the price we could get!" Scarlet said, his eyes widening. Robin could see that in his mind Will had already started spending his treasure. "It would buy land and a manor. For each of us!"

Robin shared a look with Little John, and wondered how best to rein in Will's ambitions.

At that moment, though, Robin heard a weak call of "Help," from a man he had assumed was dead.

He strode over to the man, Little John just behind him. He recognized the fallen knight immediately: Robert Loxley, the king's man. A lance protruded from his stomach, and the ground around him was soaked with blood. Robin exchanged another look with John, who gave a small shake of his head. Robin knelt and, while John held the lance steady, he gingerly examined the wound. He then checked the man for other wounds. He had just the one, but that would be enough to kill him.

Blood now flowed slowly from around the lance, but most of the man's life had already bled away.

Loxley seemed to realize this. He grabbed Robin's arm and squeezed. Robin had the sense that the man was gripping him as hard as he could, but there was barely any pressure at all.

"My name is Robert Loxley," the man said.

Robin nodded.

"My sword," Loxley said, the word coming out as faint as a breath. He tried to lift his head, clearly intent on finding his weapon.

Robin saw it sticking point down in the earth just a few feet away. He glanced at Allan, who pulled it free and brought it to him. Robin tried to place the hilt of the weapon in Loxley's hands, but the knight wouldn't take it. Instead, he wrapped his hands around Robin's so that they were holding the sword together. The man's fingers were icy cold, as if death already had him in its grip. Robin tried gently to extricate his hands, but the knight held him with all of his remaining strength.

"Its value to me is great," Loxley said, looking up into Robin's face. "It belongs to my father, Walter Loxley. Of Nottingham. Do you know it?"

Robin nodded. "Aye, I have heard of Nottingham. I was born in Barnsdale, to the south and east."

A faint smile touched Loxley's lips, which had started to turn blue. "Then fate smiles on me," he said. "You must take the sword to him."

The man's hands tightened on Robin's, and the archer felt a stinging pain in his palm. It seemed Loxley would spend his last ounce of strength forcing Robin's hands to grip that blade. He wanted to refuse. God knew he did. But here at the end of Loxley's journey, he couldn't bring himself to say the words.

Robin exhaled heavily. "I will."

That small smile returned to Loxley's face, and he slumped back, sightless eyes fixed on the sky. His hands fell away, leaving Robin holding the sword. Another man's quest; another man's folly. Robin looked at his palm, the one that had stung before. There in the center was a small speck of blood.

"An oath sworn in blood, Robin," Allan said in a hushed voice.

Robin wiped the blood away. "No. It's a scratch, Allan. And that's all it is."

King Richard's charger nickered and stomped a hoof. Will, still standing beside the creature, stroked its nose.

"And how much are you worth, you handsome thing?"

Robin started to stand, then noticed a pouch that Loxley wore around his neck. Curious, he opened it and pulled out a map. Unfolding it, he saw that it showed the coasts of Northern France and Southern England. A spot was marked on the French coast just to the east of Calais.

Surprised and pleased at his discovery, Robin looked up at Will in time to see his friend try on Richard's crown.

"Take it off," he said.

Will's face fell. But when Robin next looked around at the treasure lying at their feet and said, "And fill it to the brim," Will's smile returned. Robin felt something stirring in his mind: a plan. He grinned at Will, who didn't look pleased at all. Robin held up the map. "Loxley was making for the coast," he said, loudly enough for Little John and Allan to hear, too. "To meet a ship! That crown will be our passage home."

Allan looked unconvinced. "Robin, we're common archers. If we arrive at the king's ship with his crown, we'll be accused of murder."

But Robin wasn't about to be deterred so easily. "You've seen enough of them to know that there's little difference between a knight and any other man, apart from what he wears. We all bleed. We all die. And we're all at fault."

Robin stood and looked at the bodies and personal items scattered over the forest road. "All we need is about us. Armor, helmets. And we'll make England with horses, chain mail, and gold."

Out of the corner of his eye, Robin saw Will cross himself, but he didn't care. They would follow him, and they would see.

"Fate has smiled upon us at last," he said. "I, for one, will not turn my back on her."

They began the gruesome task of disguising themselves. Will, Allan, and Little John found knights whose clothes would fit them, and donned their armor and surcoats. This was not easy for Little John, but he managed to squeeze into garb without looking too ridiculous, all the while complaining about "wee knights" and their armor. Robin, who was about Loxley's size, put on Sir Robert's coat of mail and the surcoat bearing the noble's coat of arms, taking care to cover what he could of the blood. The rest he would clean off when they reached the coast, before they met the ship to England.

When they were ready to go, they returned to the spot where they had buried Jimoen and stood over the lad's grave for a few moments, their heads bowed, each of them praying silently. At the head of the grave, Robin placed a helmet upon the freshly turned earth and silently bid the boy farewell.

They turned from the grave and set off for the coast a short time later, Robin astride King Richard's charger, the other three sitting horses that had belonged to Loxley's knights. Robin was surprised by how convincing they looked. Dressed in the armor and surcoats of the English knights, Will, Allan, and John actually looked like noble warriors. He knew, though, that the real test would come when they reached the waters of the English Channel and had to convince the ship's captain that they were who they were supposed to be.

Before long, he tasted brine in the air and spotted white gulls wheeling overhead. They cut over to the water and Robin washed Loxley's blood from the knight's clothes. The four companions then continued along the coast until they came to the place indicated on Loxley's map.

Robin spotted the ship resting on the mudflats exposed by the low tide, not very far from the shoreline. Several crewmen and perhaps half a dozen English soldiers stood on the deck, no doubt watching for their arrival. He picked out the captain, even as he saw the man point in their direction and mouth "There."

The ship's crew jumped to life. Several of them lowered rope ladders from the deck, while others readied the ship to set sail once more. The captain was joined on the deck by two others, one of them well dressed—possibly an emissary from Richard's court.

Robin and his companions rode to the ship, their horses' hooves splashing in the shallows. Muttering another prayer under his breath, Robin halted by the vessel and looked up at the captain and the king's emissary. The ship's captain, in turn, regarded Robin warily before looking at the others, his gaze lingering on Little John, whose armor was so tight it made him appear even larger than usual.

"Sir," he said, addressing Robin. "We were told to expect twelve riders. And the king."

"The king is dead," Robin told him.

The captain and the emissary exchanged glances, both of them looking as if they had been kicked in the stomach. This was just as Robin had hoped. In their shock and grief, the men might not think to question the identities of Robin and his men.

"His Majesty was killed in battle," he went on, pressing his advantage. "We're to take the word home."

"Long live the king," the captain and court man said in unison.

The nobleman regarded Robin, gathering himself. "And you are, sir?"

Robin didn't hesitate. "I am Sir Robert Loxley of Nottingham. And you, sir?"

The man blinked. "I am the king's equerry, sir."

"Come aboard, gentlemen," the captain said. "Before the tide floats her. It's coming in fast."

Robin looked back at the others and flashed a quick grin. Their ruse had worked. They were going back to England. They were going home.

He and the lads dismounted and uncinched their horses, the incoming tide swirling around their boots. Then they climbed onto the ship, bearing the king's crown. The ship's crew lowered a gangplank and with some effort brought their horses aboard the vessel.

Once all were on board, the captain ordered the men to raise the covered sail, and soon the ship was moving away from the French coast. But only when they reached the open waters of the channel, did the captain order the men to uncover the sail cloth.

A pair of crewmen scrambled up the mast, crept out on the scaffolding and untied the cover. Down it fell, billowing in the wind and revealing the three

Plantagenet leopards, gold on a red field, glowing in the afternoon sun. With the canvas cover gone, wind filled the sail and the ship leaped forward, carving through the surf toward England. Staring up at Richard's crest, Robin's hand strayed to the hilt of Loxley's sword. It was headed home, too.

CHAPTER

EIGHT

In the fields of Peper Harrow, Marion and Gaffer Tom watched grimly as Old Paul, the farmer who had tended the Loxley crops for a generation, struggled behind the plow. The man was half crippled, the land was none too easy to work, and the brown and white dray pulling the plow stood eighteen hands high and weighed a hundred and thirty stone if it weighed an ounce.

Still, Paul, always in good cheer, glanced over at them and offered a toothless grin as he staggered past.

"Goliath's got the soil turning nicely, but for what? Nettles?"

"Possibly," Marion said, in a wry tone. "Nettle soup and dandelion salad to keep us alive until . . ." She trailed off, searching for the right word.

"Until there's a miracle," Tom finished grimly.

Paul reached the end of the row and tried to turn the dray. He hadn't the strength though, and the horse resisted his efforts. Heedless of her dress and her shoes, Marion hurried to the horse's side and grabbed its harness.

"This way," she said soothingly to the beast. "Come, Goliath."

Together, she and Paul got the horse and plow turned around. Paul started down the next row and flashed another grin her way.

"Marion," Tom called, drawing her gaze.

Marion looked back at the gaffer, who wore a deep frown on his ruddy face. He gave a small jerk of his head, directing her gaze down the lane.

"The sheriff," he said.

Marion saw him, too. Nottingham's sheriff rode toward them at a leisurely pace, trailed by two of his toughs. His long brown hair was unruly, his beard poorly trimmed, his face too long, too horselike. He wore a brown cloak with thick fur at the collar and shoulders, and studded riding breeches. He rode a fine bay with an elaborate leather bridle. Of the two, rider and mount, the latter was definitely the more attractive. Still the sheriff carried himself with the supreme confidence of a man who passed his days blissfully ignorant of his many shortcomings. He wore a smile that was both cruel and mocking, and that, though distasteful, did seem to fit his features perfectly.

Marion stepped forward to meet him, conscious of the plainness of her brown dress and slate blue smock, and of the old beige cloth she had used to tie back her hair.

"I have been at Peper Harrow, Marion," he drawled,

"waiting in vain for Sir Walter to receive me. Kindly inform him that I have better things to do than haunt his threshold."

"That you have, while there are robbers roaming free in Sherwood! That's sheriff's business; why don't you see to it?"

Tom snickered.

The sheriff's face turned beet red. "Tell the old man the next time I'll break down his door!"

Marion eyed him suspiciously. "What have you got to say to Sir Walter that he should disturb himself for you?"

The man drew himself up, looking even more haughty than usual. "That in Nottingham I stand for England's exchequer, and if he thinks himself too proud to pay what's due—"

"He is not too proud!" Marion broke in. "But too poor! In the name of King Richard you have stripped our wealth to pay for foreign adventures, while at home the Church in the name of a merciful God has reaped without mercy the larger share of what we have sown to feed ourselves. Between a sheriff and a bishop, I wouldn't care to judge who's the greater curse on honest English folk!"

She expected that he would redden and splutter in his anger, as he had before. But he remained composed as he guided his mount closer to her. Marion stood her ground, though she sensed that Tom had grown tense behind her. Paul had halted in the field.

The sheriff leered at her. He smelled of too-sweet perfume and she thought she caught the scent of wine on his breath.

"That's talk to get a woman locked in the keep," he said, his voice low and oily. "Why make an enemy of me, Miss Marion, when you have the means to make me your protector?" His gaze dropped briefly to the laces that tied the bodice of her dress.

"What means?" she demanded.

The sheriff's hand reached out, as quick as lightning. Grabbing hold of her bodice, he pulled her roughly toward him, leaned down, and kissed her full on the mouth. She should have endured the kiss; though his manners were common, the power he wielded was real. But in her fury and her revulsion Marion couldn't help herself. She bit his lip as hard as she could.

The sheriff thrust her away so forcefully that she nearly stumbled. He put his hand to his lip, testing it for blood. Marion spat.

"Like being kissed by a putrid fish," she said, her voice shaking with rage. "If you leave now, I will lengthen your life by not telling my husband when he returns home."

The sheriff laughed coldly. "Your husband? After ten years? If he's not dead, he's rutting his way through the brothels of the Barbary Coast."

If she'd had a sword, he would have been dead already. "Go. Now."

He remained just where he was, grinning. "Think on it, Miss Marion. Sir Walter is dying without an heir, so Peper Harrow will belong to the Crown, and you will be living in the hedgerow. You'll be glad to come to me then."

He laughed again, wheeled his horse, and rode away, his ruffians trailing behind him.

Marion turned and walked quickly back to the house, too furious to say anything to Tom or Old Paul.

* * *

THE WINDS ON the English Channel had died
down at dusk, leaving the ship to drift slowly toward
England. Robin and the others were awake belowdecks, their small chamber lit dimly by candlelight.
Allan sat on a barrel, plucking at the strings of his
lute, while Will and Little John drank wine and sang
along, their voices slightly off-key.

Robin sat apart from the others, lost in thought,
staring at the palm of his hand, at the small mark
that had been left there by the hilt of Loxley's sword.
Allan had said something about a blood oath, but
Robin knew better. This mark hadn't been made by
anything so mystical. He still remembered the sting
of it. Thinking this, he pulled the sword from the
scabbard on his belt and examined the hilt closely.
There was copper wire there, holding a leather grip in
place. It was wound around the hilt, its sharp end pro-
truding slightly. He gripped the hilt as he had before,
when Loxley had put it in his hands. Yes, that was
the spot.

He leaned forward a bit, allowing the candlelight to
fall more fully on the sword. The grip had a tear in it,
and Robin could see that there was writing engraved
on the hilt beneath it. He unwound the copper and
pushed the leather aside, trying to read more of the
inscription. He uncovered a single word: Lions.

Lions. Something stirred in the deepest recesses of
his memory, like a bear waking after a long winter's
slumber. He pulled off more of the wire and stripped
away the leather grip until he could see the entire
inscription.

"Rise and rise again," it said, *"until lambs become
lions."*

He stared at the candle burning before him, and he repeated the words to himself over and over. *Rise and rise again, until lambs become lions.* Yes, he had heard this before. But where, and when? And why would a sword owned by a dead knight, a man to whom he had never spoken before the events of the past few days, bear words that should remind him so strongly of . . . of what?

There were gaps in his memories, dark periods from his childhood that he had never been able to recall. These words seemed to take him back to those lost years. Like a small flame on a murky night, they hinted at something beyond his seeing, casting shadows upon shadows. The harder Robin tried to summon the images, the more elusive they became. Still, he knew of them now. *Rise and rise again* . . . Perhaps with time, the phrase would shine brighter in the recesses of his mind, and those shadows would be revealed.

And still he gazed at the candle flame, Loxley's sword lying across his lap. Robin rubbed his palm, thinking once more of the oath he swore to the knight, and of Allan's words. *An oath sworn in blood* . . . Perhaps there had been more to the day's events after all. What were the chances that they would take precisely that route through Broceliande Forest, that they should happen upon the forest road just when they did? Had it been fate that led Robin to kneel at the side of a dying knight, that led that man to place his sword in Robin's palm, that led Robin back to a memory so remote he hadn't considered it in years? What other explanation could there be?

Robin considered this as he unwound what was left

of the wire and removed the rest of that leather grip. Nearby, Allan still played his lute, singing softly. Little John and Will were playing a drinking game that Will was destined to lose.

"How do we get off this ride?" John asked eventually, his words running together slightly.

Robin looked over at him. "This boat docks first at Gravesend on its way to London. We'll leave the honor of delivering the crown to them, and we'll be gone."

Little John raised an eyebrow. "Where?"

"North," Robin said.

The big man nodded once. "Suits me." He took another drink and handed the bottle to Will. It seemed even the drinking game had grown too complicated for them. Best simply to drink.

Robin grinned, joined them. No sense in letting them drink all the good stuff.

ROBIN AWOKE BELOWDECKS with a pounding headache and a mouth so dry that his tongue felt like wood and his teeth seemed to be covered with fur. His stomach felt sour and tight.

The boat moved steadily. Robin could hear the sweeps cutting rhythmically through the water. *The sweeps.*

His mind stumbled on that thought and he sat bolt upright in his small pallet. Not a good idea. His head spinning, he forced himself to his feet, stumbled out of their cramped quarters and made his way over to the ladder leading up out of the hold. With some effort he managed to climb out onto the deck.

Shielding his eyes from the too-bright sun, Robin

refused to believe what he saw. It couldn't be. They were headed to Gravesend. That was where he and the boys were going to make their escape. That couldn't be the Thames in front of them, winding toward the port of London. Although that looked suspiciously like the famed Tower in the distance.

Seeing him, the captain raised a hand in greeting. "Make ready, Sir Robert. We will dock in twenty minutes."

"Gravesend?" Robin asked weakly, hoping that he was mistaking some other port for the royal city. As if he could mistake the White Tower for anything else in England.

The captain frowned at Robin, as if he thought him simple, or still drunk. "No, M'Lord, the Palace Dock. The Tower of London."

Robin turned quickly and lurched back to the hatch. He practically fell down the ladder and scurried back to the quarters where the others still slept.

"Wake up!" Robin shouted at them.

Little John stirred but didn't open his eyes. "Right!" he said sleepily. "I think I'll breakfast on twelve oysters and a quart of ale."

Robin shook Will and Allan.

"Where are we?" Allan asked, rubbing his eyes.

Robin shook Will again. "London!"

Will's eyes flew open. "Holy Christ!" Robin and the others washed and tried make themselves look the part. As they did, though, Robin wondered how they had ever managed to fool the captain and the king's man, and how they could possibly hope to deceive Lady Eleanor of Aquataine, Richard's mother. They didn't look like knights; they looked like ruffians, road thieves.

"Be ready to ride as soon as it's done," Robin said, crossing to his pack.

"What if Loxley was known to the king's mother, or brother, or *any* of them?" Will asked.

Robin glanced up at him. "Then we'll be riding for our lives."

CHAPTER

NINE

Over the last ten years, Robin had faced the Saracens and the French in battle. He had endured hardships most men could hardly imagine, and had found courage within his heart he hadn't known he possessed. But he could not recall ever being as nervous about anything as he was about telling Eleanor of Aquitaine that her son was dead.

It wasn't that he feared for his life, though Will, Allan, and Little John seemed fairly certain that they would all end their day as prisoners in the White Tower. Rather, he was awed by the mere fact that he was about to meet the great lady. Eleanor had been Queen Consort of England for as long as Robin had been alive. Longer, actually. She was the most famous, powerful, notorious woman in all the world. She was also said to be the most beautiful, even now, well into her seventies.

And so it was that he stood at the prow of the ship, staring toward the dock, watching as people gathered to greet the vessel. All around him, the ship's crew rushed to and fro, preparing to dock. Will and Allan stood with their feet planted, their faces pale, their hands on the hilts of their swords. The ship bumped into the dock and two men jumped onto the quay to tie her in.

Robin had thought that he would have trouble spotting the queen consort; he should have known better. As bells pealed from the towers of the palace, the royal entourage emerged from the palace gate. The crowd parted. An older woman led the royal procession down toward the dock. She was tall, regal. The sun lit her handsome face. Surely this had to be Eleanor. She was accompanied by a knight, also tall, with a mane of red and silver hair. Behind them came a younger pair, the man with dark curls and a trim beard, and on his arm a young woman of surpassing beauty. Was this Prince John then?

No sooner had Robin asked himself the question than the thought came to him unbidden and as unforgiving as stone. No, not prince. This was the new king.

GODFREY AND BELVEDERE steered their mounts through the filthy lanes of London toward the walls of the great White Tower. They had crossed the channel in the dark of night and had ridden hard to the city. Godfrey's face still ached where the arrow had hit him, but he would be damned if he was going to let a simple wound disrupt his plans.

As they neared the tower, church bells began to toll throughout the city. Belvedere shot Godfrey a puzzled

look. Godfrey shrugged. The two men rode into the
stable yard and dismounted, leaving their horses to
the White Tower's grooms. Within the tower walls,
men and women rushed in every direction, as if preparing for a wedding or a feast.

"What is this?" Godfrey asked one of the grooms.

"M'Lord! King Richard returns from France,
M'Lord."

Godfrey looked at Belvedere again, his mind reel-
ing. Richard was dead. That was what Loxley had
told them, practically with his dying breath. They
hurried toward the water gate, pushing their way past
a growing throng. Still unable to see, they climbed
the saddling stones to get a better view.

There on the Thames, already at the dock, was the
king's ship.

"Did Loxley deceive us?" Belvedere asked, keeping his voice low.

Godfrey shrugged, his eyes fixed on the vessel.

THE SHIP HAD been secured, the gangplank swung
out and positioned so that Robin could disembark.
One of the servants who had accompanied the king's
equerry handed Robin the box that held Richard's
crown. The equerry himself then stepped forward and
draped over the box a cloth bearing the Plantagenet
leopards. Robin stepped onto the plank, feeling hundreds of pairs of eyes upon him, and walked down to
the dock.

For Robin, though, this was no longer an act. He
could see Eleanor clearly now. Her face was lined,
but her eyes remained clear and brilliant, like blue
gems. They were fixed on him. While others in the
crowd continued to search for Richard, she did not.

She marked Robin's approach, saw what he carried, and already she grieved. For an instant, it seemed that her knees buckled. The color had drained from her cheeks and she briefly closed her eyes and appeared to whisper a prayer.

Then she was watching him again, composed somehow. Robin couldn't help but admire her strength.

He stopped just in front of her, holding the box before him. Eleanor pulled the cloth from the box, opened it, and removed the crown, which gleamed in the sunlight. Her hands were steady, her expression impassive, save for the mournful look in her eyes.

She turned to John and said, "Kneel."

Shock registered on the young man's face as he finally seemed to understand what had happened and what it meant for him. He slowly lowered himself to one knee.

Eleanor placed the crown on his head. "I wish you long life, my son," she said.

She then knelt in turn and every person on the dock followed her example, kneeling with rustles of silk and brocade that made the air around them hum, as if charged.

"The king is dead!" Eleanor announced, her voice as clear and loud as a church bell. "Long live the king!"

All around them the crowd repeated the words. "Long live the king!" They said it a second time, their voices growing louder. The third time, they shouted it, the sound building to a crescendo that threatened to topple the White Tower itself.

John looked around him, still pale, but seeming already to warm to his new office. "Rise!" he commanded, his voice carrying over the dock.

The people stood once more, murmured conversations sweeping through the assembled masses. The Lionheart was dead; John was their king.

The young girl standing with John took his hand, her gaze drawn again and again to the golden crown he now wore.

The queen consort seemed to have reached the limits of her endurance. She leaned on the knight beside her for support, and looked deathly pale.

"You!" the king said. "Come closer."

It took Robin a moment to realize that John was speaking to him.

Robin stood and approached the king. John was eyeing him closely.

"I don't know you," John said.

"Robert Loxley, Sire, of Nottingham." The lie came easily to Robin's lips. Speaking to Eleanor of Aquitaine had nearly been more than he could manage, but John was another matter.

The king nodded. "Welcome, then. Forgive me. I don't know any of you; you've been at war so long."

"We have, sir."

"And how did my brother die?"

"By exposing himself to danger, sir," Robin said. "As was his way."

"As was his way," John mimicked, his tone mocking, his expression turning sour.

Eleanor, standing nearby, glowered at him, her right hand opened and rigid and trembling. For a second, Robin thought that she would slap him, heedless of the crown he now wore. But after regarding him briefly with manifest contempt, she turned sharply and strode back toward the tower. Through it all, John appeared oblivious.

"You shall be rewarded," John said, still facing

Robin. He thought for a moment, then regarded the
many rings on his hand. Choosing one, he tried to
remove it. At first he couldn't pull it past the knuckle,
but after a bit more effort, he managed to twist it free.
He reached out to drop it in Robin's hand, but then
hesitated.

"Nottingham, you say?" John asked.

"Yes, my lord," Robin answered.

John smiled thinly. "Your father, Sir Walter, owes
the Crown tax." He tapped the ring on his crown. "My
Crown. We'll start with this."

He returned the ring to his finger, glanced at Robin
once more, that same acid smile on his lips, and swept
away. The crowd parted for him as if he were a ship
carving through still waters. Men bowed, women
curtsied. John seemed to enjoy it all. Eleanor's youngest might have been shocked to find himself elevated
to the throne on this day, but he had recovered all too
quickly. If this was the man who was to lead England,
Robin grieved for the realm.

STANDING WITH BELVEDERE, watching as John
claimed Richard the Lionheart's crown, Godfrey
found his gaze straying repeatedly to the knight who
had stepped off the king's ship carrying the pannier.
He knew the man. He was sure of it. But from where?

He saw the man speak to Eleanor, and then to the
new king, and he burned to know what they said.
Regardless of his identity, he had somehow come to
possess Richard's crown, which Godfrey very nearly
had in his grasp.

This stranger was his enemy.

He absently reached a hand up to the throbbing

wound on his cheek, his eyes still fixed on the man. How familiar he looked . . .

Prince John—*King* John—spoke to the man a moment longer before turning away from him and starting back toward White Tower. He parted the crowd of onlookers with a small gesture and strode past them. Even from a distance, Godfrey could tell that John was enjoying himself. Others followed him back to the Tower—the exchequer and justiciar, William Marshal and the cardinal.

As John neared the Tower gate, he spotted Godfrey. A huge smile lit his face, and he opened his arms in greeting, walking to where Godfrey and Belvedere waited.

"Godfrey, my friend!" the king said, his voice carrying.

Godfrey and Belvedere stepped forward to receive the king's greeting. Belvedere kneeled, but Godfrey remained standing.

As he drew near, John noticed the scar on Godfrey's cheek. His smile faded. "Your face?"

Godfrey grinned as if the wound was nothing. "A hunting accident."

John studied the scar critically for a second. "Call it dueling. The ladies will love you even more."

Godfrey's laugh was genuine. "I bow to your knowledge of ladies, Sire!"

John laughed in turn, and Belvedere joined in.

The king walked on toward the castle, though not before glancing back at Belvedere and saying "You may get up now," his voice tinged with amusement.

Belvedere stood. Godfrey, meanwhile, had turned his attention back to the stranger on the dock. He

knew him now. The archer from the forest in France.
The scar on Godfrey's cheek burned. The man had
known enough to recover Richard's crown and bring
it to London. He might well recognize Godfrey as
Robert Loxley's killer. He was a threat to everything
Godfrey hoped to accomplish.

"He knows too much," Godfrey said to Belvedere,
still watching the man. "Get rid of him."

Belvedere nodded, a small smile on his lips.

ROBIN HELPED LEAD King Richard's charger off the
ship and then waited as Will, Allan, and Little John
brought their mounts ashore as well. The time had
come for them to leave London and make their way to
Nottingham, and none too soon, as far as Robin was
concerned. Their ruse had worked, and it seemed that
no one would be putting them in the stocks or fitting
nooses to their necks. Still, he'd had quite enough of
pretending to be someone he wasn't.

As he and others started off the dock, though, he
heard someone call to him. "Sir Robert."

Robin halted, and cast a wary eye at the man approaching him. After a moment he recognized him
as the knight who had stood with Eleanor when first
Robin came off the ship. He was an older man, though
he didn't appear to have conceded much to age. He
was lean and tall, and he moved with the easy grace
of a swordsman. His eyes were pale, and his mane of
reddish gold hair was shot through with white.

"I am William Marshal," the man said stopping in
front of Robin. "The husband of Lady Isabel de Clare.
You will know of me perhaps. Your father and I were
young men together. He will remember."

Robin knew of William Marshal. Who in England

hadn't heard tales of the famed knight's valor in battle and his exploits in the tournament ring? Of course, Robin knew nothing of the man's friendship with Loxley's father, and so he kept his mouth shut, and simply nodded, acknowledging what Marshal had told him.

"Tell him I will come to see him soon," Marshal went on. "On Spring's first black night. I may have need of him . . ."

The knight stopped himself, smiling reflexively. Robin had the sense that he had been about to say more than he intended.

"I'll tell him," Robin said.

He bowed his head to the man and moved on. He could feel Marshal watching him as he walked, and he wondered if the knight suspected that Robin wasn't who he claimed to be. Robin didn't look back.

CHAPTER

TEN

It was late afternoon, and Marion sat with Sir Walter by the ruined arch at the entrance to Peper Harrow. Sir Walter enjoyed getting out, particularly at this time of day. He could no longer see the golden sunlight shining on the walls of his ancestral home and warming the surrounding fields, but he often told her that it remained his favorite time of day. It was Marion's as well, and she was glad to indulge his desire to sit outside as dusk approached. The air was growing chill with the sun's descent, and Marion retrieved the old man's brown woolen cloak from the cart. While there, she put on her own as well. Returning to Walter, she wrapped the cloak around his shoulders. The old man caught her hand in his own and gave it a small squeeze, favoring her with a grateful smile. She sat beside him, her face tipped toward the setting sun, savoring its warm caress. Walter inhaled deeply.

"My nose has learned something since my eyes

failed me," he said. "So—mark this, Marion—here between the myrtle and the wild strawberry patch, make my funeral pyre. Strip the turf east-west a foot deep—"

"This is mere mischief," Marion broke in, trying to make light of what the old man had said. "Frightening me with your funeral talk. I'll laugh at you when you're a hundred." Despite her brave words, though, Marion felt an odd chill. Shivering, she pulled her wrap tighter around her shoulders.

Walter gave a small laugh, but when he spoke again, it was in the same dark vein. "Lay a platform of slow-burning hardwood, spaces between to make a good draft. Then, pine laid crosswise—the sap will heat body and bones to vapor and to ash, which I will have scattered—"

"Stop!" Marion said. She stood and turned away from him, huddling ever deeper within her cloak. "Is this a funeral for a good Christian gentleman?" She tried once more to turn this into a jest. "I'll tell on you as a pagan to Robert when he returns from his campaigns."

"Robert is dead, Marion."

She spun toward him, feeling the blood drain from her face. "Who says so?"

"Robert," the old man said levelly. "He told me himself."

"In a dream?" Marion demanded, her voice spiraling upward. She rarely allowed herself to grow angry with Walter. He had been so kind to her; he had cared for her as if she was his own daughter for all the years Robert had been away. But this was too much! Frightening her so with his superstitions and foolish pronouncements.

Sir Walter shook his head slowly. "No. A visitation in my sleep. I've lived long enough to know the difference."

"Well, he didn't tell me!" Marion could hear the petulance in her own voice, but she couldn't help herself. Her entire body trembled and her stomach felt hollow and tight.

Walter reached out a hand, searching for hers. Reluctantly, she grasped it.

"I'm so sorry, Marion. I brought you here to know what I know. Your husband is not coming home."

He pulled her close to him and embraced her. Marion resisted, not yet ready to credit what he was telling her; not yet ready to give in to the grief that threatened to overwhelm her.

"And this is why you thought to instruct me about your last resting place?" she asked in a softer voice. "Because your son will not be here to be instructed?"

Walter swallowed, then nodded. His dead eyes brimmed with tears.

Marion bent and kissed his forehead. "Then I grieve for you. But do not grieve for me yet. I also know what I know. Sir Robert Loxley will ride out of Peper Harrow once again and through the streets of Nottingham with me at his side. May the forest gods grant me that, or I swear, I'll go and live in the greenwood if they will have me."

Sir Walter pulled her close again, and this time she returned the old man's embrace.

Come home to me, Robert, she pleaded silently. *Come home to this man who loves you so.*

* * *

ROBIN AND HIS companions rode at a leisurely pace through the rolling hills of the English countryside, the fields and farmlands bathed in the deepening glow of the late day sun. The road they followed skirted the edge of a grand and ancient forest, its shadows darkening by the moment. The air was still, and a thrush sang from within the wood.

Robin kept a wary eye on the line of trees, and glanced back at the others periodically to see that they were keeping watch, too. Little John rode at the rear, holding his stave across his legs and checking the road behind them now and again. This was good land, their ride thus far had been uneventful, but none of them had any doubt that Godfrey's men would be coming for them.

They stopped with the sun still up so that they would have time to set up camp before darkness fell. While Allan and Little John gathered wood for a fire, Robin and Will wandered deeper into the forest to hunt for their supper. They returned just as the first stars appeared in the sky, carrying a brace of rabbits. Little John grinned at the sight, and took it upon himself to prepare the meat, making it clear that he didn't trust Robin or Will to do so without ruining their meal.

Naturally, Will took offense and insisted that he and John cook the rabbits together. For his part, Robin had other matters to which he needed to attend.

As the last light of the twilight sky gave way to the bright glow of their fire, Allan pulled out his lute and began to play. Will and John skinned the rabbits. And Robin, his back to the others, pulled out a different sort of loot: the spoils from the forest road in

France. They had gathered the coins and jewels of the dead hastily before riding on to the coast. Now, Robin took it upon himself to divide what they had found as evenly as he could into four piles.

Allan began to sing.

Sadness, sadness,
Can only lead to madness.
You have to count your gold.
The living king of sermons.
Was delivered from his evil,
But he couldn't talk his last,
Because God took out his throat.
God's crossbow took out his throat.

"By Christ!" Scarlet said, glancing over at his friend. "Can you not sing a happy tune? We've made England with our hides and gold intact." He turned back to the rabbit he was skinning. "Sing a foot stomper about adventure and daring and courage, and how handsome I look in armor."

"What about a song called 'By the Grace of God Go I'?" Robin said, without looking up from his work.

Little John shook his head, a grin on his face. "No. Sing something about a woman. A large woman."

Allan laughed at that and began to play something new, a song they had learned in France from some of the other soldiers. It was a somewhat less pious piece than the first one Allan had played, concerned as it was with the generous assets of a serving girl. Little John laughed out loud and began to sing along, as did Will.

Robin distributed the last of their riches and

covered the piles with his cloak before turning to the others.

"I'm done," he announced.

Immediately, Allan stopped playing and they all turned their attention to Robin. He lifted his cloak from the piles and the other three gathered closer, gazing at the loot, eyes wide, mouths open.

"The money is divided," Robin said. "And so should we be."

"Where will you go?" Will asked.

"I think there is something we owe for such good fortune. I mean to give it back, Will."

"How so?" Little John asked.

Robin's hand moved to the hilt of Loxley's weapon. "The sword," he said. "Its inscription entices something in my memory. Maybe it is just a trick of my imagination. I don't know." He took a breath, knowing how the others would react to what he had in mind. "I intend to deliver it to its rightful owner, to fulfill the request of his dying son. To repay good luck with bad grace is to invite darkness."

John regarded him for several moments, firelight shining in his dark eyes. "Well," he said at last. "I'll go with you."

Allan gave a decisive nod. "And I, Robin."

"Yes," Will said.

But Robin shook his head. "No. Tonight is our last in company. Tomorrow we must go our own way. Pack up your share. We eat and sleep. Will, you have the first watch."

Will and Allan both looked like they might argue further, but Little John stopped them with a sharp look and a shake of his head. He turned his attention back to the rabbits, and after a few moments, Will did the same. Allan took up his lute again, but he didn't sing, and the tune that he played was slow and somber.

They cooked and ate their meal in silence, and bedded down soon after. A chilling mist had risen in the wood and Robin pulled his blanket up around his neck, positioning himself as close to the fire as he dared.

The forest seemed unusually still this night. As he lay huddled in his blanket Robin heard no owls, no wolves; only the occasional pop of the fire and the slow settling of the coals. Robin knew that he had been right in what he said. After their escapes from the stocks, the others would be safer on their own rather than together. Godfrey wanted him. But he couldn't help thinking that the road to Nottingham would seem longer without his companions.

He stared at the dying flames and he waited for sleep to take him.

ROBIN WASN'T CERTAIN what had awakened him. Something off in the deep of the wood, perhaps. He had heard a nightjar close by, and then had noticed snoring. Will's snoring. Some watchman. He looked up through the branches to see if he could spot that bird, but there was nothing there.

Cursing Will's carelessness under his breath, he sat up and rubbed a hand over his face. The moon had risen, and that cold mist lingered around the camp. Will had not only neglected the watch, he'd also neglected the fire. It was damn cold.

He got up, grabbed a thick bough from the wood pile, and threw it onto the fire. Sparks flared, twisting upward into the darkness . . .

And illuminating the faces of six men standing in

a circle around Robin and the others. Startled, Robin shouted a warning, then leaped back just in time to avoid a sword blade as it whistled past his face.

Robin drew his sword just in time to block the man's next assault, their blades meeting with a loud clash. He heard the others shouting as well, heard swords drawn and the *whoosh* of Little John's stave as it carved through the night air. But he kept his eyes fixed on the man in front of him.

The man attacked again, their swords meeting once more and the two of them coming face to face. The man's gaze flicked toward something behind Robin and to the right. Robin pushed the man away, swung his sword back in a tight, quick arc, plunging it into the chest of a cutthroat who had snuck up behind him, and then pulled it free so that he could meet the next assault from the first attacker.

The man's eyes widened slightly and he backed away, giving Robin an opportunity to check quickly on his friends.

Little John was swinging his stave so fast that it was a humming blur in the moonlight. He hit one man in the ribs, the bones popping like the campfire, and then hit another in the skull. This man dropped to the ground and lay utterly still; Robin thought it likely that he was dead before he hit the forest floor.

Will and Allan fought back to back, their swords dancing and ringing against those of their foes. In moments, they had dispatched both men.

Before long, only the first swordsman and one last cutthroat remained standing. The men shared a look and then bounded away from the camp and through the wood like startled deer. Robin ran after them, his sword still in hand. He heard a bow thrum and saw an arrow bury itself in a tree just beside the first man. The men kept running, but Robin closed the distance quickly. The cutthroat looked back at him, fear in his eyes. Just as he did, he tripped a line Robin hadn't seen. Robin heard something that sounded like a tree falling. Leaves flew into the air and a crude gate of sharpened wooden spikes snapped up from where it had lain hidden on the ground.

A hunter's trap. The cutthroat couldn't stop in time. He ran into the gate at full speed, impaling his chest on the spikes with a sharp, liquid grunt, and then hanging from them like a string puppet.

Robin, with Will right behind him, continued on after the swordsman, but they soon lost sight of him among the trees. Robin slowed then stopped. Will halted next to him.

Robin spat another curse, and then he and Will walked back to the cutthroat. Robin would have liked to question the man, but just as they reached him, he gave one last gasp and was still, blood dripping down the spikes and trickling from his mouth.

Allan and Little John had stopped next to the man, too.

"Careful where you step," John said, admiring the trap.

Robin stared off through the trees, hoping against hope to catch a glimpse of the man he had been chasing. "One of them got away. He was on the road in France where Loxley died."

"They work for John?" Allan asked.

"No, not John," Robin said. "I saw his face at the dock when he realized that Richard was dead. He was more surprised than anybody."

Will looked from Little John to Robin. "Who else would benefit from Richard's death?"

"The French would benefit from Richard's death," Robin said. "No leader. No army. They can walk in."

"Robin, it can't be the French," Will said.

"Why's that, Will?"

Will had been staring at the ground, as if still thinking it through. But now he looked Robin in the eye. "The one you shot in the face," he said. "He's English."

He was right, of course; Robin was annoyed he hadn't realized this himself.

But that was beside the point. If the assassins weren't working for John, and they weren't agents of the French, who was he working for?

Robin and Little John shared a glance, the big man looking every bit as troubled as Robin felt.

CHAPTER

◦━❈━◦

ELEVEN

Daylight poured into the throne room of the White Tower through high arched windows, flooding the chamber. John sat upon his throne, resplendent in a robe of embroidered blue velvet, toying with an emerald necklace, and wearing the golden crown of England's kings. His mother, Eleanor, stood to the king's left, eschewing the throne beside him, and looking austere in a simple blue gown and white wimple. William Marshal stood before the throne dais looking every bit the warrior in his armor, his sword hanging from his belt, the white in his mane of hair illuminated by the sun, accenting his age. To the king's right sat Princess Isabella, looking lovely in a satin dress that shone like pearls. She said nothing, but watched the others with a wary eye.

Godfrey chose to do the same, at least for the moment. He stood in a shadowed recess to the side of the thrones where he could see and hear everything, but where the others were less likely to take notice of him. For now he would play the role of spider, and allow Eleanor and William to buzz around the king's head, harrying him. He was sure it wouldn't be long before they managed to get themselves tangled in John's pride and stubbornness and uncertainty. When they did, Godfrey would be ready.

Guards stood at attention on either side of the dais, a trio of Eleanor's ladies stood off to the side, as did the exchequer and other members of the Privy Council, who attended the king and hung on his every word, as bound to him as the dogs leashed and held by John's sentries.

"Richard's army is coming home," John said, still playing with the necklace, and sounding both bored and petulant. "To keep it together costs money. Marshal, you speak for the money."

"I do, Sire, and there's not much to speak of."

Marshal didn't flinch from the truth. Godfrey had to give him that. But the great knight was too used to serving men like Henry and Richard. The truth wouldn't get him far with John.

"But to disband the army," Marshal went on, "could cost more than to keep it."

Godfrey suppressed a smile, amused by what he saw on the king's face. John was as easy to read as a child. He heard the truth in what Marshal was telling him. Whatever else John might have been, he wasn't stupid. He had too much of his father in him to be oblivious to what was happening to the realm. But while he already knew much of what Marshal had told him, he didn't wish to admit as much, either to the knight or to himself. And he surely didn't want to acknowledge it in front of his mother.

Isabella, on the other hand, appeared puzzled by what Marshal had said, and unlike John's wife, the Countess of Gloucester, whom she had displaced, she had just enough nerve and confidence to inject herself into the conversation despite her ignorance.

"Pourquoi, Chancellor?" she asked. Why, Chancellor?

Godfrey could see that the question itself infuriated Eleanor, who had yet to accept this woman as a proper consort for her son. She glared at the girl, as if she might will her from the chamber with her eyes. William appeared to be just as offended by the presence of the French princess. His eyes flicked in her direction for an instant, but he refused to dignify her question by answering.

All of this Godfrey saw. All of it worked to his benefit. For he could see as well the resentment building in John's eyes: anger at his mother for not honoring his decision to throw Isabel aside and take this French princess as his wife; distrust of Marshal, who John believed remained more devoted to Eleanor and the memory of Richard than to the current occupant of the throne. Godfrey understood all of this, Marshal none of it; which was why the old knight didn't stand a chance.

"As Your Majesty understands," Marshal said, "it would put a rabble at loose in the kingdom looking for a paymaster. At the same time, your lands and castles over the water will look ripe for picking and your alliances for unpicking."

"And yet the cupboard is bare," John said, sounding bitter. And this, too, Godfrey understood. How much of England's treasure had been spent to fund Richard's ill-fated crusade and to ransom the Lionheart from Trifels?

Marshal, however, had yet to learn the mind of his new liege, and so stepped right into a snare of his own making. "King Richard's campaigns were costly," he said. "And the expected rewards, unfortunately—"

"What is that to me?" the king demanded, his ire suddenly bared. "My brother's troubles are over. You are *my* minister now, not his. And you tell me I am destitute."

Once more, Marshal appeared offended, even hurt. He had served two kings prior to John, and Godfrey would have wagered the worth of John's crown that neither man had ever spoken to Marshal in this way.

Right then, Marshal knew that he would have no influence with this king. Godfrey saw the realization hit him, smiled inwardly as the man seemed to sag. But still Godfrey waited. William Marshal was too resilient and wily a warrior to be dismissed so quickly. And at the moment, he was doing more to destroy himself than Godfrey could have done.

The king regarded Marshal archly. "So," he said, "taxation!"

"Taxation?" Eleanor repeated, disbelief in her rising voice. "Milking a dry udder gets you nothing but kicked off the milking stool."

"Mother, spare me your farmyard memories. You have none, and I don't understand them."

The princess grinned; Godfrey suppressed a laugh. He caught the young girl's eye and they shared a smile. Of all the people in this chamber, aside from the king, of course, she was likely to be the most valuable ally he could cultivate.

"Rebellion then," Eleanor said, clearly miffed at being spoken to so. "Do you understand that?"

John shot her a dark look. As before, he knew that

she was right, and didn't wish to admit it. If she continued this way, she would lose whatever sway she still held with her son. By the end of this day, Godfrey could be rid of his two most formidable rivals for the king's ear.

Marshal cleared his throat, drawing the king's gaze once more. "These are difficult times. They call for restraint on both sides of the ledger: taxing and spending. We can buy time, or rather borrow for it. I can send envoys to secure loans where they may. There's money chests from Sicily to Normandy if you know where to look."

And in that moment Godfrey saw the opening he had been waiting for.

He stepped forward, emerging from shadow into the warm light that angled through the fine haze of dust hanging in the throne room air.

"Cap in hand to moneylenders," he said, his voice dripping with contempt, his eyes fixed on Marshal. "Your master is a king."

King John smiled at this. He might even have nodded. Godfrey kept his attention on the old knight. Marshal bowed, as if acknowledging a blow from an opponent in a battle tournament, and stepped aside, leaving the floor in front of the king's throne to Godfrey.

"The Crown is owed money at home," John said. "The northern barons plead poverty, but that's always been the song of rich men. While King Richard took himself abroad for years to look after our Lord Jesus, Baldwin, Fitzrobert, Loxley, and the rest have looked after themselves. The king's tax collectors have been cheated, gulled, bribed, robbed, and sent on their way with piss-pots emptied from the battlements."

He looked at Godfrey expectantly. "So, what's to be done?"

John had led himself exactly where Godfrey had hoped he would go. Flies, all of them; and Godfrey the spider.

"Give me leave, Sire, to go north with a company of mounted men. I'll have merchants and landowners fill your coffers or their coffins."

Marshal looked scandalized. "Englishmen killing Englishmen?"

Godfrey glanced at him, but his response was directed at the king. "No man loyal to the Crown has anything to fear. But loyalty means paying your share in the defense of the realm."

John nodded, clearly pleased. "That's well said! Don't you think, Marshal? Mother?"

Eleanor gave her son a withering look. "Richard commanded loyalty not by threats but by example. It would take only a miracle for you to follow it—if you could live as a warrior saint like your brother."

John was out of his throne and down the steps of the dais almost before the last word had crossed her lips. Godfrey was certain that the king meant to strike his mother. Isabella gave a little gasp. Marshal took a quick step forward. One of Eleanor's ladies stifled a warning cry. Only Eleanor herself didn't move. She glared imperiously at her son, as he halted in front of her, breathing hard.

"Your sainted son was an imbecile," he said. "And you supported him in every folly from here to Jerusalem and back. You worshiped him while the warrior lost territories hard won by his father. You kissed his picture while England had to pay four years' revenue to ransom him when he was captured." John's gestures became more animated by the moment, and his voice grew louder with every word. "You are as much to blame as anyone for the wreckage which is my inheritance. You're in grief for a fantasy, Mother, and you're too wise not to know it."

Eleanor struck him across the cheek so hard that the sound of the blow echoed through the chamber and a spot of blood appeared on John's face. No one spoke. No one so much as took a breath. Isabella gaped at them both, her eyes flicking back and forth between mother and son. At last, John dabbed at the blood with the cuff of his sleeve. His movement seemed to break a spell. Eleanor turned away and walked briskly from the room. John watched her leave, a smile on lips.

"I broke her skin more than she did mine," he said, looking from Godfrey to Marshal. He stepped back onto the dais and lowered himself into his throne. "Now, Marshal," he said, his voice crisp, "you served my brother faithfully, and my father before him. I think you've spent enough time with my family, and no doubt would like to spend more with your own. Therefore, and with regret, I accept your resignation from all your offices and the cares of the state. Farewell."

Godfrey nearly laughed aloud at what he saw on Marshal's face. The man looked like he had been slapped, too, his eyes round, his cheeks ashen. To his credit, though, the old knight managed to keep his dignity. The king held out a hand. Marshal stared at it for a moment before pulling his signet ring from his finger and dropping it into the king's palm. He bowed deeply to the king and said, "Your Majesty," in a level voice that betrayed none of the emotion written so clearly on his face. Then he turned, and left the chamber, much as Eleanor had done moments before.

John turned to Godfrey. "How many men do you need?"

Godfrey schooled his features and faced his liege.

BY THE TIME he finally left the throne room, Godfrey had gotten from the king nearly everything he wanted. He had John's trust, he had been promised all the men he needed, and he had every confidence that the king would take to heart whatever counsel he offered. William Marshal had managed to discredit himself, and John's mother had completely alienated her son, leaving Godfrey as the king's sole adviser. Not a bad afternoon's work.

He walked down the corridor of the White Tower, feeling rather pleased with himself and confident that he had already completed the most difficult part of his plan. Even as he formed the thought, though, a figure stepped out of the shadows ahead of him and planted itself in the middle of the hallway. Godfrey slowed.

He recognized the man standing before him as Marshal, but he couldn't figure out what the old knight had in mind. He stood still, doing nothing, saying nothing, his back to Godfrey.

But as Godfrey resumed his pace, Marshal suddenly thrust his arms out to the sides, his fists clenched, his back fully exposed to Godfrey.

"Choose carefully, Godfrey, the spot where you would place your dagger."

Godfrey smirked. Such drama in a single gesture. The old man had much to learn about subtlety. Still, Godfrey couldn't deny that his blade hand itched just a bit. His work would be that much easier with Marshal dead rather than just cast aside. The old knight still had Eleanor's trust, and only a fool would have underestimated either the knight or the queen consort, much less the pair of them.

But he would not tip his hand by being impatient. This was neither the time nor the place for Marshal's murder. Godfrey stared at the man's back, imagining what it would feel like to pierce its center with the blade he carried, but he stepped past the man without slowing, or even glancing at his face.

Marshal called after him, "For I will choose carefully as well."

Godfrey didn't look back. He didn't break stride. But he did thrust out his arms in turn, showing the knight the full of his back, and making certain that Marshal could see the signet ring that now adorned his hand. *Take your best shot, old man*, he thought. *I fear neither you nor your blade.*

He returned to the quarters in which he had been staying and packed what few belongings he carried with him. Then he made his way down to the Tower kitchen and got himself a small bite to eat. By the time he finished and returned to the bailey, his tax collection force was already gathered. Fifty men, armed, mounted, and clothed in the uniforms of the king's guard, all waiting for his command. They didn't appear to be England's finest soldiers, but they would suit his purposes, as would the iron-plated wagon that would carry whatever revenue they collected. John might have been a naif and fool, but he was efficient. Or perhaps the efficiency of the Tower was an artifact from Richard's rule. That struck Godfrey as more likely.

Amused by the thought, he swung himself onto the back of his black charger and led the men out of the Tower grounds.

THE SUN STOOD balanced on its edge at the western horizon, huge and orange and ovate. The eastern sky was already growing dark, a few bright stars gleaming faintly in a vast field of indigo. And in between, directly over the man's head, the heavens had taken on hues of pale purple, the color of an uncertain future.

Small breakers rolled in off the channel, lapping at the pink sands of a beach that was deserted save for him. Gulls glided over the shoreline, crying plaintively, searching for one last catch that would tide them over until morning. Cormorants flew low over the channel swells, black as coal against the slate-colored waters.

The man wore a cloak about his shoulders, its hood drawn over his head. From where he watched, half-hidden, he could see the boats as they made their landing on the beach, but the men aboard couldn't see him.

There were at least half a dozen craft, all of them on sweeps, and they carved through the water in near silence. The soldiers on board wore helmets and armor, and carried lances that gleamed as if blood-stained in the dying light of the sun.

The craft scraped up onto the sand, the doors at their front fell open, and the men began to step off onto the shores of England. Two hundred strong, bristling with weaponry, moving quietly and in unison, they responded with alacrity to the barked commands of their leader: commands spoken in French.

In mere moments, it was over. The craft slid back

into the channel and moved away from the shore back toward France. The men formed up and began their march inland.

And the man, who had seen it all, returned to where his horse waited for him. Behind the saddle was a small box that held two carrier pigeons. The man began to compose his message.

CHAPTER

❧❦❧

TWELVE

Robin, Will, Allan, and Little John rode into Nottingham just as the sun was going down. After the attack on their camp the night before, they had decided to ride together a bit longer. They had shed their armor, no longer needing to pretend that they were knights. For much of the day, an odd tightness had been building in Robin's chest and his emotions had been roiled in ways he couldn't explain. Entering this town served only to make those feelings more intense.

There wasn't much to the place: low buildings of wood and stone and mortar, many of them with uneven roofs of shingle and thatch, men and women in simple, drab garb, returning home from the fields, some leading old work horses, others carrying buckets of water, or bundles of firewood for a cooking fire. He saw few smiles on their faces. These people were weary, not merely from a day's work, but from worrying their way through a hard winter.

And yet, despite the grimness of Nottingham, Robin couldn't help but feel that he belonged here, that he had come home in a way. He couldn't decide if this was merely because he carried Loxley's sword, or if there was some deeper connection at work. He looked around the small village, and for the first time since crossing the channel, he felt that he was truly back in England.

"Nottingham," Will said, as all four of them dismounted in the lane that ran through town. "Is this your people, Robin?"

Robin considered the question. "Maybe."

Will looked around, a frown on his young face. "They don't look like much, these middle-Englanders."

Little John grinned. "I hear you Welsh boys live on leeks and cohabit with sheep." The big man made a sound like a sheep bleating.

"Right!" Scarlet said, his face turning crimson. For a moment Robin thought he would actually take a swing at John.

Before he could, though, a voice that sounded very much like that of a cross parent said, "Hush!"

They all turned and saw a strange figure by the side of the lane. It looked to be a man, a rotund one at that. He was wrapped almost entirely in gauze, and he stood surrounded by small straw hives amidst a cloud of buzzing bees.

"You wouldn't want to annoy a beehive with your noise," the man said, tending to his skeps.

The four of them approached the man cautiously.

The man paused and looked them over. "Your swords wouldn't help you if you did, gentlemen!"

"You're the town beekeeper?" Robin asked, keeping a wary eye on the swarm.

"Bless you, no!" the man said. "The friar. Tuck is the name."

"Well, Friar Tuck, would you know where I might find Sir Walter today?"

"If he's not at Peper Harrow . . ." The friar pointed up a nearby hill at a home that appeared to be larger and sturdier than those in the town.

Robin stared up at the house, feeling once more that his presence here was more than coincidence, more than simply the result of a dying man's last wish.

"How long will your business take?" Will asked him.

Robin shrugged. "If you're gone, you're gone." He nodded to his companions, and then to the friar as well. "And God go with you."

Will, Allan, and John exchanged looks, all of them clearly surprised by the abruptness of Robin's farewell. They had journeyed together for miles, fought and killed side by side.

"That's it?" Will said. "After ten years?"

"Something's with him," Allan said.

"Aye," Little John agreed. "Changed him."

The others nodded. Then Allan turned to Tuck.

"Good friar, where can a man get moderately insensible with drink around here?"

"Allan!" Little John said, clearly scandalized. "He's a man of the cloth!"

But Tuck looked at them appraisingly, a sly grin on his face. "Have you tried the honey-liquor we call mead?" he asked. "It gives a man a halo, does mead."

* * *

WITH DAYLIGHT FAILING and the air turning cold, Robin rode through the gates of Peper Harrow. He had paused halfway between the village and Loxley's house to remove the Loxley family crest and wreath from the tabard he was wearing, the tabard that had belonged to Sir Robert. He was dressed once more in the garb of a simple soldier and he carried Loxley's sword sheathed in its scabbard and wrapped in the knight's belt.

As he passed through the gate, he saw a serving girl standing beside a huge brown and white dray. Her back was to Robin and she was holding one of the horse's hooves under her arm, digging away caked mud. She wore a simple blue dress and over it a sleeveless linen smock that was begrimed and loose-fitting. Still, Robin could tell that she was tall and willowy.

"Girl," Robin called.

She turned. Her face was dirty, and though she had tied a cloth over her head to keep her hair from her face, several long, auburn strands had fallen loose and hung over her brow. She swiped at them impatiently with a muddy hand.

"Are you the keeper of this house?" he asked.

She stared back at him brazenly, as if trying to decide whether he deserved an answer.

"In a manner of speaking, yes," she said at last, her voice deeper and stronger than he had expected.

He nodded once, looking around the courtyard. It was unkempt—more yard than court. "I wish to see Sir Walter Loxley," he told her.

"And you are?"

Robin looked at her again. Brazen indeed, for a servant. "Robin Longstride."

She raised an eyebrow. "Plain Robin Longstride? No 'Sir'?"

He smiled thinly. "No, ma'am. No 'Sir.'"

"Are you here about the tax?" she asked.

He held up Loxley's sword. "I return the property of his son Robert, who is dead."

The woman paled at that, and for a moment she stood utterly still, seemingly at a loss as to what to say. Then, "This way."

She wiped her hands on the smock and walked away, crossing through the center of the courtyard toward the house. Robin dismounted and led the white charger after her, still taking in his surroundings. Chickens clucked nearby, foraging in the mud and dirt, and dogs scrounged for scraps of food. The serving girl's shoes echoed through the yard, but otherwise she made not a sound, nor did she look back at him. He had questions for her, but all of them died on his tongue. She seemed deeply shaken by word of her master's death, and Robin thought it best to keep silent.

EVERY BREATH WAS too shallow and left her gasping for more air. Her heart labored in her breast; her throat felt tight, as if some taloned hand had taken hold of her and refused to let go.

I return the property of his son Robert, who is dead.

Walter had tried to warn her. He had told her that her husband was gone, that Robert himself had told him so. Marion had refused to believe him. But there could be no denying the word of this solemn stranger. Her husband was dead.

She led the man into the large hall of the house, kicked off her shoes just inside the door, and crossed to Margaret, who stood waiting for her holding a towel and a copper basin of water. Marion sat on the stool and the girl cleaned the mud and muck from her feet. When Margaret had finished, Marion began to towel them off.

"Maggie!" Walter called from another room. "Where is she?"

The maid glanced over at the stranger before looking up at Marion. "Ma'am, Sir Walter calls for you."

"Yes, Margaret, I hear him." Her voice sounded shaky to her own ears. "Tell him we have a guest."

Margaret hurried away. Marion stood and stepped into the braided slippers the girl had left for her. Then she pulled on a house coat that, though old and worn, was a far sight better than the smock she had been wearing. Feeling more herself, her emotions under control at least for the moment, she turned once more to the stranger—this Robin Longstride—who now regarded her with a mix of shock and chagrin that might have been comical under other circumstances.

"I am Marion Loxley, wife of Robert," she said. "I thank you for taking the time to deliver the news here."

The man opened and closed his mouth several times before finally managing to say, "M'Lady, I owe you an apology. If I had known—"

"Bad news is bad news," Marion said. "There's no joy or comfort in how it comes." She hesitated. "Did you serve alongside my husband?"

"Yes."

"Did he die proudly?" she asked, surprised at the ease with which she could speak those words.

"Killed in an ambush, ma'am." He said this as if it were routine, as if he spoke of such things all the time.

For all she knew, he did. "He was the man chosen to return King Richard's crown."

It took a moment for those words to sink in. King Richard was dead, too. It seemed too high a price, even for a king's crusade. "I am glad for him," she said at last, feeling that Longstride expected her to say something. The man chosen to return the dead king's crown . . . Was this how soldiers honored one another?

"Marion, who's here?" Walter called.

"A traveler, Walter," she called back. She met the stranger's gaze. "This news will be very hard on him," she said quickly, keeping her voice low. "Do you understand?"

"Well, bring him in!" the old man said.

"Yes, yes . . ." she answered. She turned back to Longstride. "Tell him Robert is in Jerusalem and sends his love and will return soon."

"I am here to return the sword," the man said. "I do not need to say anything else."

Damn him and his soldiers' creed! "No! Let Walter see out his days thinking his son loves him and yearns to see him again."

Before the stranger could respond, Walter appeared in the doorway, leaning on his staff, a smile on his wizened face. Somehow, despite his blindness, he turned directly toward her, a gentle rebuke in his expression.

"Marion, our traveler will be thirsty. Travelers are always thirsty." He turned unerringly to face the soldier. "Is that not so? . . . Your name, sir?"

"Longstride. Robin Longstride."

Walter's smile faltered at the sound of the name, and

he seemed to grip his staff more tightly. "Do you mock me?" he asked, his voice dropping to a whisper.

Marion looked back and forth between the two men. She didn't understand what was happening, but she was now even more wary of the stranger than she had been a moment before.

She could see, though, that Longstride had no more idea of what Walter meant than she did. The soldier appeared to be taken aback at the old man's reaction.

"Sir?" he said.

Walter looked more frightened than she had ever seen him. "Are you here to exact revenge?"

Longstride frowned, but then appeared to remember his purpose in coming. "Your son asked me to return this sword to you."

The old man blinked, realization crashing over him. He slowly held out a shaking hand. The soldier placed the sword in Walter's hand, but before he could release it, Walter placed his hands over Longstride's, holding them there for a moment. The soldier gazed down at their hands, and then looked up into the man's face, recognition in his pale eyes.

In the next moment, Walter moved his hands, running them over the pommel and hilt of the weapon.

"How does Robert defend himself if he has no sword?" the old man said. "The prodigal son will not return after all?"

Longstride said nothing.

"No tears or forgiveness from his father," Walter went on quietly. "No amends to be made."

Marion felt a tear run down her cheek, her chest tight once more.

"Did you see him die?" Walter asked the man.

"I was with him as he passed," Longstride said. "His last words were for the love and bond between a father and son."

"Forgive my rudeness. My grief has been waiting for this day." Walter put down the sword. "Come, so that I may see you."

Walter reached out for the man's face. At first, Longstride flinched, clearly uncomfortable with being "seen" this way. But after that initial reluctance, he held himself still and allowed Walter's fingers to travel lightly over his strong features. For his part, Walter seemed almost to recognize something in the feel of the man's face. His fingers lingered longer over Longstride's eyes and brow and nose, than they had with others Marion had seen him "look" at.

"Robin Longstride," Walter said, his voice low again. "A common enough, but noble Saxon name. So, you will dine with us." He stepped back and wrinkled his nose, winking at Marion as he did. "But first you must bathe, sir. You stink."

LOXLEY'S WIDOW LED Robin to a bathing chamber near the back of the house. It was a small room, the walls paneled with dark wood. A candle burned near a copper tub newly filled with steaming water. As Robin followed Marion into the room, another maid was placing towels near the tub. That done, she slipped out the door, leaving Robin and Marion alone. Marion dipped a hand in the tub, testing the water.

"I have laid out some of my husband's clothes. I hope you don't find that too disconcerting."

Robin thought it best not to tell her that her

husband's clothes and armor had won him passage across the channel and an audience with the new king and Eleanor of Aquitaine.

When he didn't answer, Marion started to leave.

"My lady," Robin said, stopping her. "I cannot remove this chain mail by myself. I will need help."

"Jane!" Marion called. "Madge!"

She waited several moments, but no answer came. Appearing to steel herself, Marion helped Robin pull off his tabard. Then she began to unlace his coat of mail. Robin became very conscious of just how near she was to him, of the light touch of her fingers through the mail. He also recalled what the old man had said. *You stink.* He felt his face shading to red and he kept himself from looking back at her. He bent over while she helped him pull the mail over his head and then straightened once it was off.

Her gaze strayed to his chest and arms, lingering on his many scars.

"Thank you," Robin said.

Her eyes met his briefly, and then she left the chamber.

As much as Robin welcomed the feel of hot water on his filthy and travel-weary body, he did not tarry in the bath. He got himself clean, dried off, and donned Sir Robert's clothes. Leaving the chamber, he made his way back to the main hall of the Loxley home. A fire blazed brightly in a large stone hearth, and candles burned in two large, circular chandeliers and in candelabras standing throughout the room. Straw covered the floor. Several dogs lay near the hearth, gnawing on bones.

Sir Walter was already seated at the head of a long wooden table near the hearth. Marion, dressed now in a light blue dress, laced at the front, was placing a large bowl of stew on the table as Robin walked in. She looked up at him, before quickly turning her attention back to the food.

In addition to the stew, the table was laden with cheese, wine, and bread. It was basic fare—noble families in England ate this way every night. But Robin couldn't remember the last time he'd had such a meal, and after Walter spoke a short prayer of thanks, they all began to eat. Robin was ravenous and for a long time he simply ate. At one point, Marion got up and left the hall, saying something about getting more cheese.

Walter, meanwhile, had stopped eating and was holding Loxley's sword, once again running his hands over the hilt and the scabbard.

"You have taken a long road to bring this to me," he said. "I cannot decide whether that makes you trustworthy . . ."

". . . Or manipulative?" Marion finished for him, reappearing in the doorway bearing a plate.

"Marion!" Walter said, turning toward her as she returned to the table with a rustle of cloth and set the plate near Robin. "I am merely trying to gauge the quality of the man we have as our guest. Is he handsome?"

Marion opened her mouth, closed it again, her cheeks turning bright red. Clearly this was the last thing she had expected the old man to ask.

"In the way that yeoman sometimes are," she said. "When they're sober."

Sir Walter turned back to Robin. "Entertain us with the tale of your life. We don't get many visitors anymore, except tax collectors and beggars."

"I don't know where I am from," Robin told the man. "Only where I've been."

The old man wouldn't be put off. "I am starving for news of the outside world."

Remembering his encounter with the knight on the White Tower dock, Robin said, "William Marshal sends you a message."

Walter laughed in a way that made Robin think that he wasn't at all surprised by this, that he might even already know what Marshal had told Robin to say. "Marshal, eh? What does the old wolf have to say for himself?"

"He said to look for him on Spring's first black night."

"He calls a meeting?" Walter nodded slowly. "It has been too long. I look forward to that." He paused, absently running his hands over the sword again. "Marion, what color are his eyes?"

Marion didn't bother looking up from her plate. "I don't know yet."

"I have a proposal for you, young man," Walter went on, as if he hadn't heard. "You brought me this sword, which has great meaning. Give me your time." He held up the weapon. "It is yours."

Robin considered this. It was a fine weapon, but in the end, that wasn't why he agreed. He still felt the pull of this place, and he didn't know why. He would honor Walter's request, but he would remain for his own purposes.

"I could stay a day or more," he said. "There is a question I'd like to ask."

Walter smiled, apparently not surprised by this, either. "What is your question?"

"The words on the hilt of the sword. What do they relate to?"

The old man's smile deepened and turned sly, as if they were gaming and Walter had just made a wager he knew he would win. "I think I have much I can tell you," he said. "About history. About your history."

Robin narrowed his eyes. "That is very generous of you, sir."

Walter shrugged. "Perhaps. You have not heard the other half of the contract yet. I want you to stay in Nottingham." He looked toward Marion, perhaps sensing that she was listening closely to all they said. "And for the time being become my returned son and therefore Marion's spouse." He grinned.

She scowled at the man. "To what end, Walter? You have had too much to drink." She reached forward and took the wineglass from the old man's hand.

Robin thought she might say more, but Sir Walter raised his hand, silencing her.

"Now, in reality, woman, we both know that without a husband you will lose this land when I die. Do you dispute that?"

Marion's mouth twisted sourly. "No," she conceded.

"If I say this is my son, he will be seen as that, and, so, as your husband." He turned back to Robin, and once more Robin was amazed at how this blind old man always seemed to know exactly where everyone was. "It is a fair contract," the old man said. "It is not as if I expected you to have children." Once more he grinned, clearly enjoying himself greatly.

This time Robin felt himself blushing; he didn't look for Marion's response. He thought he could imagine it.

Walter continued to eye him expectantly. "The sword for your time, Longstride. Are you in agreement?"

The three of them sat in silence for several moments. Finally, Robin said, "Yes," in a low voice.

Walter smiled.

"Marion," he said. "Go and tell the staff that my son has arrived and our home is whole again. Let them ring the church bells in celebration." He sat back, looking immensely pleased with himself, and held out a hand. "More wine, please."

Marion looked decidedly less happy, but she gave the wineglass back to him. She glanced briefly at Robin, stood, and left the hall.

CHAPTER

❦

THIRTEEN

Tuck liked these men who had just come to Nottingham. The little one with the red hair—Scarlet—always had something amusing to say, often at the expense of the enormous Little John. The other lad, Allan something, was awfully quiet, but seemed a good sort. He played the lute well and had a passable singing voice.

Little John, though, was a kindred soul. Of that, Tuck was already certain. The man appreciated all the things Tuck himself knew to be most important in this earthly life: good food, fine drink, large women. That they had already become fast friends came as no surprise to the friar.

All three men had a great thirst, as did Tuck, of course. So after allowing them to sample as much of his precious golden mead as he could bear, Tuck decided that they needed to be introduced to the Bait and Trap.

The tavern was warm inside, and the air smelled strongly of roasting meat and musty ale, of pipe smoke and sweat. A fire burned in the hearth at the center of the back wall, and candles glowed in sconces all around the inn and in a ponderous old chandelier that hung from the groaning beams of the ceiling. There were tables and chairs around the perimeter of the great room, but much of the floor had been cleared of furniture and was now crowded with dancers and musicians.

Allan and Will looked at each other, their faces like those of little boys on Christmas morning. Then, without a glance at John or the friar, they rushed forward and were swallowed by the crowd. Little John drank down the rest of his mead and placed the stone jar by the door.

"Come on!" he said, clapping a hand on Tuck's back and leading him over to the bar. "I'm still thirsty."

They bought ales. Or rather, Tuck bought ales for them. Little John tried to explain that some kind of strange small animals had stolen all the gold he and his friends had, but with the noise and the music and the effects of the mead, the friar had a hard time understanding all that the big man said. Not that it mattered in the end. These were his friends, and by the grace of God he had coin to share.

In a short time, Tuck and John were seated at a table at one end of the Bait and Trap, ales before them, good conversation between them. At the other end of the tavern, Allan had pulled out his lute, and had joined with a pair of local musicians to form a trio that drew the attention of many of the dancers, including several young women. While Allan and the others played, Will stepped a lively jig, capering from one woman to the next, dancing with none of them and all of them, much to the amusement of everyone else in the bar.

A new keg was brought out from the back, and a loud cheer went up from everyone on the floor. Tuck hoped that Will, Allan, and John were the only ones expecting him to pay their way this evening. God hadn't graced him with enough coin for all.

When he grew tired of dancing, Will joined Allan and the other musicians on a makeshift stage and lent his voice to the boisterous singing. Other players joined in, until the music was deafening.

John and Tuck continued their conversation, periodically waving the serving girls over for more ale. The friar couldn't remember the last time he'd had so much, and in fact, he couldn't quite remember how much they'd had this evening. A lot. He was sure of that.

Sipping the latest selection the girls had brought to him, the friar smacked his lips and nodded toward his cup.

"Home brew," he said. "If I wasn't the village priest I'd try for village drunkard."

ON THE OTHER side of the inn, Allan and Will had positioned themselves at the edge of the stage. The rest of the musicians were off drinking, and so Will and Allan were drinking, too. It seemed only fair. Allan continued to play his lute, but Will was surveying the room, eyeing the women, several of whom stood in a cluster nearby, eyeing Will and Allan.

LITTLE JOHN HAD lost interest in their conversation and was trading looks with a large woman who stood nearby, sipping an ale and regarding the big man coyly over the rim of her cup.

"Right," John said. "She looks like my size. I'll put a smile on her face."

Tuck frowned, discomfited by the turn the evening seemed to be taking. He was, after all, a man of the cloth.

"So," he began, hoping to change the subject, "Why do they call you Little John?"

The man swiveled sharply in his chair, his eyebrows furrowing menacingly. "What are you getting at?" he demanded.

Tuck's eyes widened. "What?" he asked innocently.

John stood, nearly toppling his chair, walked over to the girl, and danced her away.

WILL AND ALLAN were still watching the girls who had been watching them, but they hadn't made much progress in actually speaking to them. It should have been easy—they were practically the only men in the Bait and Trap. But somehow they had yet to get up their nerve.

Will tried to give Allan some pointers, though he was slow to follow his own advice.

"The secret of success," he said, "is never go for the prettiest one. Start with the homely one on the left."

Allan looked up from his lute again, nodding sagely. "Right," he said. "Which one is that?"

Will frowned at him, and they continued to stand there, watching the girls watch them. The group of girls was smaller now, though. Several of them had given up on these two and moved on.

"The main thing is," Allan said, now dispensing

advice himself, "you mustn't frighten them off. Village maidens are shy . . ."

ROBIN SAT NEAR the fireplace in the Loxley home, enjoying its warmth, watching as serving girls cleared the plates and what was left of the evening meal from the table. Sir Walter had long since bade Robin good night and, with Marion leading him back to his chamber, had gone off to bed. The dogs still lay on the floor nearby, as if unwilling to let him out of their sight.

It had been a strange night, and he stared into the fire burning in the hearth, puzzling over the bargain he had made with Loxley's father. Of course, Robin understood that the old man didn't wish to see the Crown or its agents taking this house away from Marion when he died. And he supposed that would be reason enough for Sir Walter to chance this charade he had proposed. But Robin sensed that there was more at work here than that. Walter had recognized his name, though Robin didn't know how that was possible. The old man had appeared genuinely frightened of him at first. What was it he had asked? *Are you here to exact revenge?*

Later, once Walter had convinced himself that Robin meant him no harm, he had hinted again at knowing more about Robin's past than the archer did himself. He had offered to teach Robin something of his own history.

And Loxley seemed to take great pleasure in teasing Marion with suggestions of romance between her and Robin. Were these merely the eccentricities of an old man, or confused emotions brought on by grief and the shock of bad tidings? Or was there more to Walter's teasing and riddles?

Loxley might have looked old, but his mind seemed sharp enough. There was purpose in all of this, though what it was Robin couldn't fathom.

Marion reentered the hall, hesitating briefly at the sight of him sitting in his chair, and then continuing over to the table. The dogs raised their heads and followed her with their dark eyes. She examined the table, appeared satisfied that it had been tended properly, and wandered back toward where Robin sat, now watching her.

He wasn't sure he understood her, either. Sir Robert had been dead for days, but as far as Marion was concerned, she had lost him this very afternoon. Robin could see the sadness in her eyes; he recalled how deeply she had been moved by news of the knight's death earlier in the day, though he hadn't known then who she was.

Yet the only tears he had seen in her eyes, she had shed not for her own loss, but for Sir Walter's. It almost seemed that she cared more for her husband's father, than for her husband. Perhaps that was what happened when a knight left his home and love for ten years.

He couldn't deny that she was an attractive woman. Not merely pretty like a barmaid or a country maiden; hers was an unconventional beauty. High cheekbones, waves of auburn hair, eyes that were strikingly blue and that seemed to miss nothing of what happened around her. There was both grace and strength in her body. She appeared to be as comfortable cleaning the muck from a dray's hoof as she was hosting dinner for a stranger.

And though she clearly hadn't been happy about the deal Walter had made with Robin, she hadn't refused, either. Was she merely pragmatic, or did she have her own purpose in playing along?

Too many mysteries. Robin wondered if he wouldn't be better off leaving Peper Harrow now, while he still had the chance. But he didn't rise from the chair. Curiosity held him there; the promise of learning more about his past, about his family, about the odd twists and hints of fate that had led him from King Richard's army to the warm glow of this fire, and the company of this mysterious and handsome woman.

"Walter says we're to share my chambers," she said, after a lengthy silence.

The fire popped, startling the dog nearest the hearth.

Robin didn't answer her.

"It is merely a ruse to convince the servants," she added, her tone businesslike.

Robin allowed himself a small smile. "If the aim is deception, you should address me as 'husband,' or 'my dear.' "

She scowled at him. "Don't be ridiculous." She turned, starting toward the stairs. "Let us retire now."

He didn't move. "Ask me nicely."

Without turning or pausing, Marion started up the stairs. Robin thought she would ignore him entirely, but as she climbed the steps she said in a low voice, "Please, husband, will you join me in our chambers?"

Robin pushed himself out of the chair, crossed to the stairway, and started up after her. The dogs loped along with him.

Reaching the top of the stairway, Robin and the dogs followed Marion down a narrow corridor and into her bedchamber. It was a modest room but it felt warm and comfortable. A fire had been lit in the small hearth, and a few candles burned beside the bed.

Marion closed the door and turned to face him, her expression severe. "I sleep with a dagger," she said, glowering at him. "If you so much as move to touch me I will sever your manhood. Understood?"

Robin's eyebrows went up. "Thanks for the warning."

She gestured toward a large cushion next to the hearth. Clearly this was usually intended for the dogs, but there could be no mistaking her intent. For tonight—and no doubt all the nights to follow—this was to be his bed.

Without so much as a "goodnight" she pulled closed the curtains that surrounded her bed. Robin stood where he was, watching her. She blew out the candles around her one by one, until the only light in the chamber came from the fire in the hearth.

With the candles out, Robin couldn't see past the curtains, but he heard a rustle of cloth, and imagined that Marion must be removing her dress. A thought came unbidden: It had been a long, long time since last he had lain with a woman.

Robin stepped to the hearth, sat down on the bedding and started to pull off his boots. One of the dogs trotted over to him and lay down beside him, taking up more than its fair share of the cushion. Robin couldn't help laughing. It surely wasn't the companionship he would have preferred, but it would have to do for this night.

CHAPTER

FOURTEEN

S ir Godfrey walked quietly through the camp, stepping past smoldering cooking fires and small tents and sleeping men bundled in woolen blankets. Sinuous clouds of silver gray smoke drifted among the trees of the forest like wraiths. At the edge of the encampment horses stomped and snorted, their breath steaming in the cold night air.

In one hand, Godfrey carried a leather sack filled with wine that sloshed invitingly within. In the other, he held a lantern that appeared haloed in the fine mist.

They had come a good distance from London; as far as they needed to, though, of course, his men didn't know this. He knew that Adhemar and the others were nearby, that they were watching already, waiting.

Godfrey approached the two sentries standing at the edge of the camp. They were young men; both of them looked cold and tired. They did their best to stand at attention as he approached, but they shifted from foot to foot, trying to keep warm.

"Sir," one of the men said as Godfrey drew near.

He handed the man the sack of wine and smiled disarmingly. "Turn in for an hour," he said. "It's nearly dawn. I will keep the watch."

The two guards looked at the wine and then at their commander, gratitude written on their faces. They nodded their thanks, and headed back into the center of the camp, eager to be off their feet and to warm themselves with a bit of drink.

Godfrey watched them go until they were out of sight. Then he continued deeper into the forest, away from the camp. After a time, he could no longer hear his men; the only sounds that reached him were the call of a distant owl and a wolf's howl. But he knew he wasn't alone. He halted, held up the lantern and covered its light, uncovered it, covered it again, so that it flashed in the darkness. Lowering it again, he waited. It didn't take long.

Two hundred of them rode toward him, their armor and their horses dark, so that they emerged from the forest shadows as if conjured by magic. Their mounts moved in near silence, their swords and pikes were tied down or wrapped in cloth, so that they didn't rattle and clink. The hooves of their horses, he saw, had been covered in sacking. Like creatures of the night, they came forward and then halted before Godfrey, regarding him with cool indifference. These were hard men, soldiers he would be pleased to command and call his own. They were capable and efficient. One needed only to look at them, to witness their approach, to understand this.

Thinking of the fifty men he had left at his camp, Godfrey remembered what King Philip had said to him back in France. *England under your friend John is a country with no fighting spirit. I can take London with an army of cooks.*

The soldiers John had given him were useless— poorly trained, lazy, undisciplined. And these French before him were hardly cooks.

Adhemar rode forward, separating himself from his force. Dismounting, he stood before Godfrey and shook his hand. He was somewhat taller than Godfrey, with dark hair and a matching beard, and he carried himself with the confidence of a commander who had led his men to victory time and again. He would make a formidable ally.

"Comment allez vous, mon ami?" he asked. How are you, my friend?

"They have drunk well," Godfrey told him. "They sleep well, and they await you."

Adhemar nodded once and turned back to his men. He spoke his orders quietly and in French, and the men in front passed the commands back along their lines, one man whispering to the next. They dismounted, a soft murmur of leather and cloth, and began to untie their weapons.

When they were ready, Godfrey led them back toward the camp where his men slumbered, their bellies filled with wine, their weapons lying uselessly by their sides. Adhemar's men moved with such stealth that Godfrey glanced back over his shoulder repeatedly to make sure they were still with him. They always were.

Reaching the edge of the encampment, he and Adhemar halted and waved fifty of the French soldiers past them. Their swords in hand, the men spread through the camp, stepping over and around the sleeping Englishmen. A few of the horses grew restless, but none of Godfrey's men stirred. Within a few moments, fifty French legionnaires stood over fifty sleeping English soldiers, their swords held over the men, so that the tips hovered above their chests and necks and backs. The Frenchmen kept their eyes fixed on Godfrey, waiting for his command.

Godfrey raised his hand, thumb pointed down, and made a swift downward gesture.

As one, the legionnaires stabbed downward, the whisper of steel blending with soft grunts and the sudden exhalation of fifty dying breaths.

It occurred to Godfrey that he had never seen so many men killed so quietly. A formidable ally indeed.

HE HAD FOLLOWED from the beach, keeping at a safe distance, watching as the French army wended its way through the English countryside and into the forests outside of London. He had kept to the shadows as they crept through this wood, waited with them for the signal that summoned them toward the English camp, and listened as Sir Godfrey, the new king's most trusted man, greeted the French commander as a friend.

And now, his fists clenched, his stomach knotting itself like wet rope, he had watched, helpless, horrified, as they slaughtered fifty English soldiers in their sleep. He wanted to fight them, he wanted to run them through until his sword was stained crimson and dripped blood on the forest floor. Most of all, he wanted to squeeze the life out of the traitor Godfrey with his bare hands.

Instead, he slipped away, making not a sound, and returned to where he had tethered his horse. The pigeon box was still tied behind his saddle. He had another message to send back to London.

ROBIN AWOKE THE following morning to find that Marion was already up and gone from the chamber. She had even taken the dogs. He pulled on his boots, ran a hand through his hair, and left the room in search of Sir Walter and perhaps a bite to eat.

He descended the stairs to the great hall. Sunlight streamed through the windows and a fire burned low in the hearth. Walter sat at the head of the table, eating boiled eggs and ham, and occasionally tossing a scrap of meat to the dog lying beside his chair. He hummed to himself, clearly still enjoying the fine mood that had carried him off to bed the previous night.

Walter turned his head at the sound of Robin's footsteps on the floor of the hall.

"I hear a man's step. Good morning, my son."

Robin faltered. He understood the need to maintain this pretense for the servants and those outside the Loxley home, but aside from the hound at Walter's feet, they were alone.

"Good morning, Sir Walter," Robin said.

Walter turned in his chair. "Father," he corrected.

Robin took a breath. "Father," he repeated dutifully.

The old man clapped his hands together, looking delighted.

Robin stepped quickly to the table and leaned on it, so that he stood over the old man. "What is it of my history that you know?" he asked, unable to keep the impatience from his voice. He didn't know how much of this dissembling he could endure. He had no desire to wait days upon days to learn what Walter knew.

But the old man gave a small shake of his head. "Patience. You must show yourself today." He gestured toward Sir Robert's weapon which lay upon the table. "Wear your sword." Walter turned toward the stairway again and bellowed "Marion!"

"I am here, Walter," she said, appearing at the base of the stairs. She wore a linen long-sleeve bodice, a brown riding skirt, and boots. Clearly, she already knew that Walter wanted them to spend the day out in the village. She didn't come join them at the table, or offer any sort of greeting to Robin. She simply pulled on her riding gloves, clearly annoyed, and in a temper as sour as Walter's was sweet.

"Reacquaint your husband with his village and his people," the old man said.

Marion regarded Robin coolly. He was wearing the clothes he first put on the night before. Robert's clothes—his breeches, the finely embroidered shirt, and an open, collared jacket. Without comment, she walked to the door leading outside.

"I'll see to the horses," she said.

Robin watched her go. Turning back to Walter, he saw the old man gesture for him to come closer.

"I feel invigorated," the old man said, sharing a confidence. "I woke this morning with a tumescent glow." He pointed to himself. "Eighty-four. A miracle."

Robin straightened, unsure of exactly what he ought to say in response to this.

Marion appeared in the doorway once more, shaking her head and muttering, "I have always wondered at the private conversations of men." Then, more sharply, "Husband!"

She left the house again, and Robin followed reluctantly, unsure of whether he preferred to spend the day with his "wife" or the old man. Stepping out into the bright sun of Peper Harrow's courtyard, he saw his white charger standing next to a handsome black horse he assumed was Marion's.

Marion mounted smoothly and appeared to be just as comfortable sitting a horse as she had been cleaning a dray's hoof, or hosting a stranger at her supper table. The more Robin saw of Robert Loxley's wife, the more impressed he was. She didn't wait for him, but steered her mount toward the gate and the lane leading down into Nottingham. Robin swung himself onto the charger and rode after her, pulling abreast of her just as they cleared the gate and started down the road. She still said nothing to him, and for the moment Robin held his tongue as well. From the perspective of the hill on which Peper Harrow was perched, the town of Nottingham looked smaller than it had the day before. The fields surrounding the town appeared green enough, as if they should have yielded healthy crops, but several of the plots remained uncultivated.

The town itself looked as though it once had been prosperous—its buildings were well-constructed, the road leading to and from the village gates was relatively broad and well-traveled. But like the fields, the town seemed to have suffered as of late. Prosperity was but a memory now. Hard times had come and stayed.

Robin glanced at Marion and found that she was watching him, as if gauging his responses to what he saw. She faced forward again, maintaining her silence. He looked beyond the fields to the vast forest looming at their edge, its shadows seeming to swallow the morning light.

"What wood is that?" he asked, pointing.

"That is Sherwood Forest."

"Sherwood," he repeated in a whisper. The name stirred his memory, though he couldn't say why.

They continued down the hill into Nottingham and steered their horses to the center of the small village.

As they did, Robin spotted three familiar forms in the street, walking gingerly and squinting hard at the morning light. None of them showed any sign of being able to walk a straight line, or, for that matter, to clothe himself properly. Will Scarlet carried his boots and shirt. Allan A'Dayle's shirt was on, barely, but he seemed to be holding up his breeches with one hand and carrying his lute with the other. And Little John seemed to be wearing everything backward, or at least sideways. Taken together, they made quite a sight. A moment later several girls emerged from a nearby building, their clothes nearly as disheveled as those of Robin's friends. As soon as they spotted Marion, however, they retreated back inside.

John made his way over to a horse trough and began to splash water over his head and face. The others paused to wait for him.

Chuckling at the sight, Robin started toward them. "You still here?" he said. "I thought I'd seen the back of you." He glanced at Marion, who had followed. "My men at arms. This is about as courtly as they get. Will Scarlet, Allan A'Dayle, and Little John."

John waved at her from the trough. Will and Allan sketched bows.

Marion looked them over. Robin expected her to be scandalized, to refuse even to acknowledge them, but she surprised him.

She nodded to the men, an ironic smile on her lips. "I trust you had . . . an historic evening."

"Gentlemen," Robin said. "Lady Marion Loxley." He paused, but only for a moment. "My wife."

Will dropped his boots. Allan nearly dropped his breeches. Little John straightened and walked back to where the others stood. They exchanged looks and then turned as one toward Marion, and regarded her for several moments.

She endured their stares as best she could, though after a few seconds her gaze began to flick toward Robin, as if she was hoping he would make them stop looking at her.

"A little rash perhaps," Will said at last, out of the side of his mouth. "But well played, Robin."

Robin raised his eyebrows at the three of them. Taking his hint, they bowed to Marion and offered greetings.

"G'day, ma'am."

"How do you do?"

"Pleasure to make your acquaintance."

Robin cleared his throat. "Also, it may be best to address me as Robert." When the three of them looked his way again, skepticism on their faces, he added, "For the time being."

"Really?" Will said.

Little John nodded solemnly, clearly suppressing a smile. "Right you are, Robin!"

Allan bowed deeply to him. "Sir Bob . . ."

Following his lead, Will and Little John began to bow as well, and soon the three of them were practically falling over one another trying to see who could bow the lowest and grovel the best.

"That's the way," Robin said, grinning at them.

As he and Marion turned their horses to continue through the town, Robin could tell that Marion was trying to keep herself from laughing. He also had the sense that she liked the boys, and again, this surprised him.

For his part, Robin realized that he was relieved and pleased that Will, Allan, and Little John hadn't left Nottingham. He liked having them around, and since it now seemed that he would be living in this town for some time, he felt better knowing that he had allies here.

Just a bit farther up the lane, past scrabbling chickens and pigs rooting through dirt and rotten leaves, Marion and Robin came to a cluster of villagers who, it soon became apparent, had been waiting for a chance to welcome "Robert Loxley" back to his home. They called greetings and bowed to Robin, their hands clasped, their knuckles held to their foreheads. Robin felt himself growing vaguely uncomfortable. He could accept having to pretend to be Loxley in front of the house servants and townspeople. But pretending that he deserved their obeisance in this way—he had to resist the urge to jump off his horse and pull them up off their knees.

"This is rare respect for a foot soldier," he muttered so that only Marion could hear.

"Then bear yourself like a knight, sir," she said, an edge to her voice. "Your people look to you."

"My people . . ." Robin looked at the townsfolk

a second time. They weren't groveling out of fear; in fact, they seemed genuinely pleased to have their lord back in Nottingham. *My people* . . . He sat a little straighter in his saddle, and he belatedly acknowledged the greetings they offered. He didn't put on airs, or act superior as he had seen some nobles do. But he nodded to them, the way an army commander might answer the shouted greetings of his men.

Marion nodded her approval and actually graced him with a smile. "Like that," she said quietly. She eyed a white-haired woman and her husband, standing slightly apart from the others. These two bowed as well, but they eyed Robin keenly, their brows furrowed. "Now even the older folk who remember Robert—"

"They know something's amiss here . . ." Robin said, watching the couple as well.

"Sir Walter is their lord," Marion said, her voice still lowered, but her tone firm. "I am their ladyship. And you are Robert returned if we say so and act so."

As if to prove her point, another gentleman, even older than the two who had been watching Robin, stepped forward and saluted him, standing as straight as his old body would allow.

"Sir Robert!" he called. "You remember me! Tom Chamberlain—the pig man!"

Robin smiled at the gentleman. "And you don't look a day older, Tom!"

Marion glanced at Robin quickly, surprise and approval in her expression. He smiled back.

They rode on slowly, waving, smiling, nodding, accepting greetings and offering some of their own. This all felt strange to him, but he could see now that he didn't have to be false to himself in order to "be" Loxley, and perhaps he couldn't ask for more than that on his first day in Nottingham.

Riding around a bend in the lane, Robin and Marion came to what Robin guessed was Nottingham's tithe barn. Most every town in England had one; the bishops of York had to have their grain, just as the realm's kings demanded their gold. The heavyset friar Robin and his companions had encountered the day before stood outside the barn beside a wagon that had been loaded with grain. Nearby, eight guards and their horses waited to escort the wagon northward. All of them wore the bright red and white livery of York's bishop, and looked every bit as competent as any soldier of the realm.

"Friar Tuck is new here," Marion told him, indicating the priest. "You will be Robert for sure."

Tuck looked over at them as they approached and raised a hand in greeting. If Robin hadn't known better he would have sworn that the good friar looked every bit as hungover as Will, Allan, and Little John had been. His eyes were red, and though he favored Marion with a smile that appeared genuine, it obviously took a great effort.

He stepped forward to meet them. "Ahh, Marion. Good word travels from Peper Harrow this morning." He turned his gaze to Robin. "Sir Robert, you should have made yourself known when we met in the fields. Welcome home."

Before Robin could reply, a second wagon rolled out of the tithe barn. It, too, was loaded with grain. A deacon of the church followed it out into the sunlight, a ledger in his hand. He took little notice of Robin and Marion.

"Yes," Robin said, acknowledging Tuck's greeting. "Forgive me, Friar. What goes on here?"

"We are moving the grain to York at the bishop's request," the friar said. "Some politics out of London I hear."

Marion gave the friar a reproachful look, and the man wilted some under her gaze. In fairness to Tuck, Robin didn't think he looked too happy about sending the grain away. But if the bishop had called for a shipment, there was nothing Tuck could do. Even as he formed this thought, Robin felt the kernel of a plan forming in the back of his mind. He kept it there for now, but he smiled inwardly at the notion that had come into his head.

"This is our grain," Marion was saying, scolding Tuck as if he was a wayward child and she his parent. "It belongs in the soil."

"Lady Marion, I but follow the demands of my superiors, and abide by their saying and their rule." He sounded truly distressed, and Robin found himself feeling some sympathy for the man. Some.

Marion said not another word. She looked straight ahead, as if Tuck had become invisible to her, and rode away. Robin steered his horse closer to the man.

"Does his holiness know of your wealth in honey?" Robin asked in a voice only loud enough for Tuck to hear. "Should the bishop not be told of that bounty, too, so that the righteous may spread Nottingham honey on Nottingham bread?"

Tuck's eyes went wide, and he licked his lips, clearly understanding that he was caught between his bishop and his lord. "There are wolves in York, Sir Robert. Voracious wolves. These bees are my family. I am a procreator by design and need." He paused licking his lips a second time and shuffling closer to Robin's horse. "A great need. I am not a 'churchy' friar, never have been. I prefer to preach on the highways and byways—the spray of wildflowers from Poppleton to Dover and back to here I take some humble credit for. The bees bring life. They are my life, Sir Robert."

Robin decided then and there that he liked this friar. He leaned closer to the man. "Then the bees need not be spoken of." He raised his voice a bit, glancing at the deacon. "This place needs all the life it can get, do you not agree?"

The church's man shot Robin a filthy look.

Tuck, though, smiled conspiratorially. "Easily said for you, sir, but who will protect the friar from the wrath of his bishop? The bees bring life," Tuck said again, the words laden with meaning this time. "They are my life, Sir Robert."

Robin leaned close to the man again. "Should the grain not find it's way to York, then the bees need not be spoken of." He nodded to the friar and spurred his mount after Marion, who had ridden far ahead. Robin felt confident that he and Tuck had reached an agreement, and they would soon be fast friends.

CHAPTER

FIFTEEN

Robin caught up with Marion at the edge of town. She regarded him oddly as he pulled abreast of her once more, but she didn't ask what he had said to Tuck. She led him back around the town and up onto the hill, so that soon they were riding through the fields just outside of Peper Harrow. As before, Robin was struck by the richness of the surrounding lands. It all looked lush and fertile. Had he been a farmer, he would have been drawn to the deep living green of these lands. He looked around him, his puzzlement growing by the moment.

"This is rich country," he said at last. "Where are your cattle? Your sheep?"

Marion took a breath, looking over the lands in turn. "Sold," she said. "Eaten, stolen, traded. We have had seven lean years in the shire. Our meat is rabbit, or a wild pig on a lucky day."

Robin looked toward the forest. "And deer?"

"If you're willing to risk your neck to the king's executioner!" Marion said. "Every deer in the land belongs to his majesty."

He hadn't known. That didn't seem any more just than the church claiming these people's grain. No meat, no bread. How were they supposed to eat?

"The lives of kings and bishops depend on their people," Robin said, as much to himself as to Marion. "So why do the people believe it's the other way about?"

Marion eyed him curiously, clearly not knowing what to make of what he had said. In truth, Robin wasn't sure what to make of it either. He had never said such a thing before, at least not so that others could hear. It wasn't really the kind of thing he was used to thinking. He'd spent the last ten years as a soldier, worrying about his own survival and that of the men fighting beside him. He took Loxley's sword and armor as much to get himself back to England as to honor Sir Robert's last request. But this . . . this had been an odd day. First he had ridden through town as a lord, and had found himself warming to the feel of it. Now he had spoken as if trying to incite a rabble. Who was this Robert Loxley he had become? For that matter, who was the Robin Longstride whom Sir Walter claimed to know?

Robin turned to look back down at Nottingham below them. And doing so, he saw the grain carts rattling away along the road, the bishop's guards riding on either side of them. The kernel had sprouted roots and taken hold.

He and Marion resumed their ride. Passing through the fields, they saw two men working the land, one of them bent and ancient looking, the other only slightly younger, with a ruddy, pleasant face. Marion whispered their names to him as they drew near the pair: the younger man was known as Gaffer Tom; the old one was Paul, a farmer who had worked the Loxley lands for years upon years.

When they had drawn even with the men, Gaffer Tom took off his hat.

"Welcome home, sir!" he called.

Paul raised a gnarled knuckle to his forehead. "An honor, sir!"

Robin nodded back to the men, and as they returned to their labors, Robin and Marion continued their ride. She told him more about the history of the land and the Loxley family. Robin listened, trying to hang on to every bit of information she offered. All the while, they kept to the hill, so that every few moments Robin was offered a different perspective on the town below and fields around them. Eventually, Marion's narrative came around to her own story.

"I was an old maid when Robert courted me," she told him with a smile. "Twenty-four! And ripe for a nunnery. The daughter of a respectable widow with"—she held her thumb and forefinger just a little bit apart—"a thimbleful of noble blood. He saw me in church at Ely and I was betrothed in a week. A week later, he was seduced by King Richard to join ship for France and Jerusalem. So we were wed, and he left at daybreak to ride south. That was my married life, with a man I hardly knew."

"A good knight," Robin said, thinking of what it must have been like for Sir Robert to leave his new bride the morning after his wedding.

"Short, but oh, so sweet," Marion said, staring off over the fields.

It took Robin a moment. "No," he said, trying to keep from laughing. "A good—"

"Oh!" Marion said, raising a hand to her mouth, her face coloring.

Robin grinned. "A knight-in-arms. A brave soldier."

He had to give her credit; she recovered quickly, making the best of her embarrassment. "My knight-in-arms even so," she said, smiling as well. "And I in his." She looked at him sidelong. "And you?"

Robin shrugged looking straight ahead. "I am what I am: an archer as soon as I could bend a bow and, ever since, on the march for pay, with nothing to offer a woman."

The words sounded harsh and bitter to his own ears, and he smiled at her to soften what he had said.

"Least of all a lady," he continued. "I barely spoke English before I learned to speak French. I was brought up by strangers among olive groves in Southern France. I can't remember my mother or my father."

Saying this, his thoughts turned once more to the promise Sir Walter had made the night before. Somehow, the old man knew the secrets of his past. It seemed Marion's thoughts had taken a similar turn. She looked at him, a question in her eyes.

Robin met and held her gaze. "I think when Robert Loxley gave me his sword, it was not for the sword's destiny, but for mine."

Marion opened her mouth to say something, but at that moment, they heard a commotion coming from near the mill house in the distance. They spurred their mounts forward and soon came to a good-sized bog. Several women stood along the edge of the water, trying to reach a ram that had wandered in and gotten itself stuck. The creature bleated piteously and thrashed about, desperate to keep its head above the rank water. Mill weed floated at the surface of the bog and Robin could see from how the animal struggled that the bottom was heavy with mud and muck. The women were trying to get a rope around the animal's neck in order to pull it to safety. But the creature fought them as well as the bog, making matters worse for itself by the moment.

"Stop!" Marion shouted at the women, riding to the edge of the water. "You'll break its neck!"

She leaped off her horse, started to step into the bog, but stopped herself. She searched around the water's edge, and soon spotted a hoe. Taking hold of it, she hiked up her skirt so that her legs were bare to the thighs. She waded into the water, using the hoe to test the bottom of the bog before each step. Slowly, she made her way toward the bleating ram.

Robin had halted his horse beside Marion's and watched her as she sank deeper and deeper into the bog, heedless of her clothes and of exposing her legs. He wasn't sure whether to be amused or impressed, and in the end decided that he could be both. He certainly understood why Loxley had been so taken with the woman upon seeing her in that church in Ely. Robin had never met anyone quite like her.

In the next moment, though, matters took a turn for the worse. Marion had nearly reached the ram, which was sinking faster and faster. But as she tested the bottom in front of her, the hoe suddenly plunged all the way into the mud, and it nearly took Marion with it. She pinwheeled her arms to keep from falling forward and managed to right herself. But the hoe was lost, and the ram nearly so. The creature thrashed ever more wildly, and now Marion was helpless to do anything about it.

Robin threw himself off his horse and grabbed a rope as he ran toward the water's edge.

As he ran past the village women, he shouted for them to take hold of the other end of the rope.

He didn't pause to see if they had done as he asked. Reaching the bog he launched himself into the water, landing knee-deep in the mud and wading toward where Marion still stood.

"I'm on the edge of the shelf," she called to him.

"Go back to the side."

She shook her head. "I can't move my legs."

That was an unfortunate complication. But looking at Marion, Robin could see that she was all right. She didn't appear to be in any danger of sinking deeper into the mud, and while she no longer had the hoe, he knew that she could go back to the edge without difficulty when eventually she freed her legs.

She smiled at him, clearly relieved to see him coming toward her. She held out her arm to him so that he could pull her out.

"Thank you, my—"

Robin continued past her toward the ram.

Her face fell. "—lord . . ."

He pitched himself forward, diving headlong toward the ram, his arms outstretched. The creature gave one last terrified cry and then went under, disappearing from view save for its horns. Robin grabbed for them and managed to grip one and then the other. He felt tension in the rope and hoped it meant that the women had a firm grip on it. He shouted to them to pull.

At first nothing happened, and Robin realized that he was starting to sink along with the animal, which continued to flail about in the muck. But then he felt a tug on the rope and a moment later he was being pulled back from the deepest part of the bog. Holding fast to the ram, he got its head above water again and dragged it along with him. Soon, he was back on the shelf. Getting his feet under him, Robin stood. He let go of the ram, which was free of the mud now. The creature made its way to the safety of the edge, heaved itself out of the water and ran back to join its flock.

"Thank you, my lord," Marion said archly, though with a smile. "Is it my turn now?"

Robin waded back to where she was standing, still waist deep in the water. He took her hands in his and pulled her toward him.

"Hold tight," he told her.

She wrapped her arms around him.

Once more he called for the villagers to pull on the rope, and once more he felt himself being tugged back toward the water's edge. This time he pulled Marion with him. Within moments they were out of the bog and back on solid ground. Marion released him, though not before looking up into his eyes for just the briefest moment.

Robin dropped the rope.

As he did, he heard someone clapping behind him. Turning, he saw a bearded man sitting a large bay. He wore a cloak with a broad furred collar and studded riding breeches. His hair was long and unruly, and though he wore a smile, there was something unpleasant about the man's expression.

The women, who but a moment before had been chattering excitedly about Robin and Marion's rescue of the ram, had fallen silent at the sight of this man. Marion, who had walked back to her horse, didn't appear pleased to see him either. She regarded him with poorly concealed distaste and then looked to Robin, a warning in her eyes.

"Nicely done, sir!" the man said to Robin, smiling still.

Marion remounted, holding her boots in her hand, her skirt bunched up so that some of her leg was still bared.

The man, Robin noticed, leered at her in a manner that would have made even a dead husband jealous.

"And to see Lady Marion Loxley's legs naked to the breeze was beyond my hopes this morning."

Robin looked to Marion, his eyebrows up, as if to ask if he had her permission to punch this lout in the mouth.

He thought she would be scowling at the man, but really she seemed quite amused as she said, "I think you do not know my husband, Sir Robert." She turned to Robin. "Allow me, my lord, to present the Sheriff of Nottingham."

Robin swung himself back into his saddle, so that when he faced the sheriff again, they were eye-to-eye. On most occasions Robin was not given to snap judgments about any man, but he had taken an effortless dislike to the sheriff. He had met men like this one countless times before—in the army, on ships, in taverns. All of them were the same, and none was worth a damn. This sheriff had already shown himself to be boorish; that he reeked of arrogance and ambition, of selfishness and pride, came as no surprise. Robin had never understood how men of this sort always managed to land themselves in positions of power, but he'd seen it happen too many times to think it a coincidence.

Holding the man's gaze, Robin offered a slight nod by way of acknowledgment, which the sheriff returned with a sneer, apparently no more taken with Robin than Robin was with him.

"I had the honor of succeeding to this office not long after you left for the Holy Land," the man said. "Welcome home, Sir Robert. You make your mark quickly, saving the king's ram from drowning."

"What is this?" Marion demanded, her eyes blazing.

An unctuous smile curled the sheriff's lips. "What is owed in coin I have the right to take in goods or livestock in King Richard's name."

"King Richard died a soldier," Robin said. "King John is our master now."

The sheriff seemed surprised by these tidings, though he showed no sign of being moved by them. "That's news indeed. Long live the king."

"Aye," Robin said, remembering his encounter with the new king, and thinking that John and the sheriff deserved each other. "If God wills it."

He reached back into a pouch than hung from his saddle and pulled out a coin. He held it up for the sheriff to see and then tossed it to the man the way he might have thrown alms to a common beggar. The sheriff caught it and looked at it.

"Here's a ram's worth of tax for the exchequer."

The sheriff glared at him.

"We'll meet again, Sheriff of Nottingham." Robin smiled thinly. "I'll not forget your compliment to Lady Marion."

Robin turned his horse, and Marion did the same alongside. As she did, Robin glanced down at her legs. "Beyond my hopes this morning, too . . ." he murmured, just loud enough for her to hear.

She followed the line of his gaze and then shot him a look that would have kindled damp wood. Husband or no, apparently there were certain lines he wasn't yet allowed to cross. Hiding a grin, Robin followed her away from the bog and the sheriff.

THE SHERIFF WATCHED Lady Marion and her husband ride off, his sword hand itching. Without taking his eyes off the couple he bit down on the coin Loxley had given him. It seemed real enough. He pocketed it and took hold of his reins, his hands trembling with rage.

Loxley might have been a soldier, he might have been a lord, but that didn't give the man the right to speak to him that way. He was the king's man—whichever king. This was his bailiwick, and no crusader could change that.

He had met men like Loxley before: superior, disdainful, utterly convinced of their own infallibility. He had also brought down bigger men than Loxley, with the law if he could, with a blade if he had to. This one would be no different.

"Aye, we'll meet again, Robert Loxley," he said, nodding decisively. "Be sure of it."

CHAPTER

SIXTEEN

Night fell over Peper Harrow, and after an ample but simple meal like the one they had enjoyed the night before, Sir Walter retired, claiming to be unusually weary. Robin sat before the hearth again, enjoying the warmth of another blaze. He hadn't been sitting long, however, when one of the servants appeared saying that Sir Walter had sent her.

Marion was on her feet immediately, but the girl explained, somewhat sheepishly, that the old man had asked not for her, but for Sir Robert. Robin thought that Marion regarded him with a touch of resentment as he stood, puzzled himself, and followed the girl up the stairs to Walter's bedchambers.

The room was dark when Robin entered. He could barely make out the old man's bed, which appeared plain and ancient. Moonlight filtering in through the window alighted gently on the blankets and pillows so that he could see the old man was lying on his back, as still as death. He couldn't see if Walter's eyes were open or closed, and after waiting for some time for the man to speak, he began to wonder if perhaps in the few minutes it had taken the servant to fetch him, the old knight had fallen asleep. He was just about to turn and quietly let himself out of the chamber, when Walter stirred.

"Longstride," he said. As always he turned his head directly toward Robin. Not for the first time, Robin wondered if the man was only feigning his blindness, or if his hearing had grown so acute that he no longer needed his eyes to know what everyone around him was doing.

"You need to know what I know," the old man went on. "Your father was a stonemason." Robin saw him smile in the darkness. "Is that pleasing to you?"

Robin took a breath and nodded. Then, realizing the man could not see his gesture, he said, "Yes, it is. A mason . . ."

He trailed off, silenced by the onset of a memory . . .

HE IS IN Barnsdale, his childhood home. In the village center. The cross of the Celts stands in the middle of the square, gleaming in the sun beneath a sky of purest blue. He feels himself rising and falling. He is being thrown. Exhilarated, scared, laughing. He soars up toward the blue, falls back. And is caught in strong arms, only to be thrown again. Rising, falling, laughing until he can't catch his breath.

Finally, those powerful arms catch him one last time and set him on his feet. Robin looks up into the clear blue eyes of his father. He knows those eyes. He has seen them reflected in a looking glass, and in the gleaming armor of the knights who sometimes come to his town. They are his eyes, too. Clear and blue and honest.

His father kneels down before him and grips his arm gently. "Always keep this day in your memory, and in your heart."

The cross behind his father has a small gap, a single spot where one last stone has yet to be set. His father leads Robin to the base of the cross and trowels cement into the gap where this last stone will be placed. He takes hold of Robin's hand and presses it into the wet cement, making an imprint. He smiles at Robin, who smiles back. Then the stonemason presses his own hand into the cement beside Robin's imprint.

Two other men, standing with a cluster of soldiers, separate themselves from the group and join Robin and his father next to the cross. They press their hands into the cement, too.

The older Robin, the man in a darkened bedchamber in Peper Harrow, who is watching his childhood self and wondering at this long-forgotten image from his boyhood, knows these men. He can almost name them, but that knowledge flutters just beyond his reach, like a butterfly on a summer day, and then it is gone.

Robin's father now walks to where the last stone rests, a chisel nearby. Robin follows, and so sees the words carved into the stone on one side. Words that Robin has committed to memory with his father's help.

"Rise and rise again, until lambs become lions."

His father hefts the stone, carries it to the cross, and sets it in the gap, the inscription facing in, so that only those who have come to witness the completion of the cross will know that it is there. The words, resting forever beside the handprints.

The stonemason turns to his son and smiles, and Robin grins back at him, thinking what a wonder it is to have a father who could have fashioned such a great cross.

ROBIN STOOD IN the darkness of Sir Walter's room. *My father was a stonemason.* These words echoed in his mind, like rolling thunder on a summer evening. Such a small thing, and yet he knew so little of his family, of his past, that it seemed huge, like a man's sword in the hands of a child.

"But he was more than that," Sir Walter said from his bed. "He was a visionary."

"What did he see?" Robin asked in a hushed voice.

"That kings have need of their subjects no less than their subjects have need of kings. A dangerous idea! Politics!"

Robin had said much the same thing to Marion earlier this day, and hadn't known at the time what to make of his own words. Had those been his father's words, sent to him across time and over miles and through the boundary between life and death, between thought and memory? Or did such sentiments simply run in his blood? Was he finally learning what it meant to be a Longstride? Strange that the lesson should only be brought home now, when he had taken on another man's name.

Robin looked at the old man, eager now to know the rest of the stonemason's tale. "What happened to him?"

"Put out your hand."

Slowly, Robin reached toward the bed. Walter groped for his hand for a moment before finding it.

He gripped tightly; there was strength still in those old fingers. Robin stood just by the bed now. Looking down into Walter's rheumy eyes, he saw that they looked almost white in the moonlight.

"A blind man can see things in the dark," the old knight said. "Do you understand me?"

He swallowed. "Yes."

"Close your eyes," Walter told him. "Leave the remembering to me."

Robin did as the old man said, waiting for whatever Walter had in store for him. Suddenly he felt the old man's body convulse, as if Walter had been struck by lightning. The old knight's grip tightened painfully on Robin's hand, until Robin felt that his bones were being ground to dust. At the same time, Robin doubled over, as if he, too, had been struck. He wanted to cry out, to ask what was happening. But in that instant, he saw.

THEY ARE BACK in Barnsdale. Robin, his father, other men. Soldiers. So many soldiers. The cross looms above them. Dull now, almost gray, beneath a brooding sky. The soldiers hold his father, pinning his arms. Robin is yelling for them to let his father go. Tears stream down his face and he struggles to break free of the hands that hold him back. He wants to go to his father, to help him get away from the soldiers. But he's held fast and so can only watch.

A soldier steps to where his father is held, a sword in hand. And with a single powerful stroke, he cleaves the mason's body. Blood blossoms from the wound. His father's legs buckle beneath him, his head lolls; only the grasp of the other soldiers keeps him from collapsing to the ground. A scream is ripped from

Robin's throat. Then the world begins to spin. The blood, the soldiers, the cross. And all is black.

ROBIN OPENED HIS eyes in the darkness, his hand still in Walter's crushing grip. He remembered it all. The memories coursed through him, as though a dam had cracked and given way. Walter dropped his hand, and Robin staggered briefly before regaining his balance. His chest ached with the memory of that sword stroke. His head spun, as it had when he was boy. When he had witnessed the murder of his father.

"Who?" he asked, breathing hard.

"Think!" Walter told him, his voice harsh in the still, dark room. "King Henry's soldiers! You were there. You saw it. Do you remember what happened after that?"

Robin closed his eyes again, reaching back for that memory as well. But though he scoured his mind for any hint as to what followed the horrors he had just seen, nothing came. At last he opened his eyes again and shook his head.

"Almost nothing before I was young in Normandy, brought up among farming folk."

"You were taken there by two men," Walter told him. "Noblemen. Sympathizers. They took you out of danger, and hid you with a family in France."

"You!" Robin said, comprehension crashing over him like a wave. And with that understanding came a vague memory of two men standing with Robin and his father by the cross in Barnsdale.

"Yes," the old man said. "The other was a nobleman, my best friend since my youth."

Robin shook his head slowly, trying to keep up

with all that the knight had told him. "I don't understand. Noblemen, led by a stonemason joined in . . .
in what?"

"An appeal to justice," Walter said, his voice growing stronger, his eyes open wide in the darkness and
shining with moonlight. "And one without bloodshed.
He was a philosopher, and he had a way of speaking
that took you by the ears." He paused, as if savoring
the memory. "Finally, hundreds listened, who took up
his call for the rights of all ranks, from baron to serf,
and many a nobleman saw the right of it."

A visionary, Walter had called his father. And yet
what was left of the stonemason's dream? The hidden memories of a little boy, and the dreams of an
old knight.

"His call died with him," Robin said softly.

But Walter grabbed for his hand again and gripped
it hard. "Not dead!" the man said. "Not now!"

Robin considered this, staring at their hands in the
ghostly light. "You and I and others, Sir Walter."

The old knight nodded, staring at Robin intently
through sightless eyes. Robin stared out the window
toward the fields and the shadowed wood beyond.
The notion that had come into his head earlier in the
day returned now. Not exactly his father's way, perhaps, but certainly his own.

WILLIAM MARSHAL SAT at the writing table in his
chamber, gazing out an open window at the roof-
tops of London. The sun was just up in the east, and
the waters of the Thames glittered with its light, as
if diamonds had been strewn across its surface. He
smiled bitterly at the thought. Strange that such rank

waters should look so lovely at a distance. He shifted his gaze toward the White Tower, which gleamed in the morning sun. Something dark and rank festered within its walls as well.

It had only been a matter of days since John had banished him from the throne room and the halls of power, but already William felt like a stranger in the city. He had served kings most of his life. To have that taken from him by the likes of Godfrey and Richard's wastrel of a brother . . .

A knock at his door roused him from his dark thoughts. A servant entered, carrying a small rolled piece of parchment, sealed with wax. A message from his man in the north.

Marshal broke the seal and unrolled the parchment.

The message scrawled in that familiar hand was chillingly brief. "200 French arrive at night at Hampton Bays."

Marshal took a long breath and gazed once more toward the White Tower.

GODFREY HAD NEVER been to Peterborough before, and after today he didn't imagine he would ever want to return. Not that there would be much left of the village once Adhemar's men were done with it, but even if the French were to be more gentle in their collection of taxes than they had been in other towns, he couldn't think of why anyone would come here. There was dung and mud and a few patches of grass and not much else to speak of. Still, if anyone could wring blood from this stone, it was Godfrey.

He signaled to Adhemar, who waved his men forward, giving instructions solely with hand gestures. No words. That had been the sole condition he had placed on the French commander and his legionnaires. The men started toward the village gate, pulling the iron-clad tax wagon with them. The legionnaires entered the village like vikings, breaking down doors and ransacking houses, pulling out into the street anything that looked even vaguely valuable. If they didn't find anything upon their initial search of a house, they ripped apart walls, searching for hidden caches.

From nearly every house came the frightened wails of children and the screams of women. One man tried to keep the soldiers from seizing two of his chickens. The soldiers clubbed him until he fell to the ground, blood running from his head. Another tried to block the doorway to his house, but was overwhelmed by the legionnaires, who forced him back inside. Godfrey didn't see the man after that, but he heard the soldiers beating him, heard the man's wife sobbing and begging them to stop.

It was strange, even eerie in a way. The screams of the villagers, the sounds of furniture being smashed, and houses being destroyed, and not a word from the soldiers. These were disciplined men. Once more, Godfrey was impressed.

Yet, despite the best efforts of Adhemar's men, they added few coins to the tax wagon. There simply wasn't enough wealth in these godforsaken villages. Even taking everything, they didn't wind up with much.

Adhemar had walked the length of the lane running through the village—not a great distance, really—and had come back to stand beside Godfrey as the Englishman watched the soldiers move from house to house. Adhemar looked into the wagon and frowned. He scooped up the small pile of coins that had been added to their plunder and then tossed it back into the wagon contemptuously. He looked at Godfrey, scowling, as if to say, "So much work and this is all?" Godfrey was sure though that they would be able to wring more treasure from the cities and hamlets to the south.

CHAPTER

SEVENTEEN

Robin found the boys in the shed where Friar Tuck brewed his mead. Between Will, Allan, and Little John, the snoring should have been enough to wake the entire village of Nottingham, but somehow the three of them slept. He retrieved a bucket of water from the nearby well, returned to the shed, and tossed the water onto his friends. They sputtered and groaned, but at least they were awake.

"All right, lads," he said, tossing the bucket aside. "You should have left while you had the chance. Something's afoot. Off we go."

He glanced at the friar, who looked both startled and amused. Nodding once, Robin left the shed, with Tuck following. He could hear the boys grumbling.

THE DEACON COULDN'T help but be pleased. Not one, but two wagons filled with grain. The bishop would be delighted, perhaps delighted enough to elevate him to the priesthood and give him his own tenancy. And not down here in the hinterlands, either. A tenancy near to York, where he might win the favor of the bishop and thus advance his career more quickly.

That fool, Tuck, had too much charity for the people in his little hamlet. The bishop had far more important matters on his mind than plantings and harvests in the countryside. Which was why the deacon would be elevated to abbot before long, while the friar remained exactly what he was, where he was.

The sun was setting in the west, and the shadows of the wood were beginning to bring a chill to the air when the deacon steered his cart around a bend in the road. He sat up straighter, pulled from his reverie by a strange sight. A hooded man sat on a stool in the middle of the lane, looking very much like a man in a tavern waiting for an ale. The two carts rumbled closer to him, but the man didn't so much as look up. He simply sat there, almost as if he were asleep, right in the center of the road. The deacon didn't see any way to go around him, and he had no wish to run the man over.

Drawing closer, the deacon saw that the man wore leather breeches and a woolen cloak about his shoulders. He didn't appear to have any armor, but he held a bow across his lap and had an arrow loosely nocked to the string.

Finally, the deacon had no choice but to stop the carts. He raised a hand signaling a halt to the driver behind him. He pulled back on the reins and shouted "Whoa!" to his horse. The wagons slowed to a stop. The deacon stood up in the front of his wagon, peering through the dimming light, trying to get a better look at the man sitting before him.

"You there!" he called.

The man looked up at him, though the hood continued to shroud most of his face. "Do you speak to me?" he asked, brazenly.

"Do you see anyone else, you insolent wretch?" the deacon demanded. Could the man not see that he wore the bishop's colors? Did he not recognize the Church's grain carts?

"I do not," the hooded man said. "But perhaps if I were sitting high, like you . . ."

The deacon had had quite enough. "By God, you'll be sitting in the stocks at York! Move aside!"

"No one may pass who can't answer the riddle," the man said.

The deacon opened his mouth to respond, but then stopped himself, smiling and feeling a bit more at ease. A riddle. The man had to be a lunatic, but if all he wanted was to play at riddles, he was probably harmless enough. But the hooded man still hadn't moved, and the daylight was failing, and the deacon's patience wasn't infinite. He glanced back at his pikemen, sharing the joke with them.

"Moon-mad," he whispered. The soldiers laughed. Facing the hooded man again, he said, with just a hint of impatience in his voice, "And what is the riddle?"

"What did the thief say to the honest man?" the stranger asked.

The deacon shrugged. "Let me pass, you loon. I'm on Church business."

"Oh," the hooded man said, sounding disappointed. "You've heard it before. I'll ask you another."

It took the deacon a second to realize that he had been insulted. He straightened, glaring at the stranger. Then he turned to look back at the three guards behind him and nodded once.

The soldiers climbed down off the wagon carrying long pikes, and advanced on the man slowly, shoulder to shoulder, their weapons leveled at the stranger.

The hooded man gave no indication that he feared the guards. In fact, he crossed his legs as if making himself more comfortable. When the guards were almost upon him, he sighed heavily.

"What has six legs and isn't going anywhere?" he asked, sounding bored.

The pikemen glanced at each other, grinning, looking supremely confident. The deacon didn't consider himself a cruel man, but he looked forward to watching the guards teach this troublemaker a lesson. The guards stopped in front of the man and prepared to move him bodily from his stool.

And that was when everything started to go horribly wrong.

The deacon heard a sound behind him, and twisting around saw a second hooded man, this one with impossibly broad shoulders and a long wooden stave. This man swung himself upside down from a low branch over the second cart. He tapped the shoulders of both the driver and the soldier beside, and when they turned to look, he flipped himself onto his feet, and in the same motion whirled his stave in a blurring circle. The two guards tried to fight him off, but this hooded man was too fast for them. In the span of perhaps two heartbeats, he had knocked both men off that wagon and onto the forest floor, where they lay senseless.

At the same time, the last two guards in the deacon's cart drew their swords. And as soon as they did, two archers stepped out from behind trees and fired their arrows. *Thunk, thunk!* Before the deacon could turn to see what these darts had done, the two men nocked and fired two more. *Thunk, thunk!* The arrows had pierced the tunics of the two guards—one arrow each at the wrist and the collar—and pinned the men to the wooden frame of the wagon. Neither man appeared to have been hurt, though both of them looked astonished, not to mention terrified.

"Near misses," said the hooded man on the road. "They won't miss again if you move!"

Facing forward again, the deacon saw his three pikemen turn to watch what was happening to their fellow soldiers. They had raised their pikes and now, without warning, their weapons were jerked out of their hands and hurled into the forest, as if . . . the deacon swallowed . . . as if by magic.

The pikemen looked around, clearly unnerved by this, and began to move away from the hooded stranger, back toward the wagon.

The deacon supposed he should have been scared, too, but he didn't run; he *refused* to run. His hands trembling with rage, his chest rising and falling with each breath, he glared at this common thief standing in the road. He could see that the hooded man was grinning, but his eyes remained hidden. Still, the deacon thought he knew the man, though he couldn't say from where.

"I demand to know who you are!" he said, his voice quavering.

The hooded man's smile broadened. "Men of the hood," he said, "Fare thee well."

From the corner of his eye, the deacon saw a movement behind him, and too late he realized that he had allowed another of the hooligans to creep onto his cart. He felt a hard blow to his head and started to fall.

Looking back as he tumbled off the wagon, he had the strangest sense that he also knew the hooded man who had hit him. But before he could figure out why this one looked so terribly familiar, he hit the ground and blacked out.

THE DEACON LANDED with a thud and gave a low groan. But he didn't move, and he didn't open his eyes. Out cold.

Robin threw back his hood and looked up at Friar Tuck, who had knocked the bishop's man on the head. The priest pulled back his hood as well, and grinned down at him. Clearly Tuck was enjoying himself. He was right: he definitely was not a "churchy" friar.

"The Lord giveth . . ." Tuck said.

Robin climbed up onto the cart with him. ". . . And the Lord taketh away."

Allan and Will joined Robin and Tuck on the first wagon, still laughing about the way they had used their looped ropes to snatch the lances out of the guards' hands and fling them into the wood. Robin had to laugh, too. The men had looked terrified.

Little John settled himself onto the second wagon, and nodded to Robin, indicating that he was ready to go. Tuck flicked the reins and clicked his tongue at the horses, working to get the wagon turned around on the forest lane. It took some maneuvering to get both carts headed back in the right direction, but soon they were rattling southward again, toward Nottingham.

"My advice is to plant it now," the friar said, once they were on their way.

Robin glanced at him. "Why is that, good Tuck?"

A mischievous grin spread across the priest's face.

"When it sprouts, I can claim it as a miracle from God. The Church in York won't dare deny a miracle."

Robin laughed. He couldn't remember the last time his spirits were this high. He didn't know if his father would have approved of what he had done, or if this was what Sir Walter had in mind. But at the moment he didn't care. He and his companions had struck a blow against the wealthy and powerful on behalf of those who had neither riches nor influence. All in all, it seemed a good day's work.

As they continued down the road, Allan began to strum his lute and Will began to sing, his voice loud and merry, if slightly off key.

> *Oh gather 'round me, people,*
> *A story I will tell,*
> *About the Sherwood outlaw,*
> *The farmers knew him well.*
> *He took the Church grain,*
> *And hid it in the ground,*
> *And in a few short weeks,*
> *Green treasure could be found!*

As he started the verse again, the others joined in, their voices echoing through the trees. Thus they made their way back to Nottingham, growing quiet as night fell and they drew closer to the town.

By the time they steered the cart into the planting fields, they were taking every care to make no sound at all. Not that the people of the town would have minded—though Robin wondered what the ill-mannered sheriff would have thought of what they had done. But despite their singing and joking, all of them knew how great a risk they were taking. They had no wish to give the Church or the sheriff any excuse to punish others for their mischief.

Working quickly and in silence, they halted the carts, filled slings with as much grain as they could carry, and began to scatter the seed in the furrows Farmer Paul had made with his plow and dray. Several times they had to refill their slings, but they planted all the grain from the first of the carts they had stolen. It took hours—Robin was weary and sore by the time they finished—but again, he couldn't help thinking that he had done God's work this evening and night.

They hid the carts and horses in a barn at the far end of the field, where no one was likely to find them.

Then Robin made his way back to Peper Harrow. The house was dark and still as he crept through the courtyard and into the great hall. A fire still burned low in the hearth, and the hall was warm and smelled of stew. Robin's stomach growled loudly and he realized that he hadn't eaten anything for hours. Still, his fatigue was more powerful than his hunger.

Rather than chance disturbing Marion, he found a blanket by the chair near the fireplace. He sat, wrapped the blanket around his shoulders, and within moments had fallen asleep.

Some time later, he awoke to the soft padding of footsteps on the stone. Looking up, he saw Marion standing beside the chair looking down at him. He shifted in the chair, tried to stretch his back a bit. The fire had burned down to nothing but glowing orange embers, and the ubiquitous dogs sat around his chair.

"I thought you had left," Marion said. It was hard to read her expression in the dim light, and she spoke softly, so he couldn't say for sure what emotion he heard in her voice. But it almost seemed to Robin that she was relieved to find him here.

"Spring planting began tonight," he told her. "The north field is sown. The south tomorrow night. I returned late and didn't want to wake you."

She quirked her head in surprise, and a half-smile touched her lips. "How did you get the seeds for sowing?"

"If you need to ask, it is not a gift," Robin said.

Her smile warmed. "If that is what it is, then thank you."

Marion regarded him a moment longer, as if she saw something in his face and his bearing that she hadn't noticed before. She turned and left him there, but he could see that she smiled still.

CHAPTER

EIGHTEEN

The Baron of York had long prided himself on his close ties to the royal house of the realm. Decades before, Baldwin's father had joined Henry the Second in his campaigns against the Irish, and Baldwin himself had fought under Henry's banner in the north to repel Scottish invaders. He had been too old to join Richard on his crusade, but as baron he had done all he could to give support to the Lionheart's march on the Holy Land. He paid his taxes to the Crown, gave grain to the bishops of York.

In every way, he had served his realm honorably and courageously. Never in his life had he uttered a seditious word, or given comfort to those who did. He considered himself a friend of the Plantagenets and had long assumed that they looked upon him as a loyal subject and a dependable ally.

Apparently, he had been mistaken all these years. Or he had been a fool. How else could he explain the army that had gathered outside his gate, demanding what remained of his treasure and threatening to sack his village and home should he refuse?

It was John's doing, he knew. Richard might have squandered England's treasure and the blood of her young men in pursuit of his wars, but he had never been a despot. He had never sacrificed the well-being of his people simply because it pleased him to fill his coffers with gold.

This new king, though, was a different matter. He would happily destroy the realm to satisfy his greed. Richard's leopards were gone, banished. Wolves now controlled England. And they were at his gates.

Baldwin was headed for the ramparts of the Barnsdale tower, the better to see just what his people faced. He tried to cinch his sword belt as he took the tower stairs two at a time, but his hands shook with fury, making it difficult for him to do much of anything. His grandson climbed the stairs behind him, trying to keep up with him, breathing heavily with the effort, and probably with fear as well. It was no small matter to face the king's army.

"This Robber King is no king of mine!" Baldwin said bravely, hoping for the lad's sake that he sounded more confident than he felt.

He reached the top of the winding stairs a moment later and stepped out onto the battlements of the town walls. There were townspeople up there already, many of them dressed in rags, looking half-starved. And these men had come for gold? Baldwin would have laughed if he hadn't been so enraged. He pushed past his people so that he could get a view of what was happening below.

The force was smaller than he had been led to believe. His grandson, panicked and inexperienced in such things had spoken as if the entire English army was at the Barnsdale gate. There couldn't have been more than two hundred men massed before the walls.

Still, Barnsdale couldn't stand long against any force, not even one half this size. His people were farmers, not warriors. His gates were intended to keep out road thieves and ruffians from the wood, not English regulars.

One of the king's men had stepped forward to the town gate and was now nailing up a notice, which, of course, Baldwin couldn't read. Not that he needed to. He could imagine well enough what it said.

"Are you Baldwin?"

The baron shifted his gaze to the man who had spoken. He wore a fine coat of mail, and, over it, a black tabard marked with a brightly colored crest Baldwin did not recognize. A black cape was draped around his shoulders, fastened at the neck with a silver chain. His head was clean-shaven, his eyes deep-set and dark, and he bore an angry scar on one cheek. He sat an impressive black stallion that seemed to complement perfectly his clothing and appearance.

"Open the gates," the man said. He spoke the words forcefully enough, but there was an insouciant quality to his voice, as if it made little difference to him whether or not Baldwin complied.

"In whose name do you come against us like Vandals and Vikings?" the baron demanded.

The man pointed to the notice his soldier had posted. "In the name of King John. Pay or burn."

Baldwin felt his face going red with anger. "We have paid in money and men for King Richard's wars, and we have no more to give!"

The bald man looked to the soldier next to him, a dark-haired, bearded man who sat tall on his mount. The two eyed each other for a moment. Then the second man gave a small shrug of his shoulders and the bald man looked up at Baldwin again.

"Burn then," he said, as if it was nothing to him.

The man turned in his saddle and nodded to the soldiers behind them. Instantly, several dozen of the men stepped forward carrying grappling hooks that dangled from the ends of thick rope. They swung them expertly and almost in unison, and sent them soaring up to the top of the wall. People fell back from the iron talons, the baron included, and then watched in horror as the soldiers pulled the ropes taut, allowing the hooks to grip the wall. The men began to climb toward the ramparts.

They climbed quickly—they were as well-trained as any English warriors the baron had ever seen. Baldwin leaped forward, drawing his sword, and began to hack at the ropes, desperate to cut them before the soldiers reached the top of the wall. Many of the townspeople fled the walls in a blind panic, but some of Baldwin's men joined him in attacking the ropes. The baron cut through one, and then another, sending the climbers tumbling back to earth, and, he hoped, to hell. Another man reached the top of the wall only to be stabbed by one of Barnsdale's guards. But farther down the wall, a soldier made it to the top, jumped onto the battlements, and began swinging his sword savagely at anyone who got in his way. A second soldier joined him, and then two more.

Within seconds, the wall was swarming with soldiers. Innocent men and women were wounded and killed before they could flee to safety. Baldwin's men tried to fight the invaders off, but they hadn't the skill to do battle with soldiers like these.

Baldwin had little choice but to call for his men to fall back and for his people to save themselves. He glanced back over the edge of the wall and saw that the bald man was still looking up at him, a smug smile on his lips.

IT DIDN'T TAKE long for Adhemar's men to gain control of the town walls, but Godfrey had never been a patient man, and even waiting those few minutes put him in a foul temper. He could hear screams rising from the ramparts and from beyond walls in the village, and he hoped that this time their work would be rewarded with more coin and treasure than it had been in Peterborough.

At last, as the screams continued, the gates to the town began slowly to swing open. Godfrey didn't wait for Adhemar's men to open them all the way. As soon as he could, he spurred his mount forward and rode into Barnsdale, wrinkling his nose at the smell of pig shit. Sheep bleated and chickens ran for safety, wings flailing, feathers flying. Another useless country village, probably with barely enough gold to make all this effort worthwhile.

The lane that carved through the village was littered with bodies. Those who were merely wounded crawled for safety, leaving trails of blood in the dirt. Others lay motionless. Soldiers moved from house to house, killing whoever got in their way, taking all that they could find. Godfrey looked back at Adhemar and nodded a second time. The Frenchman looked back at one of his men in turn and made a small gesture. Moments later, several men entered the village bearing torches and made their way toward the nearest of the thatched roofs.

Godfrey looked up at the walls, knowing that he would find Baldwin watching him, watching it all. Godfrey smiled and offered a slight shrug. He had given the baron a choice, and Baldwin had chosen poorly.

FROM BARNSDALE, GODFREY led his army toward the city of York, where he knew that their take would be far greater than it had been in the smaller villages of the northern baronies. The Church had spent the last several months gathering grain from its parishes. Now Godfrey, in the king's name, of course, would gather grain and gold from them. It wouldn't be long before John had lost not only the support of his nobles, but also of the bishops. The land would be rife with civil conflict and ripe for conquest.

They made their way through the streets of the city to York Minster. Godfrey was not much given to religiosity, but even he could not help but be impressed by the cathedral, with its Norman-style spires and enormous colored glass windows. He had seen the great cathedral at Canterbury, and thought that this one compared not unfavorably. But he wasn't here to admire architecture, and he definitely hadn't come to pray.

He sent in some of his men—on horseback—to deal with the curate Father Tancred and his monks.

He could hear the commotion from out on the street: pews being thrown over, glass shattering, men dying. When at last the sound abated, Godfrey spurred his own mount up the stairs and into the abbey, his sword in hand.

Monks still ran for cover, arms thrown over their heads as they were chased by soldiers. The interior of the church was a mess. Altars had been shattered, blood stained the floors, several fires burned, blackening the stone walls.

And at the center of it all stood Tancred, his robes singed, his begrimed cheeks streaked with tears, his eyes wide and wild with disbelief and outrage and terror. He clutched a golden chalice to his chest with shaking hands, looking like a mother guarding her babe. He looked around him, desperate to stop the destruction of his church, but helpless to do more than watch. How hard that must have been for him, Godfrey thought, enjoying the moment. A man in his position couldn't have been used to feeling powerless; before this day, he had probably never feared for his life. How the mighty had fallen.

Seeing Godfrey, Tancred took a step back, gripping his chalice even tighter.

"Why?" the abbot demanded, his forlorn voice echoing off the walls and ceiling. *Why? Why? Why?* "Tell me why!" *Why! Why! . . .*

Godfrey didn't answer him. He hefted his sword and advanced on the man slowly, a smile on his lips. Catching the eyes of two of his horsemen, he signaled them to help. They rode toward the abbot as well, the hooves of their mounts clicking loudly on the stone floor and resounding through the chapel.

They herded the man, driving him back toward the great altar. Tancred stumbled once, but righted himself. He tripped a second time and went down hard on his back. Still Godfrey and the other two riders advanced. Tancred scrabbled backward, climbed clumsily to his feet, and continued to back away. At last the abbot reached the steps leading up to the altar. Once more he fell, but he crawled up the stairs, his wide, terrified eyes never leaving Godfrey's face.

"Is God not watching?" Tancred asked, his voice barely more than a whisper.

Godfrey spied a rope tied to a cleat on the wall. Following it, he saw that it led to a massive iron chandelier.

"I don't know," he said, raising his blade. "Go and ask him."

He sliced through the rope, so that the chandelier smashed down upon the abbot, the crash of iron on stone and Tancred's dying cry reverberating through every corner of the abbey.

Sheathing his weapon, Godfrey looked at the French soldier nearest to him and nodded toward the abbot's body. The legionnaire dismounted, stepped over the wreckage and plucked the golden chalice from Tancred's fingers. Godfrey motioned for it impatiently and the man brought it to him.

Godfrey turned his horse and rode back outside to the lane. The tax wagon sat in front of York Minster, guarded by several men, not that anyone would have dared come near it. He was pleased to see that it was loaded high with Church grain. Godfrey considered the chalice for a moment, and then threw it in with the rest of what they had collected.

* * *

BLOODIED, GRIM, MORE angry and determined than
he had been in all his days, Baldwin led the survi-
vors of King John's assault toward the crossroads at
Northumbria. Only fifty or so had been fit enough
to make the journey with him. A few were soldiers.
Most were farmers, humble craftsmen, even house
servants. They were old and gray, they were too
young to shave, they were fathers, husbands, sons.
But they had come this far with him; after what they
had all been through, he knew that they would follow
him anywhere. Most of them wore bandages, others
bore bruises and burns, several had limped all the
way from Barnsdale. And every one of them carried
a weapon of one sort or another: a sword or a battle
pike, a hammer or an axe, a pitchfork or a hoe.

They had passed others like them on the road.
Driven from their homes, robbed of whatever meager
wealth they once could claim, hell-bent on exacting a
measure of revenge.

They saw more and more of them the closer they
drew to Northumbria, and as the crossroads came
into view, Baldwin realized that refugees were con-
verging on the place from every direction. The king's
tax collectors had been busy; now John would reap
what they had sown in his name. As Baldwin and his
followers neared the meeting place, one man in par-
ticular caught the baron's eye. He was broad in the
shoulders and chest, and the years had given him an
ample gut as well, so that he cut quite an imposing
figure on his charger.

Baldwin and Baron Fitzrobert had never been
friends, nor had they been enemies. They were rivals
of a sort, in the way that all nobles were rivals for

their king's favor. But they also shared a certain respect for each other. At least Baldwin respected Fitzrobert; he assumed the large man felt the same way about him. Fitzrobert had fought the Scottish invaders as well, and had been a fearsome warrior, swinging his two-handed bastard sword as if it were a weapon half that size.

But the two of them were here now, a long way from the battlefields of the north and years removed from Henry's reign. They had been driven to it—Baldwin didn't see that they had any choice. Still, the fact remained that they had come to the crossroads to plot treason.

"Fitzrobert!" Baldwin called when he was close enough to make himself heard.

The big man raised a hand in greeting, but his expression was wary. "Baldwin!"

Baldwin halted his horse in front of Fitzrobert and for several moments the two barons eyed one another, as if each was trying to determine if the other could be trusted.

At last, Fitzrobert nodded once, seeming to come to a decision. "We'll make an army of the north to march on London," he said, loudly enough for all to hear.

The men who had accompanied Baldwin let out a ragged cheer, as did the other refugees around them. The sound gladdened Baldwin's heart, though his expression remained grim. Avenging the attack on his town would be sweet, but there could be no mistaking the gravity of this endeavor. He saw his own misgivings mirrored in Fitzrobert's pale eyes.

"Send word through your shires," Baldwin said. "We'll rally on the road to London."

"Where?" Fitzrobert asked.

He didn't need to consider; the answer came to him immediately. "There is only one place for this meeting."

At that, the big man grinned. "Yes!"

Another cheer went up from the men around them, at least those old enough to remember. Baldwin had to smile as well. Treason or no, they had waited many years for this.

Baldwin and Fitzrobert quickly set to work scribbling messages to the lords in their baronies, as well as to other barons. Once their missives were written, they chose the best riders from among their small bands of followers to carry their messages forth from the crossroads. If they were to do this, it would have to be arranged quickly and quietly. If word of their intentions reached the White Tower, all was lost, and Baldwin and Fitzrobert would likely wind up with nooses around their necks.

Yet, as Baldwin watched their messengers ride off, scattering in all directions like silken seeds carried on a late summer breeze, he did not feel fear, but rather something that King John's henchmen could never steal from the heart of an Englishman: Hope.

ELEANOR OF AQUITAINE stood on the lush grounds of the White Tower, the battlements of the fortress at her back, the royal forests spreading over the countryside before her. She wore a black velvet gown and a heavy cloak about her shoulders. Her head was uncovered, her hair bound back in a single long plait.

The morning had dawned clear and cool, and Eleanor had wanted nothing so much as to leave the confines of the castle. Henry and Richard were gone, and though the years had been kinder to her than they were to most, she felt old. Each day it took her longer to work the cold of night out of her ancient bones. Each day she felt herself being shunted to the periphery of all that happened within the Tower walls.

She came here because the forest still called to her, because she took far more pleasure in flying her owl, in watching as the great bird glided through the wood on silent, still wings, than she did in watching her son rule England.

She heard footsteps behind her and knew without turning who had come. Word of William Marshal's dismissal had reached her the day it happened. At the time, Eleanor had still felt the sting of her own confrontation with John too acutely to give much thought to Marshal. Only later did she realize that in a single day, her son had severed ties to the only two people left in the White Tower who had served not only Richard, but Henry as well. Who would he turn to now? Sir Godfrey? His little French princess? She feared for her son; she grieved for England.

Marshal halted beside her and bowed. He followed the direction of her gaze and watched the Eagle Owl for a moment or two before facing her once more.

The years had been kind to Marshal as well. There were lines around his mouth and eyes, and there was now as much white as red in the leonine mane that framed his face, but he still looked as though he could win a sword tournament or lead an army into battle.

"Your Majesty," he said, "I have lost the confidence of King John, but he may still listen to you."

Eleanor smiled bitterly. "Allow me to know better, Sir William."

"Then you are wiser than your owl."

She laughed at that. "I dare say. I have lived longer."

He inclined his head, acknowledging her point. She and Marshal had known each other for more years than she cared to count. They had not always been friends, or even allies in the ever-shifting politics of England's royal house. But she considered him both friend and ally now; there was no one in the realm she trusted more. And she knew the man well enough to understand that he cared not a whit for his own standing in the king's court.

Marshal took a long breath now, looking out toward the forest again. "Alas, Richard was no Henry, and John *not* Richard, Your Majesty. But it is the Throne I serve, and this must endure."

"Speak plainly, Marshal. What is troubling you?"

His brow furrowed, and there was an expression of real pain in his eyes. "The Crown is in peril." He met her gaze. "Godfrey has been plotting with Philip of France. French troops have already landed on our shores, and they are murdering Englishmen in the name of King John. The northern barons will make civil war against the Throne. They are assembled to march on London, leaving our coast defenseless against the invasion which is certainly coming."

Eleanor's first instinct was to question Marshal's information, but she quickly dismissed whatever doubts she harbored. Marshal would not have been here, saying such things to her, if he hadn't been certain. She knew little about this man Godfrey, but she had mistrusted him from the start. And Philip, the French king, had repeatedly shown himself capable of the most insidious deceptions. She put nothing past him.

She felt weary. Not too many years ago, she might have seen an opportunity in such circumstance, a chance to reclaim her influence. But she no longer cared to fight battles like these. It seemed, though, that God had his own plan for her.

CHAPTER

NINETEEN

The more Eleanor considered what Marshal
had told her, the more she came to see that she
could not be the one to deliver these tidings
to John. His suspicions of her ran too deep, and she
supposed that was her fault. She had not been a loving
mother with any of her children; such was not in her
nature. More to the point, she had made little effort to
hide her disappointment in John, or her preference for
Richard. It was small wonder her youngest hated her.

And so she had no choice but to swallow her pride
and call on the one person she knew could help her,
the one person John trusted above all others.

Once she finally sent word, she did not have to wait
long for a reply.

As before, Eleanor was struck by how pretty
Princess Isabella was. She wore a satin dress of
beige, printed in blue and embroidered with gold at
the neck and sleeves. She had a tiara in her hair, a

looping necklace of diamonds at her throat, and rings on several of her fingers, so that she appeared to sparkle with the light of the candles that illuminated Eleanor's room.

Watching the girl watch her, Eleanor again had the sense that the princess felt intimidated in her presence. She had to resist the urge to relish the feeling. She had called the girl here in order to enlist her help; she had to remember that. But she also couldn't help but remind herself that the father of her first husband was this child's great grandfather. Between the two of them, they had witnessed the sweep of Europe's history over the past sixty years.

Eleanor had never been good at begging for help from others. She took it as a sign of how far she had fallen and how desperate matters had grown that she should be so dependent on this . . . child.

She had no choice, though, so she plunged in. "My son has an enemy in his court, closer to him than any friend. An English traitor, a paid agent for France."

The girl's eyes widened in what Eleanor took to be unfeigned surprise, but her voice when she spoke remained even. "You know this for certain?"

"Yes."

"How?"

Eleanor took a breath. They had reached the crux of the matter, though Isabella couldn't have known this. To win the girl's trust she had to be as forthright as possible. But the same truth she shared with the princess here, could well keep John from acting, if the girl betrayed her confidence.

"The treachery has been discovered by the only man among us whose wisdom I respect. And the king has banished him from his presence."

"William Marshal?" Isabella said, without missing a beat.

Clever indeed.

"William Marshal." Eleanor placed her cup on the table and stepped closer to the fire, her arms crossed over her chest. "Marshal lost his office, but kept his informants—sightings reported, letters intercepted—and he kept his eyes and ears open on his travels. He has no doubt. England is in danger, and one man is at the center of the plot." She turned to look at the girl, who still sat, her hands twisting nervously in her lap. "Tell me, do you trust me?"

"All my trust is in John," Isabella said. "If I had more to give, I might give it to you."

A reflexive smile touched Eleanor's face and vanished. "I envy you. I have trust for no one. But this time there is too much at risk to ignore Marshal's warning." She hesitated, but only for an instant. "The traitor is Godfrey. He has gone north to provoke the barons against the Throne. While England is at war with itself, the French army will land unopposed, and—"

"Why are you telling me, when you must tell the king?" Isabella broke in.

"Because it is you who must do that," Eleanor told her. The girl blanched, and Eleanor felt a pang of sympathy for her. She moved ruthlessly to crush it. The realm was at risk; either the girl was true to John and would do as Eleanor told her, or she wouldn't and all would be lost. Either way, compassion was not something they could afford just then.

She pressed on. "Tell King John that you have received word from France—from Philip himself, if you like—to return home to safety, and why."

"Why not tell him the truth?" the princess asked, her composure clearly shaken. "That William Marshal—"

"A mother he distrusts, bringing him the word of a man in disfavor?" Eleanor shook her head, smiling sadly. "No. If you hope to be queen, you must save John and England."

Isabella sat for a long time, saying nothing, gazing into the flames, seeming to consider what Eleanor had said. At last, still silent, she stood, dropped a quick curtsy, and left the chamber. Eleanor could but hope that she had managed to convince the girl.

JOHN SAT SPRAWLED in a low chair, his back to the fire blazing in his hearth, a sconce of burning candles beside the fireplace, the rest of his throne room in shadow. His evening meal sat on the table beside him, forgotten for the moment. Isabella had knocked at his door moments before, and at his summons to enter, had stepped into the chamber tentatively, as if afraid to speak with him. She had looked first to the throne and, not seeing him there, had turned a full circle before spotting him by the fire.

Still she had kept her distance, and at first he had found her diffidence charming. He had to remind himself sometimes that she was still but a girl, beautiful and alluring though she was.

But then, her words began to reach him. She had not come to chat idly or to seduce. She spoke of things she shouldn't have known; things that couldn't possibly be true. Listening, staring at her, John raised a hand to his face and began to rub it over his mouth. The other hand balled itself into a fist. And still the words rolled over him, like breakers blown onto shore by a winter storm. His mother, Godfrey, the northern barons. His heart pounded; his chest heaved with each breath.

Her face a mask of worry, Isabella came forward at last, dropping to her knees in front of him and taking his fist in her hands. And still she tried to explain.

He thrust himself out of his chair, yanking his hand free of her grasp. At first he paced, his rage building with every step, until he could no longer contain it. He swept everything off the table with a single violent gesture, roaring his frustration.

"Godfrey! Bloody Judas!"

Glasses smashed against a stone pillar, a pitcher of wine shattered on the floor, leaving a dark stain that glistened in the candlelight like blood. He grabbed hold of the table and threw it over, the wood cracking loudly. Isabella cowered beside his chair, but at that moment he didn't care.

He wanted to rage at his mother and at Marshal. Who were they to meddle in his affairs? Richard was dead; the realm was his now! Didn't they understand that?

But he knew that he wasn't really angry with them. It was Godfrey! The man had betrayed him! He wanted to deny it, but his heart told him it was true. Marshal had been a part of the royal house for longer than John had been alive. Godfrey, on the other hand, had been John's man from the start. John himself had brought him into the White Tower. He had been weak and foolish. Godfrey had known exactly what he wanted to hear, and like a fool John had mistaken the man's truckling for wisdom. Now he was paying the price.

The worst part of it was that his mother had known, and had tried to warn him. So had Marshal. Yes, he wanted to rail at them, but their only crime was that they were smarter than he was. They had seen this coming and he had not. The irony was as bitter as tansy; he nearly gagged on it.

His anger had spent itself. He took a long breath and looked at Isabella once more. She was watching him, holding a dagger in her hand, its tip pressed at her breast, nearly breaking the skin just over her heart. She held his gaze as he walked to where she stood. She let him take hold of the handle of the dagger, offering him her life for the tidings she had brought.

John's hand trembled as he closed his fingers over the hilt, and for just an instant he considered how easy it would be to slide the blade home. His eyes brimmed and he felt a tear slide down his cheek. Still she looked into his eyes, so brave, so willing to accept whatever fate he chose for her. He had never known that anyone could love him this much.

He let go of the dagger and it fell to the floor, clattering harmlessly.

He touched her face with the hand that had held the knife. "There was never a beauty so wise, nor a counselor so beautiful." He kissed her softly on the lips. "Nor a wife as loyal."

John's tears flowed freely now. He took Isabella in his arms and kissed her again, deeply, passionately, clinging to her as if he might never let her go. And she kissed him back, her ardor a match for his.

WILLIAM MARSHAL WATCHED as horse and rider turned another circle in the riding ring, the bay stepping gracefully, the man sitting him deftly applying pressure with the reins. First he coaxed the horse to a canter, then to a trot, then down to a walk. He made the beast step high, then dance to the side. William turned with them, occasionally offering a bit of instruction or a word of encouragement. Mostly though, he watched, enjoying the click of hooves and the smell of hay and horses. It had been too long since Marshal had spent time with his horses and with his people. He had spent too many years in the royal court; he had been too ensconced in politics and intrigue.

Horses, he realized, were not unlike kings. The secret was making them think that they were in control, even when they weren't. A horse would buck and rear under too heavy a hand, just as a king might ignore counsel given too adamantly. Marshal smiled ruefully at the thought. Perhaps he had learned that lesson a bit too late.

He watched as the rider steered the bay around the ring once more, making the horse step high again. As the man completed the turn, Marshal saw a group of riders approaching from the direction of the White Tower. It took him a moment to realize that the king himself rode at the fore.

Reaching the ring, John dismounted and shouted, "Marshal!" sounding panicked, even desperate.

Marshal faced the king, but remained in the ring, his rider now dancing the horse in place.

"Your Majesty," he said, his voice as calm as John's had been fraught.

"Keep that animal still! It hasn't got the palsy!"

The rider reined the horse to a stop and patted it gently on the neck. William watched John, trying to make sense of his presence here and what he had said.

"Do you think I haven't noticed how you have deserted me?" the king asked, sounding like a spoiled child.

Marshal frowned. "If Your Majesty recalls our last conversation—"

John's eyes blazed and he cut Marshal off with a sharp gesture. "At our last conversation, Philip of France was not coming our way with an invasion fleet!" He inhaled deeply, composing himself with a visible effort. "My friend Godfrey is not the friend I thought he was. Stirring up the barons against *me*. Coming south with an army. How dare they!"

"Sire," Marshal said, keeping his voice level in hopes of calming the king. "Forgotten men are dangerous men. The barons must be told that when the French come, we are all Englishmen together. Let us ride north to meet them. Wiser kings know they must let men look them in the eye, hear their voice, break bread with them. The barons need leadership."

Clearly, John heard him. He appeared to consider Marshal's words. But the truth was, John was no more a statesman than his brother, and he was far less of a warrior. He had too much pride to do what Marshal asked of him, and he was too afraid of the threat posed by the barons and the French to stay his sword. Godfrey's betrayal and all that his plotting had wrought demanded more courage, wisdom, and subtlety than John possessed. Marshal knew this, and he suspected that the king himself did as well.

"They march against their king!" John said, giving in to his anger and his fear. "I'll meet them with my militia's pikes in their gizzards! You've lost your touch, Marshal."

The king spurred his mount to a gallop and led his entourage back toward the Tower.

Marshal watched him go, frustrated with himself as much as with John. The king had come to him!

And he hadn't found the right words to sway him from what would prove a disastrous course.

He turned and saw his man standing a short distance off, tending to the pigeons, the ones Marshal kept, as well as the ones this man had sent to him from the north, after learning of Godfrey's perfidy. Marshal beckoned to the man.

"Saddle up with a spare horse. I leave immediately."

The man nodded to him.

Marshal stared off in the direction John had ridden. "I want to know where to find Godfrey."

The man nodded a second time and went to ready the horses.

CHAPTER

❦

TWENTY

The sheriff leaned back in his chair outside the town building in the center of Nottingham, watching the rabble go about their business. They complained about taxes, about the Crown and the Church taking too much, but he saw these people every day. He knew how little they worked, how much time they spent in idle pursuits. The farmers among them could easily have worked their fields more and with greater efficiency; the smiths and wheelwrights and woodcrafters could have produced more and chattered less. With a bit more industry, these people would have had more to eat, and he would have had more to send to London, to the benefit of all. But they groused endlessly, and so they suffered.

From the north edge of town, one of his rounds men approached leading a second man who kept his head covered with a hood. The sheriff sat forward and cast a questioning look at his rider, as the two stopped before him.

"Won't give his name," the roundsman said. "Demands audience with the sheriff."

The sheriff raised an eyebrow. "Demands." He turned to the hooded stranger, his hand resting on the hilt of his sword. "What have you got to say for yourself?"

"Long live the king," the stranger said smoothly. From within his cloak, the man produced a sealed letter. The sheriff stood and took it from him. He broke the seal and read. Before he was halfway through it, he looked up at his man and nodded, dismissing him.

The roundsman glanced once more at the hooded rider and then left. The sheriff finished reading the letter, and as he did, the stranger pushed back his hood, revealing a shaved head, small, widely spaced eyes, and a trim beard.

"Long live the king," the sheriff said when he finished reading. He looked the man in the eye. "You ride with Sir Godfrey?"

The stranger nodded. "Tax collection proceeds apace. Nottingham's turn is coming."

"Good," the sheriff said. At last he would have some help in putting the rabble in their place. "Tell Sir Godfrey the Sheriff of Nottingham is his man, may he put his stamp on my authority. I see trouble coming from Loxley of Peper Harrow."

The stranger laughed. "Sir Walter? A blind old man gives you trouble?"

The sheriff scowled at the man. "Aye. And his son will give more. The crusader, Robert Loxley, is returned. A week ago."

At these tidings, the man's entire bearing changed. Clearly he knew Sir Robert, or at least of him. But more than that, he appeared deeply surprised to hear of the knight's return. When the sheriff asked him what he knew of Loxley, however, the man demurred, apologized for needing to leave so soon, and rode away. Watching him go, the sheriff had the distinct impression that the stranger believed Sir Godfrey would be just as interested to hear of Sir Robert's return as he had been.

ROBIN CREPT THROUGH the most remote of Peper Harrow's fields, dew dampening his boots and breeches. He kept low and stepped carefully, creeping forward as silently as a fox, his bow held ready, an arrow already nocked. Perhaps twenty paces ahead of him, two pheasants—a brilliantly colored cock and a plump hen—foraged in the grass. Robin watched the birds for any sign that they were aware of his approach. Whenever the male stopped eating to look around, he froze.

When he was close enough, he straightened slowly, drew back his bow and loosed the arrow. Without waiting to see if the first dart struck true, he grabbed a second arrow, drew it back and fired, all in one smooth, blurringly fast motion. His first arrow struck the male in the neck; the second hit the hen's breast as she took off, knocking her back to the ground.

Robin strode to where they lay, fresh blood staining their feathers, as red as the Plantagenet crest and steaming in the cool morning air. He tied them together with a thin strand of leather, and hung them on his shoulder. Marion and he would eat well this evening.

He started back toward the house, taking the long way around the fields so that he could check on those he and his friends had sown the past two nights. They hadn't sprouted yet, of course, but still Robin took great pride in seeing the grain in its furrows. As he walked up and down the rows, he spotted a few stray seeds, and he nudged these back into the earth.

Robin had never thought of himself as anything more or less than a soldier, a man whose bow was for hire. He had surely never entertained the idea that he might tie himself to the land as a farmer. But planting this grain had changed something inside him. He hadn't given much thought to remaining in Peper Harrow for long, but a part of him wouldn't feel satisfied until he saw green shoots emerging from this rich brown soil. And another part of him wouldn't be happy until he saw this crop of grain harvested. It was an odd feeling for him.

Looking up from the grain, Robin spotted Marion in the distance. She wore a simple brown dress, a shawl wrapped around her shoulders. Her hair was unbound and she carried a broad basket, as if prepared for a picnic. Robin started to raise a hand in greeting, but realized that she wasn't walking toward him or the fields. She was headed into Sherwood Forest.

Pausing near the edge of the wood, she looked about, seeming to make certain that no one watched her. A moment later, she stepped into the shadows of the trees and disappeared from view.

This was her home and had been for more than ten years. She was entitled to come and go as she pleased. Robin knew this. But he couldn't help being puzzled by her behavior, nor could he resist the pull of his own curiosity. He hurried across the fields, and upon reaching Sherwood's fringe, hesitated but a moment before plunging into the forest.

He had tracked more wary game in his time, and so found Marion's trail with ease. He followed, quickly at first, more carefully as her path took him deeper and deeper into the wood. When at last he spotted her, he slowed to match her pace, taking great care to keep out of sight, his puzzlement growing with every step. This was no idle walk she was on. Marion made her way through the wood with purpose, following what looked to be a path she had taken before. Through a shallow hollow over a series of low hills, briefly along the banks of a stream and then into a second hollow—it would have been easy for someone less experienced with woodland travel to lose his way. But Marion never hesitated.

At one point Robin lost sight of her and paused, peering through the trees, trying to spot her again. As he searched, he heard a strange high-pitched whistling sound. It was coming at him fast and he looked up expecting to see some kind of bird.

Crack!

A throwing stick struck him hard on the side of the head, staggering him for just a moment. Before he could recover, something crashed into his side. He staggered again, but managed to stay upright. A creature—a badger at first glance. At least it had a badger head and fur on its back. But it was a boy. He had no time to see more than that. A second creature smashed into him from behind. He turned, managed to see a wolf's head and fur.

And then four more of them were on him, all boys, all dressed in fur as well, a couple of them sporting animal heads like the first two. They carried sticks, and they weren't afraid to use them. While some of his attackers pummeled him with their weapons, others grabbed at his arms and head and face with their hands, and still others punched and bit and scratched.

He had no desire to hurt children, but in mere seconds he'd had enough of these monsters. He swatted one off his leg, grabbed another from his back and threw him into the brush, shoved another one off his arm. But every time he got rid of one, two more seemed to attack. Their blows grew ever more vicious and Robin had no choice but to fight back harder, smacking one hard across the cheek with an open hand and kicking another in the stomach. And still they came. He didn't wish to use his bow or blade, but he was growing more desperate by the moment. They got him down to one knee, but Robin rallied, threw them off in quick succession, and had nearly won his way free.

But then they were on him once more, all fists and teeth and small, sharp elbows. He felt like a bear that has disturbed a beehive. He had might on his side, but these little ones could sting. He threw them off two at a time now, not caring how rough he was. And then, out of the corner of his eye, he thought he saw an actual bear. It took him a moment to realize that this was another boy, wearing dark fur and a bear's head. By the time he understood the danger, it was too late. The others had latched onto his arms and legs again. He could only watch as the cudgel rose and came down hard on his head.

And everything went dark.

* * *

WHEN ROBIN CAME around again he was still on the forest floor surrounded by the "animals." He couldn't have been out for long. The "badger" and a "fox" had started to tie his wrists and ankles with long vines. Rather than alerting them to the fact that he was awake, Robin played at still being unconscious. Through half-closed eyes, he watched the others as they gathered more vines and prepared a long pole. More boys milled all around them and from what he could see, Robin didn't think that any of them was more than ten or eleven years old.

Which wasn't to say that they couldn't do some damage. His head throbbed, and the rest of his body was covered with cuts and bruises and bite marks. Still the question remained, what were children doing in the middle of Sherwood Forest, living like the creatures whose skins they wore?

With as much care as possible, Robin tensed his wrists and ankles, so that as the boys tied him, he left himself a bit of maneuvering room. Whenever one of the boys looked his way, he closed his eyes completely, so by the time they took the pole and passed it through the spaces between his bound ankles and wrists and his body, they remained convinced that he was still out cold.

When they had the pole in position, six of the boys—three by Robin's head and three by his feet—lifted the pole onto their shoulders so that Robin hung like a trussed deer ready for cooking.

They started walking slowly through the forest, Robin swinging from the pole, his eyes closed now as much to keep from getting dizzy as to convince the boys he was unconscious. He hoped that his captors had remembered to retrieve his bow, quiver, and sword, not to mention the pheasant he had killed earlier.

Their walk through the wood seemed to take forever. Robin's wrists and ankles ached, his neck was growing stiff, and his stomach felt as though he had been at sea for too long. As they moved deeper into the forest, the number of boys walking along with the six who carried him continued to grow, until it seemed that there were dozens around him, all dressed in furs, all far too young to be living on their own in the wild.

Still viewing the world through half-closed eyes, Robin saw that the forest had thickened. The trees were taller here, more massive. Robin felt that he was being carried back in time to a primeval wood that existed before the royals had claimed these lands for their own.

The boys walked on and came at long last to a camp. Small fires burned before primitive, cavelike shelters with roofs made of branches and leaves. There were a few larger, sturdier structures as well, with walls made of animal skins. Still more boys were busy throughout the encampment. Some stood around fires stirring food in banged up pots, others worked to shore up the various shelters, and still others busied themselves with making or repairing tools and clothing and weapons. The boys he saw here looked to be older and larger than those who had attacked him, and many of them did double takes as they took note of what the smaller boys were carrying. This didn't go unnoticed by Robin's captors, who were clearly quite proud of themselves.

As the boys continued to parade him through the

camp like a trophy, Robin spotted Marion. She stood at a fire of her own, a low, broad bed of embers burning in a shallow trench. There were several boys gathered near her, and all of them appeared to be ill or injured. Several bore bandages; one stood on a crutch. A number of the boys, all of them coughing, were huddled by the fire. Four or five pots boiled there, steam rising from them in great clouds. Marion had the boys leaning over the pots, their heads covered with animal skins, so that they could breathe in the steam. Robin assumed that she was boiling herbs.

While the sick boys breathed in Marion's concoction, she had turned her attention to a wounded child. She was bent over him, dressing a small wound on his arm with medicine from a vial and a bandage seemingly made from leaves and moss. The other boys watched her closely, not the way they would a distrusted stranger, but rather as they might their own mothers.

The boys who carried Robin let out a shout, announcing their arrival to those who hadn't yet noticed. Marion looked up and, seeing that they carried a man on their pole, regarded them with alarm and disapproval. A moment later—Robin saw it happen—she realized who it was they had captured and her expression changed. She still looked concerned, but there was a hint of amusement in her eyes as well. Robin couldn't say that he blamed her.

The six who carried him finally stopped walking and dumped him unceremoniously in the middle of the camp. They milled around him for a moment or two, and Robin continued to pretend that he was unconscious.

One of the older boys walked over to them, carrying himself with the confidence of a war commander.

"Good work, men," he said, stopping in front of Robin. "Has he spoken?"

One of the other boys shook his head. "Let him hang a little, Loop. He'll taste better."

The other boys laughed. A number of the younger ones crept closer to Robin and reached out to poke his shoulder, his back, his leg. Robin opened one eye and let out a low growl. The boys jumped away again, squealing happily.

Marion joined the group gathering around Robin, a smile on her face as well.

"He were spyin', Loop," one of the boys who had captured him said to the leader.

Marion looked down at Robin, an eyebrow raised. Robin smiled weakly, admitting his guilt.

"Spying!" Marion said. "Why, I'm ashamed of you, Robert!"

"A good day to you, Lady," Robin replied.

The one named Loop turned to Marion. "Do you know him?"

Marion gestured toward the boys with an open hand. "Sir Robert," she said, as though making formal introductions, "the runaways of Sherwood." She indicated Robin. "Boys, Sir Robert Loxley, my husband."

For the first time, Loop appeared frightened. "Untie him!"

But Marion held up a hand, stopping them. "Oh, I think spies must not be let off so easily."

Robin gave her a wounded look. "That was unkind."

Loop's eyes widened as he finally seemed to understand the significance of what Marion had said. "You were a crusader?" he asked, sounding awed.

"For ten years," Robin said. "Thirty-five in the army."

"Hear that boys?" Loop called to the others. "You bested a crusader!" The younger boys beamed; the older ones looked at them with renewed respect. Loop pointed to his army. "My men are good fighters," he told Robin.

Robin considered them. "They move silent, like creatures of the forest." Looking up at Loop again, he added, "But it's only a worthy skill if you live as men, not as common thieves and poachers."

Loop's face fell. "We're soldiers," he insisted, sounding terribly young.

"True soldiers fight for a cause," Robin said. He paused, cast a quick look at Marion. "Besides, you have many skills left to learn."

"Like what?" the boy asked, a challenge in his voice.

Robin grinned. "Knots!"

Saying the word, Robin rolled onto his knees and got to his feet, pole and all, in one seamless motion. The boys gaped at him, too surprised to move. Gripping the pole in both hands, he lifted it free of the vines tied around his ankles. With the pole out of the way, the vines were so loose that he was able to step out of them with ease. Still gripping the wood, he spun, so that the pole made a swift arc. Several of the boys jumped back, just out of the way, and the stick smashed through a water gourd hanging from a nearby branch. Drops of water and shards of the gourd flew in all directions.

"Because that would have been your head," Robin said to the startled Loop.

He let go of the pole, allowing it to slip through his fingers and fall free of the ropes binding his wrists. And as with the ties at his ankles, this made the knots loose enough that he could simply throw them off. Catching the pole in his hands before it hit the ground, he gripped it like Little John would his stave and quickly backed Loop against a tree trunk, trapping the lad there with the end of the pole pressed lightly against his chest.

"And that, your breastbone," Robin went on.

He did all of this in mere seconds. Every person there stared at him, awed, shocked to silence. Even Marion. She eyed him as if he was a stranger, looking both impressed and a bit frightened. She caught his eye, and Robin gazed right back at her, letting her see that this was as true a part of him as the rest of what she had come to know these past few days. He could be a leader, as her husband had been. He could rescue a ram and steal grain back from the Church. And he could fight.

After a moment Robin stepped back and lowered the stave. "There's much I can teach you." He said. "You can find me in Nottingham."

Loop stared at him for another moment, still impressed. Then he nodded, smiling faintly.

He and his riders reached the outskirts of Nottingham just as night fell. Stars spread across the velvet blue sky, from the darkness of the east toward the waning fiery glow at the western horizon. From the rise where they halted their mounts, he could see a bonfire burning at the edge of a broad field. People converged on the blaze from other fields, and from the town at the base of the hill—it seemed that some sort of celebration was just beginning.

Good. That would give him the opportunity to approach unseen. William Marshal twisted around in his saddle to face the leader of the small escort that had ridden north with him.

"Wait for me here," he said.

The man nodded. Marshal rode alone toward the fire.

As he and Marion returned to Peper Harrow from the forest, Robin managed to shoot and kill a wild boar. That boar now turned on a spit over a great bed of coals not far from a blazing bonfire. Will Scarlet turned several birds, including Robin's pheasants, on small spits nearby. Villagers had brought cheeses and breads, greens and roots, mead and wine. King John wouldn't have thought much of the feast they were preparing, but in his brief time here, Robin had yet to see the people of Nottingham this excited. Everywhere he looked, people grinned and laughed. Robin could see, though, that Marion had been right the other day. There were few young men left in the town and fewer boys.

Allan had brought his lute and was tuning its strings. Robin saw Friar Tuck and Little John approaching, each carrying stone jars, and John rolling a keg in front of him with one foot. When they finally reached the fires, Tuck sat down behind Allan and took up a double-sided drum.

Little John hefted the keg. "Come, Allan," he said. "I'll get them drinking if you'll get them dancing."

Allan smiled and began to play a lively old drinking song. The friar beat the drum in time, and around them people began to clap their hands. Robin wondered when they had last enjoyed such an evening in this town.

Robin had joined Sir Walter, who sat bathed in the glow of the bonfire, a huge grin on his lined face, one hand slapping his thigh in time with the music.

"Music. Laughter. The crackle of a bonfire." He paused, sniffing the air. "And a roasting pig!" he said, delighted. "That unmistakable sound of people about to eat." He turned his grin on Robin. "You have returned life to us."

"And the fields planted."

Robin looked up to see that Marion had emerged from the darkness to stand with them. She held out a hand to him.

"As lord and mistress, it is expected that we dance," she said. "They will wait until we do."

Robin looked over to where Allan and the friar were playing. The townspeople were milling around the musicians and clapping, but they had yet to start dancing. And, in fact, many of the villagers kept glancing toward the two of them, clearly waiting. It would still take him some time to get used to being lord of the manor.

He looked up at Marion once more, took her offered hand, and let her lead him over to the bonfire and the musicians. Her hand felt warm in his and he was conscious suddenly of the firelight shimmering in her hair. He sensed that every pair of eyes was trained on them, but he didn't care. In that moment, all that seemed to matter was the music and the fire and the woman beside him.

Marion took hold of his other hand, nodded to him once, and they began to dance.

NOBODY APPEARED TO have noticed the sheriff as he rode up to the field, dismounted, and approached the fire. He had gotten himself a tankard of ale, but still no one spoke to him. Now, watching through the flames as Loxley and Lady Marion danced in the firelight, he raised his cup, trying to join the spirit of the evening.

"Well," he said, "here's to . . ." He trailed off. No one seemed to hear him. They didn't even seem to know he was there. He lowered his cup slowly, the smile he had fixed on his lips giving way to a scowl. Grumbling to himself, he took another drink and watched.

LITTLE JOHN HAD the keg tapped and was filling cups and tankards as quickly as they were handed to him, and occasionally draining and refilling his own.

Allan had finished his first song and was playing another one, as Tuck continued to beat on the tabor drum, occasionally taking time out to drink his honey mead. Scarlet began to sing.

If I were a minstrel,
I'd sing you six love songs,
To the whole world of the love that we share . . .

Robin had never thought much of Will's singing voice, but tonight he sounded sweeter than usual. Although that might have had more to do with the woman dancing with Robin, than with anything Will had done to improve his singing.

Once he got started, Robin realized that he liked dancing more than he thought. Then again, that might have been Marion's doing, too. The townspeople around them had joined in the dancing almost as soon as Robin and Marion began. They laughed and clapped hands, and shouted greetings to Sir Robert and Lady Marion as they spun past. Robin barely noticed them.

He did spot the Sheriff of Nottingham lurking at the edge of the firelight, a tankard in one hand and a piece of roasted fowl in the other. The sheriff appeared to be watching them dance. Robin thought that the man looked covetously at Marion, but that might have been a trick of the light, or of his own imagination. A moment later, the sheriff turned and walked away, melting into the darkness. And good riddance to him.

Will sang on.

If I were a merchant,
I'd bring you six diamonds,
With six blood red roses for my love to wear . . .

Robin had his arm around Marion's waist, and her arm was around his. Her eyes shone bright with the flames, and her color was high. A smile touched her lips as she met his gaze. He smiled in return. Her eyes held his for another beat of Tuck's drum and then she looked away self-consciously. Robin felt others watching them. They were supposed to be husband and wife, and just then he felt very much like they were. Did Marion as well? Was it too soon for her?

But I am a simple man,
A poor common farmer,
So take my six ribbons to tie back your hair.

She leaned closer to him, her body moving in concert with his, her hair close enough that he could smell rosemary and lavender. She looked up into his eyes again, then lowered her gaze, smiling still, moving her head closer to his neck.

Robin leaned in once more, inhaling, hoping to catch the scent of her hair again. As he did, though, he spotted something in the distance, near to the edge of Sherwood.

At first he thought it another trick of the light. The glow of the bonfire barely reached that far. His sight was keen; he doubted that many others would have noticed. Will perhaps, and Allan. But they were busy with their music.

Marion noticed the line of his gaze and shot him a questioning look. Still he watched the fields nearest the wood. It seemed that a deer had stepped out from the trees. But it wasn't a deer. Other animals followed. A badger, a wolf, a bear, a fox. And still more came. A line of them. Loop and his boys had come forth from the wood. They didn't approach the fire, but remained where they were, watching.

MARSHAL SLID THROUGH the crowd unnoticed, his cloak concealing his mail and tabard, his head covered. The people around him were having too good a time to take notice of a stranger, and he did nothing to draw attention to himself. He skirted the edge of the firelight and moved deliberately, making certain that he didn't appear to be in too great a hurry.

He spotted Sir Walter from a good distance. His friend sat near the bonfire, a smile lighting his face, a finger bouncing on his thigh in time to the music. Even from far away, he looked old; several years had passed since Marshal last saw him, and they had taken their toll on the man. Then again, William knew that time had left its mark on him, too. If Walter could have seen him, he surely would have told William as much.

Marshal walked a wide circle around the townspeople and their cooking fires and came at last to where Sir Walter sat. Stepping out of the flickering shadows behind his friend, he looked around to make certain he wasn't seen, and then sat beside the man.

The old man's finger stopped bouncing.

"*Agni Leones Fient,*" Walter said in a low voice. The lambs will become lions.

Marshal looked at him in amazement, a smile spreading over his face. "How did you know it was me?"

Walter grinned. From up close, in the warm glow of the blaze, he looked more himself than Marshal had imagined from far off. There was no denying that the lines in his face were deeper, or that his hair was now shot through with silver. But he sat straight-backed, and his eyes, though sightless, were still lively. And clearly his mind remained sharp.

"Who else would sit beside me uninvited?" he said. "Like a friend from the old days?" He reached for Marshal's arm, found it, and gave it a quick squeeze. "How are you, William?"

He placed a hand on Sir Walter's shoulder. "Well," he said. "And troubled."

One of the townspeople called a greeting to Sir Walter and he raised a hand acknowledging it. "And what brings you?" he asked, still speaking quietly.

"I am riding on to Barnsdale tonight." Marshal looked around once more, and when next he spoke, it was in a whisper. "I never thought to give myself such importance, Walter, but I am all that stands between the king and disaster for England."

Walter nodded at this. "I've heard something of the barons' anger against the Crown's tax collectors."

"Well," Marshal said, "anger has turned to actions. They assemble to march against the king."

"You think you can persuade the barons to turn back?" Walter asked.

"Turn back?" William shook his head. "No! To join King John against a French invasion." He leaned closer, eyeing his friend intently. "Help me, Walter. You have the barons' respect. I have been too long in the palace."

"And you speak for the king."

Marshal heard disapproval in Sir Walter's tone.

"I do," he said. "Civil war will bring no one liberty."

Walter turned his face toward William's. "I cannot go with you. I cannot speak for this king."

In the days that had passed since Marshal had resolved to stop here in Nottingham and speak with his old friend, it had never once occurred to him that Walter might refuse him. They had marched together, fought together, dreamed together of building a better England, a freer England. King John was far from the ideal ruler;

no one knew that better than he. But better a poor leader than a realm divided by civil war and conquered by Philip Augustus.

"He's the only king we have," Marshal said, pleading with his friend.

A small smile lit the old man's face. "But not the only hope!" he whispered.

William didn't bother to mask his surprise.

Sir Walter went on, speaking as earnestly as they had long ago, when freedom and the possibility of a better England had seemed more than mere fantasy. "In the time of the stonemason, we had a vision of justice. Not king's justice, but justice for all. I believe that moment has returned to us."

"Explain," William said, eager to hear more and desperate to believe him.

Walter held up a hand. "Wait," he said. "Wait for my daughter."

Marshal frowned. He had known Robert, of course, the old knight's son. But a daughter . . . ? He looked around at the faces dancing past him in the shifting golden light of the fire, and soon spotted one woman who was not laughing or celebrating with the others. She was watching him and Walter, eyeing the old man protectively, and him with obvious distrust.

She was an attractive woman—long dark hair, high cheekbones, a full, sensuous mouth, intelligent eyes. She gazed their way for another moment and then started in their direction.

"Sir Walter," she said as she drew near.

Walter turned his face up to hers, his expression untroubled. "This is my old friend William Marshal," he told her. Looking at Marshal, he added, "Lady Marion Loxley, my son's wife."

Marshal nodded to her, though he had trouble holding her gaze. He had met her husband not long ago, and had found himself wondering if the man was who he truly claimed to be.

"My lady," he said, "I was glad to see Sir Robert when he disembarked in London."

"I think you know better, Marshal," Sir Walter said. The old man turned back to Marion. "Please find him, Marion. Sir William, I know, would like to meet Robin Longstride again."

Marshal's mouth fell open. He wouldn't have been more surprised if his old friend had said that he had the King of France here in Nottingham waiting to meet him. Memories flooded his mind. Of Barnsdale, of the magnificent cross, of the stonemason Longstride, of his tragic bloody death at the hands of Henry's soldiers. And of a boy with long limbs and brown hair, who was forced to watch his father die and was then spirited away to France. Marshal had loved the father, and had grown fond of the lad, but he had never thought that he would see him again. They had left him with farming folk in Normandy knowing that he would be safe there. But when they went back for him, intending to tell him of his father and see to his education, they had been shocked to find him gone. A legacy lost.

He remembered as well that the Loxley he met on the dock in London had seemed oddly familiar, though at the time he hadn't known why. He wouldn't have guessed this in a thousand years.

Once more he began searching the faces around him and soon spotted Loxley—Longstride—speaking with the musicians and a broad-shouldered man who seemed to have taken it upon himself to provide every man and woman in the village with ale. He saw Marion join the man, and then the two of them moved off into the shadows, where he lost track of them.

The music went on, growing louder and more raucous by the moment. More wood was thrown on the fire, more food carried out into the field. The celebration showed no sign of ending before dawn. Through it all, Sir Walter sat with a joyful look on his weathered face.

As he watched the townspeople dance, William felt a light tap on his shoulder. Turning, he saw that Lady Marion had returned. She beckoned to him silently. Marshal stood and followed her a short way to where Longstride stood alone, watching the villagers.

"This is Robin Longstride," Marion said, keeping her voice down so that no one else would hear. She looked at Longstride. "William Marshal."

Looking into the younger man's face, Marshal took a breath. Knowing now who this man was, he saw the resemblance to the stonemason he had known all those years ago. The keen blue eyes, the square face, the strong profile. How could he have missed it back in London?

"We have met before," Marshal said, his voice barely more than a whisper.

Longstride stared back into his eyes. Marshal could see that he remembered, that whatever he had forgotten in the intervening years was coming back to him.

"I know," Robin said.

They continued to look at each other, each giving in to memory. After a few moments, Marshal offered a hand. Longstride gripped it and laid his other hand over their two. Marshal did the same, and they stood thus for some time, while Marion looked on.

ROBIN AND WILLIAM Marshal had sat down together apart from the others. Marion had gone to sit with Sir Walter, and the rest were too happy with the music and dancing and honey mead to notice the two men.

Sir Walter had told Robin a little bit about his father and his past, but Marshal knew so much more. Or at least he was willing to tell Robin more. He shared his own memories of the stonemason—of Thomas Longstride—and of the things he had talked about: freedom and justice, the rights of people to make their way in the world as they saw fit. He talked as well about that terrible day when the king's men killed Robin's father. His recollections weren't much different from what Robin had recently recalled, but oddly Robin found some comfort in that. None of it was easy for Robin to hear. Yet, even as his emotions churned, leaving him more out of sorts than he could remember being, he felt pieces of his life sliding into place in ways that made sense for the first time.

"How old was I?" he asked.

"Hobbyhorse age," Marshal said. "Old enough to walk astride a horse's head on a stick; young enough to make believe you had a horse!"

Robin smiled at that. Even this he could remember. Talking to Marshal had opened his mind to a flood of images. And though there was a thin line between swimming in these memories and drowning in them, for now at least Robin managed to stay afloat.

"Sir Walter and I returned from the Holy Land to fetch you home," Marshal told him, his expression sobering. "But you had gone. We had lost Thomas Longstride's son! That was a wound which never healed."

The look on Marshal's face said different, though. The wound was healing now.

CHAPTER

TWENTY-TWO

The following morning, as the rest of Nottingham awoke to a too-bright sun, and the overly loud calls of overly zealous roosters, and the type of headaches that only Tuck's mead could induce, Robin began to delve deeper into his past and the legacy of his father's politics.

Upon waking and descending the stairs of Peper Harrow to the great hall, he found Sir Walter already awake and sitting at the long wooden table, which was laden with old scrolls. Walter waved him over, grinning and gesturing grandly at the mountain of parchment.

And so Robin was introduced to the extensive writings of Thomas Longstride.

It seemed that referring to his father as a mere stonemason was akin to calling Richard the Lionheart a mere soldier. Robin's father had written at length about politics, about opposing the king and rousing the people of the realm from their torpor, and about his dreams for England. Some of what Robin read inspired him; some of it confused him, and these tracts he and Walter discussed until his father's words became clearer. Through it all, though, Robin's admiration for Thomas Longstride grew, and his understanding of his own life, of notions that over the years had struck him as if out of the blue, crystalized.

For so long he had thought of himself as rootless, a mercenary—an Englishman, to be sure, but one without any true ties to the land or its people. His father, though, had been so much more. And seeing this, reading the man's words, visualizing for himself the realm Thomas had tried to build, Robin realized that he wanted more for himself and for England. He had never been a man to indulge in regrets or self-doubt. He had chosen a soldier's life, and had lived it to its fullest. But after learning so much about his father, he could no longer be satisfied with the man he had been.

Walter seemed to understand this. At first he said little, save to answer Robin's questions and refer him first to one scroll and then to another. But as the morning wore on, Walter began to say more. He spoke of what he and William Marshal had done to help Thomas spread his teachings to others. He described the horror of watching Henry's men murder the stonemason, and of seeing Longstride's dreams, and those of the people who had followed him, die in the wake of that terrible day in Barnsdale. And at last, Walter told Robin of all he and Marshal had done to see Robin safely to France, so that one day Thomas Longstride's son might take up his cause.

Only a day or two before, Robin might have refused

to listen. *This isn't my legacy,* he might have said. *This isn't the life I want.* But not now. He listened, and he thought he could hear in the old man's words, an echo of his father's voice.

Between all that he had read and heard and thought about, Robin lost track of the time. But sometime around midday, he and Walter heard a commotion outside the house. Walter appeared alarmed, and Robin understood why. After all this talk of freedom and remaking the realm even in the face of opposition from the Throne, he couldn't help wondering for just a moment if King John's men had come for them.

As it turned out, this wasn't too far from the truth.

One of the house servants hurried into the great hall leading a messenger. The man looked exhausted; his clothes were ragged and travel stained. But he stood straight-backed before the two of them as he gave his message to Sir Walter.

"My lord," he said, "Peterborough has been burned by the king's men. Darlington and York as well. Fitzrobert gathers an army to slay King John in London! He asks the barons to gather for council at Barnsdale."

Walter turned from the messenger to Robin. The old man might have been blind, but his eyes seemed to burn deep into Robin's soul.

"Cometh the hour, cometh the man," he said. "The time for pretense is over. Hug me like a father."

Robin didn't flinch from his gaze. "Have you told me everything?"

"Your father, the mason Longstride, was the leader of our rebellion against Henry. That is why he was killed. Promise me you will avoid the same fate." Walter pointed directly at the messenger, though his eyes remained fixed on Robin. "Go with this man," he said. "You will find what you are looking for."

Robin gazed at the man and began to nod. At last his path was clear, his past made sense, his name had meaning. This was his father's cause; he was the man to lead it.

He gave Walter's arm a quick squeeze, stood, and followed the messenger out into the courtyard.

MARION STOOD ON the bottom stair, her hand resting against the cold stone wall, her head tilted slightly, so that she might hear all that Robin and Walter said to each other. She shouldn't have been listening. But the matters Robin and Walter discussed had ramifications for all of them, and she wanted to understand fully the connections between the two men.

Mostly she wanted to know more about this man who had come into their lives so suddenly and with such profound consequences for them all. Since Robin's arrival, Nottingham had been transformed. The wild boys were beginning to emerge from the shadows of the wood, music and dance and laughter had returned to the fields surrounding Peper Harrow. And despite the dark tidings he carried with him from King Richard's army, Marion felt her own heart moving past grief to a new and unlikely love.

Now it seemed that there was even more to this man—and Walter—than she had imagined. Robin's father was the leader of a rebellion to which Walter had been party. Had her Robert been involved in this, too? From the sound of it, she didn't think so. But still she wondered.

The messenger, though, had spoken quite clearly. A new rebellion had come, and the other barons looked to the house of Loxley for aid. She didn't know whether to be proud or outraged. And so she hid in the shadows, and she listened.

For several days now, they had acted at being husband and wife. But there could be no denying how powerfully they had been drawn to each other the previous night as they danced in the firelight. She had lost one love to the last crusade. Would she lose another to the barons' rebellion?

Walter turned in his chair and looked back toward the stairway.

"Marion?" he called.

She didn't want him to know that she had been listening, and she didn't trust herself to speak of Robin with anyone just now. Silently, she withdrew.

It hadn't taken Robin long to find Will, Allan, and Little John. This was something else that had changed so quickly for him in recent days. Not long ago he had been ready to bid farewell to his friends and accept that the time had come for them to go their separate ways. But they resisted, and he was glad. He couldn't imagine undertaking this journey to Barnsdale without them.

They had followed him back to Peper Harrow and waited for him now as he saddled his horse and cinched his pack. As he readied his things, the house servant he had sent to find Marion appeared in the barn doorway. She was alone.

"Where is Marion?" he asked her as he retrieved his bow.

The girl curtsied deferentially. "I couldn't find her, sir."

Robin frowned, wondering where Marion could be.

He didn't like the idea of leaving Nottingham without saying good-bye to her. By the same token, he knew that he couldn't afford to delay their departure. From what the rider had said, it seemed that Fitzrobert and the other barons were itching for a battle. Robin needed to reach Barnsdale as quickly as possible.

He thought about telling the girl to search the house for Marion again, but then thought better of it. There was too much to explain, too much he didn't yet understand—about himself, about what he was setting out to do, about what he and Marion had begun to share. In the end he merely nodded to the girl and led his friends from the barn and out of the Peper Harrow courtyard.

SHE STOOD AT her window, taking care to keep out of sight, and she watched them ride away. She wasn't sure why she had avoided the servant Robin sent for her, or why she didn't call to Robin now, to offer a word of farewell and a wish that he return to her. She recalled watching her husband ride off to Richard's war and wondered at the changes wrought by ten years of waiting. She hadn't been nearly as frightened when Robert left. She had been young and in love and convinced that he would return, that life couldn't deal her so cruel a blow as to take her husband. She knew better now, and so she prayed that fate would be gentler with her this time.

THEY HADN'T RIDDEN far before Robin reined his mount to a halt, pausing on the road to look back at Nottingham. The town had not seemed like much when first he saw it, but it had changed in the few days he had spent there. The lanes seemed to hum with activity; shops were busier, people looked happier, more at ease.

And even as he resolved to see his father's work through to its end, Robin also felt the tug of the place on his own emotions. For the first time in his memory, he had found a home in his native land, and someone with whom he could imagine spending the rest of his days.

He felt the others watching him. After a few moments, Will, who was closest to him, began to whistle softly the melody he sang the night before. Robin couldn't hear the tune without thinking of Marion; of the firelight on her face, of the way she had felt in his arms.

If I were a minstrel,
I'd sing you six love songs,
To tell the whole world of the love that we share . . .

He turned his mount once more and led the men away from Nottingham and Peper Harrow, toward Barnsdale, where a rebellion was brewing.

CHAPTER

TWENTY-THREE

They were awake with the first faint glimmerings of daylight. Adhemar's legionnaires moved about the camp with their usual quiet efficiency, their blue cloaks and tabards blending with the pale gray smoke of cooking fires and the fine, cool mist that lingered in the wood, so that they looked like ghosts drifting among the trees.

As the men around him fed themselves and prepared to break camp, Godfrey bent over a crude washbasin, splashing cold water on his face and shaved head. They had miles to ride today, as they had the previous day and the one before that. Their campaign had taken on a rhythm of sorts, one that felt comfortable to him. Word of the barons' rebellion had reached him. He hoped it had reached London, as well. The king would see in the alliance between Baldwin and Fitzrobert a threat to his power. And without Marshal there to guide him, he would meet the threat with the only tools he understood: bows and pikes and swords. By the time Philip Augustus crossed the channel, England would be neck-deep in civil war.

At the sound of his own name, Godfrey straightened and turned, drying his face with a towel that he then tossed aside. Belvedere had returned and approached him now with one of his toughs in tow. Belvedere looked travel weary, but he wore a self-satisfied smile.

"I found him, m'lord," the man said.

"Where?" Godfrey asked, resisting an urge to raise a hand to the fading scar on his cheek.

Adhemar stood nearby, and Godfrey sensed that he was listening closely to their exchange.

Belvedere smiled, as if sharing some great joke. "In plain sight, living in Nottingham as Sir Walter's son."

This was the last thing Godfrey had expected him to say. "The temerity of the man." He had to admit, though, that he admired this Loxley, or whoever he really was. Living openly in the dead knight's home? It was something Godfrey himself might have done.

He crossed to a nearby table, which held a map tracing the path he and Adhemar had burned across England. He looked to the French commander.

"Two men," he said. "Four horses. Ride hard to the coast, and then onto Paris with a message for the king."

Adhemar eyed him eagerly. "And the message?" he asked, his accent thick.

Godfrey considered, but only briefly. The moment for subtlety had long since passed. "Tell him it is time."

Adhemar hurried off. Godfrey remained by the table, staring down at the map. He traced their path, his finger gliding over Barnsdale and York, Peterborough and Darlington. At last, his finger came to rest, and he tapped the map lightly, looking up at Belvedere.

"And we to Nottingham. No prisoners and not a stone unscorched." He grinned. "By God! I'll make the place famous!"

IF NOT FOR the great cross that still stood in the center of the village, Marshal might never have known that he was in the right place. Though a modest town, Barnsdale had always been clean and welcoming, a pleasant place to visit.

But Godfrey and his henchmen had left the village in ruin. Fields and homes and shops had been burned black, and everywhere Marshal turned, he saw fresh graves marked by simple crosses.

Yet, Barnsdale had been transformed in other ways as well. Throughout the village, bright banners fluttered in the wind, bearing the sigils of baronies from throughout Northern England. Small clusters of soldiers milled about in the lanes, if these men—some older than Marshal and Sir Walter, some no more than boys—could even be called soldiers. They sharpened blades and axes, turned pitchforks and hoes into makeshift pikes. They talked among themselves, their expressions grim but determined. A few of them watched Marshal as he made his way through the lanes. Perhaps they knew who he was. Perhaps they saw that he wore the colors of the Plantagenet and assumed that he was the king's man and thus an enemy of their cause.

Horses grazed where they could find food. Dust drifted through the streets, occasionally swirled with leaves and bits of straw in tiny whirlwinds.

Marshal made his way to a large canvas pavilion in the center of the village, where most of the barons and their men had gathered. A smith, working at what was left of the village forge, made new shoes for horses. Cooking fires burned and men waited in line for thin broth and scraps of bread. Most of those who had gathered here looked no more like soldiers than those Marshal had passed in the street, but they were being drilled by more experienced fighters. Nearby, an armorer distributed weapons from a wagon laden with rusted swords, lances, and old battle axes. Clearly, the barons and their men were in earnest. And few men knew better than William Marshal what an army of committed soldiers could accomplish, regardless of their training or the state of their weapons and armor.

Marshal entered the pavilion and immediately all conversations ceased, and every man looked in his direction. He recognized Baldwin and Fitzrobert right away. He had known the former for years. They had served together, fought together, gotten drunk together. Once he had counted the baron as a friend, though he could tell from the way Baldwin regarded him now that those days were gone. Fitzrobert, he didn't know as well, but there were few barons in all of England as formidable in appearance. He was a mountain of a man, and he glowered at Marshal with manifest hostility.

There were about two dozen other barons in the pavilion. Some of them Marshal knew as well as he did Baldwin; others he had never seen before. But he sensed that Baldwin and Fitzrobert were the leaders of the group and he focused his attention on them. The two men were angry to the point of bitterness, and Marshal could hardly blame them. He had seen what Godfrey and his men had done to Barnsdale, Baldwin's home, and it seemed that the home villages of these other barons had suffered similar fates. Had William been in their position, he would have been eager for blood, too.

But in this case their calls for vengeance were misplaced. They needed to understand that King John wasn't their enemy; Godfrey and his French allies were. He soon realized, though, that Godfrey had planned all too well. Such was their rage at the king, that they would not listen to anything he said. Each time Marshal responded to their grievances he was shouted down. In their eyes, John was a villain, and Marshal was the king's man.

"I speak for all here," Baldwin said, raising his hands to silence the other barons, and addressing Marshal. "As regent, John was vain and dissolute, but now a crown on his head makes him a despot. You have spent too much time in the palace, William."

William opened his hands. "You must swim with sharks to understand them." The barons began to shout at him again, but Marshal raised his voice and spoke over them. "John is new to the throne— but a brigand he is not. Godfrey has betrayed the king and England. He is an agent of King Philip; his marauders are French. Do not let his barbarism blind you to the threat approaching our shores. Every minute wasted in dissension brings this country closer to its own demise."

He looked around the pavilion, hoping that some of the men might heed his warning. But even though a few appeared to recognize the truth in what he said, none of them was ready to join cause with John.

Godfrey had divided them, but John himself had sown the seeds of this rebellion with his pettiness and his lack of discipline.

"We have been bled by the Crown long before Godfrey," Fitzrobert said, drawing nods and murmurs of agreement. "Go back to London and tell the king: We will meet him on the field of his choice!"

The others roared their approval.

LONG BEFORE THEY reached the Barnsdale gate, Robin could see that the town had been attacked. The gate and town wall were blackened, and those few buildings which still stood within the walls had been damaged as well. Will, Allan, and Little John had been chattering on about the girls they had met in Nottingham, but seeing the town, they fell into a grim silence.

All was still around the town, save for a single bird that circled once overhead and then swooped down into the village. It had the look of a messenger pigeon. Robin wondered what new tidings awaited them within those scorched walls.

Crossing through the gate, Robin found the lanes of the village crowded with a ragged army of yeomen and peasants of all ages. They were armed and some wore armor, but Robin was certain that few of them had been soldiers a month ago. Many wore haunted expressions, as if they had already witnessed horrors enough to last them a lifetime.

And looking around, he had no doubt that they had. Barnsdale had been ravaged. What hadn't been torn apart had been burned. Almost no home or shop had been spared.

Robin glanced back at Will and the others before

dismounting and beginning to walk slowly through the village. His village, where he had passed the earliest days of his childhood. The place looked familiar to him and he tried to get his bearings, to recall where his home had been. He could tell that the others were following, but he didn't look back at them. The place had taken hold of him—the look of it, the smells. His blood seemed to flow through his body and into the very earth on which he walked.

You will find what you are looking for, Sir Walter had said.

Robin was close now. He knew it. The deeper into the village he walked, the more powerful the feeling grew. And so when he turned the corner, he should have been prepared for what he saw. Should have been, but wasn't.

Towering over the ruin that once had been Barnsdale's village center, stark against the blue sky, stood the Celtic cross that he remembered from his youth. The cross his father had built.

Seeing it, Robin felt as though he had been punched in the stomach. He walked toward it, unable to look away, and unable to resist the memories that washed over him once more.

HE IS TOO SMALL. Something is happening at the center of the crowd, but men's backs block his view, so that all he can see is the cross towering above all of them. The men are soldiers, he realizes. They wear chain mail and tabards bearing the Plantagenet leopards. But this doesn't stop him. He wants to see, *has* to see, and he can't. And so he begins to push his way through, snaking between and around and under when all else fails. He pushes past a forest of legs and swords hanging from belts, and comes at last to the front of the army that has gathered in the center of the village.

His father stands straight and tall before the cross, facing the king's men, dignified and strong, as unmovable as the cross itself. If he is afraid, he shows no sign of it. But Robin is afraid. And he sees fear written on the faces of those who look on.

Thomas Longstride draws his sword slowly, his eyes still on the soldiers. There is no menace in the gesture, no threat. He pulls the weapon free and then turns it so that he can offer the hilt to the nearest of the soldiers. It is an act of goodwill, a peace offering. Any fool can see that.

ROBIN DIDN'T WANT to remember any of this. He knew the ending as well as he did his own name. He had seen it, he had remembered it once. He wanted only to turn away, to leave this place. But still he walked on toward the cross, breathing quickly and hard now. And still the images came, inexorable as the tide.

THE KING'S MEN have grabbed hold of Thomas Longstride. They grip his arms, holding them outstretched so that he is defenseless. Around them, the people shout that he has done nothing wrong. Robin screams for them to let his father go. But the guards won't listen. The man who has taken the stonemason's sword raises it and strikes. . . .

ROBIN STAGGERED AND cried out as if taking the remembered blow himself. He nearly fell, but righted himself, his eyes unseeing. . . .

* * *

HE SCREAMS, SWOONS, collapses to the ground, and for a moment is lost to the darkness. But soon he feels powerful hands lift him. He tries to fight them off, to kick and punch and bite. His father is dead; he will not be taken, too.

But through half-lidded eyes he sees that it is not the king's men who have taken him, but two others. Young men, grim and determined.

And from a distance of too many years, the older Robin, the man walking through the streets of his youth, recognizes these two. Sir Walter, his eyes whole and clear, and William Marshal, his mane of red hair untouched by silver. They spirit him away through the village, away from blood and murder and his father's cross.

ROBIN PAUSED IN the lane, looked back up at the cross. This was where he had watched it happen, where he had fallen. He knelt, touching the ground, trying to slow his heart and catch his breath. Looking up again, he stopped breathing altogether. Thomas Longstride knelt before him, alive, untouched by the sword, his dark eyes boring into Robin's.

Robin felt a sob ripped from his chest. He closed his eyes tight and took several deep breaths to compose himself. When he opened his eyes once more, the vision of his father was gone. He was alone in the street again, watched by the soldiers before him and his friends, who stood just behind. He climbed to his feet, weary, frightened by what was happening to him, and walked the remaining distance to the base of the cross.

Reaching it he knelt again at the place his father had fallen.

"Robin?" Little John's voice. He sounded worried.

"Journey's end," Robin said without turning.

The stone before him was covered with soot, bloodied, weathered by storms and wind and thirty-five winters. But he could see the chisel work, and he reached out tentatively to brush his fingers against the blocks. Blocks his father had cut and shaped. He pulled his sword free, and pressing it to the base of the flagstone on the stone step, he pried the block loose. There was a scroll there, as he had known there would be and he opened it, revealing the words he remembered from his youth, words he had read on the hilt of a sword not so very long ago and yet seemingly a lifetime.

Then, again using his sword, he lifted a second stone to reveal handprints. One clearly belonged to a boy. It was tiny, the impression in the dried cement shallow, tentative. The one just beside it was that of a man, firmer, deeper. Robin placed his hand over that one. His palm and fingers fit it perfectly.

He stood and looked toward the pavilion where soldiers, townspeople, and nobles had gathered beneath brightly colored banners. There were hundreds of them; perhaps a thousand.

Looking to the far end of the lane, Robin saw riders approaching the pavilion. They were dressed as soldiers, their horses armored, and they rode with precision. It took him a moment to recognize the lead rider and another to convince himself that he wasn't mistaken.

King John had come to Barnsdale.

CHAPTER

TWENTY-FOUR

Marshal had continued to argue with the barons long past the point where he still believed he could turn their minds. He knew he should have given up, but he had served the realm for too long to surrender so easily.

The barons were set on their course, and refused to believe that Godfrey was anything more than just another overzealous servant of the Throne. And how could William, a servant of that Throne himself, convince them otherwise?

"We will not fight to save John's crown," Baldwin told him with finality. "Let him rather bend the knee to us!"

The barons and their soldiers cheered this. If he had accomplished nothing else, William had at least given the nobles ample opportunity to inspire their men.

A commotion at the back of the pavilion silenced

the crowd, and a moment later Marshal heard shouts of "Make way for the king."

Scarcely believing it possible that John could be here, Marshal tried to see past the men before him, shifting to one side and then the other. Finally, as the last of the men parted to let the newcomers through, he saw that the king had in fact come.

Whatever John's shortcomings as a leader, Marshal could not help thinking in that moment that he did at least look the part. He wore battle garb—chain mail and a brilliant tabard bearing the Plantagenet crest—and he carried his golden battle crown tucked under one arm. He smiled confidently as he walked, his dark curls shining, his eyes sweeping over the mob imperiously.

Stopping before Baldwin, John drew his sword, flipped it over in one quick motion, and caught it deftly by the blade. Then he presented the hilt to Baldwin.

"I'll do more than that, Lord Baldwin," he said in a voice loud enough for all to hear. "I'll bear my breast for your sword-point."

Marshal wasn't sure what to make of the king's ostentatious display. He thought it possible that it might impress the barons enough to make them listen to reason. Or it might come across as mocking and arrogant, like so much of what the king did and said, and serve only to anger them further.

Clearly the barons were no less bemused than he. Several bowed reflexively. Some began to kneel, but then straightened quickly, seeming to remember that they were supposed to be in rebellion.

John, not done yet, tossed his crown to the ground so that it rolled to a stop at Baldwin's feet.

"Is this what you want?" John asked. "I'd rather give it to you than have it taken by the French."

Baldwin glanced down at the crown, but made no move to pick it up. Of all the men in the pavilion, he appeared least impressed with the king's antics.

"You mistake me, Sire," he said. "I have no right and no ambition to wear this. But," he went on, raising a finger, "let the rightful wearer beware! From now, we will be subject only to law which we have a hand in making. We are not sheep to be made mutton by your butchers."

John frowned. "Godfrey set himself to turn you against me."

"Then he did more than was needed to accomplish that," Fitzrobert answered.

The other barons had recovered from the initial impact of John's arrival. They shouted angrily in agreement. A few laughed ironically.

"We are men of means," Fitzrobert said, drawing himself up to his full height, and appearing to take up half the pavilion. "And we control our own lot. But the only law is your law. No longer!"

Shouts of "Aye! Aye!" filled the pavilion. John glanced around, clearly less confident than he had been only moments before.

WHILE JOHN AND the barons argued back and forth, Robin strode through the pavilion, stepping past nobles until he stood directly in front of the king. Few took notice of him, dressed as he was in common garb. A few of the barons scowled at him. William Marshal, on the other hand, couldn't have appeared more pleased. He beamed at Robin, looking like a half-drowned man who had just been thrown a rope. The king, on the other hand, barely spared him a glance. Belatedly, Robin realized that he was a commoner among nobles and knights, a stonemason's son come to address a king.

"I am here to speak on behalf of Sir Walter Loxley," he said.

John was eyeing Robin closely, his eyes narrowed. Robin wondered if the king recognized him from the dock in London.

"Speak if you must," he said disdainfully.

"If you are trying to build for the future, your foundation must be strong," Robin said. "This land enslaves its people to the king, one who demands loyalty, yet offers nothing in return."

Several of the barons nodded and voiced their agreement.

"I've marched from France to Palestine and back," Robin told them. "And I know that in tyranny lies only failure. You build a country like a cathedral, from the ground up. Acknowledge the rights of every man and you will gain strength."

The barons nodded their agreement with this, as well, and then turned as one to John.

The king regarded Robin shrewdly, the way he might an opponent in a knife fight. "Who could object to such reasonable words?" He smiled disarmingly and gave a small shrug. "But my dilemma is this: A king cannot bargain for the loyalty every subject owes him. Without that loyalty, there can be no kingdom."

Robin considered this for a few seconds. "Then offer justice in the form of a charter, allowing every man to forage for the hearth, hunt for the pot; to be safe from eviction without cause or prison without charge; to work, eat, and live merry as he may on the sweat of his own brow. Then, a king that great and wise will not only receive loyalty from his people, but their love as well."

For just an instant, it seemed to Robin that he could feel his father's presence there in the pavilion, that he had spoken these words with the stonemason's voice.

John gave a small chuckle in response to what Robin had said. "What would you ask?" the king said. "Every man his own castle?"

"Every Englishman's home is his castle," Robin answered. "All we ask for is liberty and law. You, Sire, have the chance to unite your subjects both high and low. It is all on your nod."

As Robin spoke, he saw a man emerge from the crowd, make his way to William Marshal's side, and speak to Marshal in low tones. Marshal's eyes widened at what he heard, and he stepped forward to stand beside Robin.

"Your Majesty!" he said. "My lords! The French fleet is in the Channel!"

Silence fell over the pavilion. The barons stared hard at the king, who looked back at them, perhaps searching their faces for even one ally who might come to his defense. Seeing none, a thin smile crossed his lips. "I have only to nod?" he said. "I can do better than that. I give my word that I will sign this charter. On my mother's life, I swear it."

A deafening roar went up from the barons, knights, and soldiers. John had clearly been reluctant to agree to the charter, but he smiled at the response he'd evoked, his color rising.

Robin couldn't help but feel proud of what he had unleashed, but he knew that the coming battle would be a difficult one, and that the future of the realm hung in the balance. It seemed though that there was even more at stake than he had guessed.

Marshal stepped closer to him.

"Godfrey makes for Nottingham," he said, keeping his voice low. "I must stay with the king. I will send Baldwin and Fitzrobert with you, and we will meet at the White Horse when you are done."

Robin nodded and turned, determined to reach Peper Harrow in time to stop Godfrey's assault.

Marion could not remember a finer day in Nottingham. Yes, Robin was gone, but she believed with all her heart that he would return. And signs of what the man had brought to the hamlet were all around. The village bustled as it hadn't in years.

Everywhere, townspeople went about their chores wearing smiles and greeting one another cheerfully. Farmers sold vegetables and fowl from carts. Older children played marbles and bowling hoops in the lanes, while their younger siblings rode hobbyhorses or followed their mothers from cart to cart.

As Marion made her way through the town market, she thought she heard music playing. A fife and a flute, and at least one drum; more likely two. Itinerant musicians often traveled the countryside this time of year, but it seemed a bit odd to her. Until recently there had been little music of any sort in Nottingham.

Now, only a few days after the dance by the bonfire, musicians had come to the hamlet.

Hearing the music, some of the children gave up their games and ran to investigate. Marion watched them go, smiling at the glee she saw in their faces.

And then she heard another kind of drumming. Hoofbeats. Of many horses. Dozens of them, perhaps hundreds.

Lifting her skirts, Marion hurried down the lane toward the village gate to get a better look. What she saw froze her blood. An army of nearly two hundred men was approaching Nottingham through the fields. At least half the men were mounted, and all of them well armed.

Townspeople had gathered around her, and others were coming forward to see for themselves what was happening. The smiles Marion had seen on their faces only moments before were now gone. They looked scared, grim, as if every one of them sensed in the soldiers' appearance a return to the dark times from which the village had so recently emerged.

Marion watched the soldiers for another moment before turning and fighting her way back through the villagers toward the alarm bell in the village center. Reaching it, she pulled the rope, and the bell began to peal, echoing loudly through the lanes. But she knew better than to expect that anyone would come to their aid; Robin and his friends were too far away to help them. The men and women of the village would have to protect themselves.

THE SHERIFF OF Nottingham had just lathered his face to shave when he heard the commotion outside his home. Holding his razor in hand, he walked to his door and stepped outside to see what was happening.

He recognized Godfrey's men right away, saw the king's tax collection force fanning out through the village, and he grinned at the sight. The rabble in this town had ignored him and mocked him in equal measure. They had refused to submit themselves to his authority, and had dismissed him as a man of little consequence. And none had shown him less respect than the troublemakers up in Peper Harrow.

Well, their time of reckoning had arrived at last. The sheriff was a loyal servant of His Majesty, King John. Few others in Nottingham could claim as much. He would enjoy watching them get their comeuppance.

He watched as Belvedere walked through the village, directing his men, and shouting to the villagers.

"Tax collection! Valuations free! No exceptions!"

Belvedere seemed to be enjoying himself. He grinned broadly, and nodded his approval as the soldiers moved from house to house, taking what they could.

The sheriff leaned against the door frame and grinned as well. Yes, he would enjoy watching this.

TUCK COULD HEAR the tax collectors' cries from within the Church of Saint Edmund, and he hurried around his small nave hiding what he could from King John's men. He had little time, and with Loxley and his friends gone for the time being, it fell to him to protect the people of his parish as best he could.

He went to the church door and peered outside. A group of soldiers marched his way. Tuck barely had time to close the door again and sit down in the nave. He tried to look nonchalant, but when the soldiers kicked in his door, he started and jumped to his feet.

The men swarmed into his church and quickly discovered his stash of mead. They began to help themselves. Tuck mourned the loss of his golden drink, and he feared what the men would do to the chapel. But he also recognized an opportunity when it presented itself. As the soldiers drank, he slipped out of his church.

GODFREY HAD TAKEN thirty of Adhemar's men and led them up the lane to the manor on the hill. Loxley's home. The fading scar on his cheek itched as they approached the stone gates of the house. He was looking forward to avenging the wound.

Entering the courtyard, which was little more than a dusty feeding ground for pigs and chickens, Godfrey swung himself off his mount, sword in hand.

"Loxley!" he shouted. "Show your lying face."

His men spread out and advanced across the yard, weapons drawn, searching for the impostor shamelessly claiming to be the man Godfrey himself had killed. Apparently he wasn't done killing Loxleys. He was fine with that.

ONE OF THE leaders had set up a long table, using broad wooden boards set on barrels. This man was now overseeing the collection of what seemed to be every piece of property the people of Nottingham owned. And Marion, caught in a collection line with the others, could do nothing about it. She had a small blade in her belt; she always did. But these men were armed with lances and swords. Any attempt she made to fight them off would end in her own death.

So she watched and grieved as the people of her village—all of them of modest means—stepped up to the table one by one and handed over spoons and knives, tools and silver needles, mementos and heirlooms that could never be replaced and which never should have been taken in the first place.

After some time, Marion couldn't even bring herself to watch. She couldn't remember feeling so helpless. And yet, moments later matters turned far worse.

She reached the table and the soldier there didn't even look up at her.

"Name?" he demanded.

"Loxley," she said, refusing to give in to the feelings of humiliation she read on the faces of her friends and neighbors.

"Christian name?"

"Marion."

"Land?"

"Five thousand acres."

Upon overhearing this, a man sitting at the end of the table stood and approached her. He was her height, with a clean-shaven head, a trim beard, and small, widely-spaced eyes. She hadn't seen him before this day, but she had heard others calling him Belvedere, and she had watched him as he oversaw this brutal "tax collection."

He came around the table and took her by the arm none too gently.

"Lady Marion," he said with an unctuous smile, "this is no place for you."

She tried to pull her arm out of his grasp, but he tightened his grip.

"Let go of me!" she said.

Belvedere ignored her and beckoned to one of his

men; a rough-looking sort who bore more resemblance to a highway thief than to a soldier. The ruffian strode over and the tax collector whispered something to him. Marion heard little of what he said, though she did make out the word "barn."

The ruffian leered at her and then dragged her away from the village center, his hand viselike on her arm. Marion shouted at the man to let go of her, but he might as well have been deaf. The villagers stared after her, but none of them came to her defense. Nor could she blame them. They were as helpless against these hooligans as she.

The ruffian pulled her down a deserted lane to an empty barn. He thrust her inside, and for an instant Marion feared that he meant to force himself on her. But the man merely leered again and then shut the barn door. She rushed to the door and tried to push it open, but he had already barred it. She searched frantically for another way out, but found none. She was trapped.

AT FIRST NO ONE responded to Godfrey's challenge. He and his men stood in the courtyard of the manor, waiting, until Godfrey began to wonder if all the Loxleys had abandoned the place.

But at last a door opened and a man stepped into the daylight. It wasn't the man Godfrey had expected. Rather it was an ancient knight, his face deeply lined. Godfrey did notice though, that the man wore a sword on his belt. He also appeared to be blind. He didn't look directly at any of them, but instead held his head high and said, "Who calls here?"

Godfrey took a step to the side, so that he was far from the area where the old man was looking. His soldiers laughed.

"You mean here?" Godfrey asked, in a mocking tone. He sobered quickly. He had a man to kill. "I call for Robert Loxley."

"My son is not here to answer you," the old man said.

"That's the truth. Your son is dead in a French ditch."

The old man's hand flew to the hilt of his sword. "And who are you to say so, sir?" he demanded, steel in his voice.

Godfrey had started to move as the codger spoke, and made his way behind the man. As he finished his question, Godfrey shoved him to the ground.

"I, sir?" he said. "I am the man who killed him."

The absence of Sir Robert, or whoever the man really was, disappointed Godfrey, but at least he had the old man for a bit of sport. And it seemed that the ancient knight had no intention of being dispatched without a fight. He climbed to his feet and, amazingly, drew his sword.

"Fight me, who dares!" he roared.

Godfrey glanced at his men. "Lord have mercy upon us," he said, feigning abject terror. This earned him another laugh from the soldiers.

"Amen to that!" said the old knight.

Godfrey raised his sword and stepped toward old Loxley from the left, attacking the knight's off hand. He swung hard, intending to end this fight with a single stroke.

Somehow though, whether because he wasn't as blind as he made out, or because he heard Godfrey's approach, Loxley managed to parry the blow at the last moment. He moved deftly, swinging his sword with the ease and grace of a younger man.

Surprised, Godfrey stepped back. Perhaps this

wouldn't be the easy kill he'd imagined. All the bet-ter. He turned his sword and slapped at the old man with the flat of the blade, toying with him. Loxley lunged for him, stumbled. He swung his sword so hard that he nearly spun himself off his feet, but Godfrey stepped away nimbly. The legionnaires laughed uproariously.

Godfrey stepped back out of the man's reach and sketched a small bow for the men. But this small move-ment seemed to be all Loxley needed to fix his position. Suddenly the old man launched himself at Godfrey, swinging his weapon with both hands. Godfrey blocked the strike, but only just. He backed away quickly, forced off balance by the power of the old man's assault.

But Loxley wasn't done. He swung his sword a second time and a third. Having located Godfrey, he fought with the skill and determination of a seasoned warrior. Godfrey parried desperately, but even so, he was unable to block one strike that caught him in the side. Only his chain mail saved him from being cleaved in two. The rings of his coat were torn open, and Godfrey stumbled down and to the side.

Which proved to be Loxley's undoing. With Godfrey no longer just in front of him, the old man blundered on straight ahead. Godfrey rolled to his side, and was up on his feet an instant later. But Loxley was past him.

After taking a step or two, Loxley halted, seeming to realize that Godfrey was no longer in front of him. Godfrey strode toward him, gripping his sword. They had wasted too much time on one old man. He pulled back his blade, and stabbed Loxley through the back. The old man's back arched; his sword clattered to the ground. Then he collapsed to his knees, toppled over, and was still.

TWENTY-SIX

The sheriff had finished shaving and had put on his finest day clothes. He opened the door of his house intending to greet the tax collectors properly and to demonstrate to all in the village that he was the Crown's chosen representative here in Nottingham. Perhaps that would earn him the sort of deference he deserved.

Upon looking out at the town, though, he couldn't help but notice that the king's men seemed to have gone a bit far in their collection of taxes. Throughout the village, bedlam reigned. People were screaming, not in outrage, but in terror. Houses burned, men and women lay dead and wounded in the street. Yes, these people needed discipline, but this struck him as too much.

Several of the French soldiers stood just in front of his house along with the bald, bearded man who had come to the town days before. The sheriff thought his name was Belvedere.

He greeted this man as if they were old friends.

"Excusez-moi!" he said. Excuse me.

Belvedere turned to look at him.

"I'm French on my mother's side," the sheriff went on in a confidential tone.

"Ah, *ouí*!" said the bald man.

The sheriff's smile broadened and he winked at the man. "Ah, *ouí*."

Another group of men hurried past, also carrying brands. Belvedere barked an order to one of them, and the man threw one of the burning brands through the window of the sheriff's house.

In moments, flames were crackling within and dark smoke began to pour from the window.

The sheriff's first thought was to rush inside and try to put out the fire. But Belvedere was watching him, and the sheriff thought better of it. If all went as planned, he would have plenty of gold to build himself a new one. Or he would take Peper Harrow as his own.

ALONE IN THE barn, Marion began to wonder if she had been singled out in recognition of her status as a landowner and the wife of a knight, or if she was being held in preparation for special ill treatment. Belvedere's comment about her not belonging in line with the others seemed to suggest the former. But everything about his manner and that of his henchman made her fear the latter.

She had been alone in her dusty prison for perhaps a quarter of an hour, when she heard someone unlocking the door. She moved quickly to the far wall, and stood with her back pressed against it. Sunlight filtered in between the boards of the walls, slanting through the barn unevenly, in broad, hazy planes. She pulled her knife free, hid it in her sleeve, and placed her hands behind her against the wall.

The door opened, and Belvedere walked in. He paused, looking her up and down and smiling in a way that made her skin crawl. After a moment, he closed the door and secured it from within. He crossed to her, regarded her once more, and then removed his belt and sword.

Marion watched him, certain now that he intended to rape her. He stepped so close to her that his chest was nearly pressed against her breasts. Looking down at the laces of her bodice, he grinned and began to untie them.

Marion turned her head to the side, as if shamed. But she allowed the blade to slip down from her sleeve into the palm of her hand. Still, she didn't move, and Belvedere pressed even closer, his breath hot on her face and neck.

She brought her arms out from behind her and as he moved to kiss her, she plunged her dagger into his back. He gasped, his mouth opening, his eyes going wide. He grabbed for her throat, but Marion leaned back against the wall and kicked at him with all her strength.

He fell hard onto his back, driving her blade deeper into his heart. His body convulsed and then was still. His eyes stared sightlessly at the ceiling.

NOTTINGHAM WAS BEING destroyed before Tuck's very eyes. Houses burned, the streets were littered with the dead; those who still lived were in flight, desperate to get away from the king's men. Tuck had done what he could to fight off the invaders, but he was but one man against so many. Still he didn't give up.

First he crept back to his church, where French soldiers still drank his mead. He carefully picked up one of his bee skeps, carried it back to the church entrance, and before the men could stop him, threw the hive inside. He slammed the door shut and secured it.

He heard shouts from within, then yelps of pain. Grinning with satisfaction, he turned away from the chapel and started back toward village center.

Seeing one of the French ruffians climb onto a thatch roof with a burning brand, Tuck followed him up, moving as stealthily as his bulk allowed.

Before the man could light the house on fire, Tuck swung his stave, catapulting the man off the roof. The Frenchman landed hard on the ground and lay still.

Tuck smiled grimly and looked around for more of the enemy to attack. Instead, he saw something from his vantage point on the house that nearly stopped his heart. The soldiers were herding villagers into the tithe barn near the church, shoving some inside, literally throwing others. At the same time, others in the tax force were splashing something onto the sides of the building. Tuck would have bet all the gold in the realm that it wasn't water or even his beloved mead. It was naphtha, or something worse. They were going to burn those poor souls alive.

ROBIN AND THE barons rode hard, thundering toward Nottingham. Robin could see smoke rising from the town and he prayed that Marion was safe.

Fitzrobert and Baldwin rode alongside him; Will,

Allan, and Little John were just behind. As they neared the village, Robin turned to the barons.

"Take the southern flank!" he said. "Circle them, and then to the west!"

Other men of their rank might have chafed at being ordered about so by a common soldier, but Fitzrobert and Baldwin understood what was at stake and were as eager to find and defeat Godfrey as Robin. They both nodded to him and led their men to the south. Robin and his friends went to the north.

WITH THE OLD man dead, Godfrey led his men back down the lane toward Nottingham. He would help Adhemar and Belvedere finish their work here, and then they would go on to the next village. But as they rode through the manor gate, Godfrey spotted a contingent of men emerging from the forest that bordered the Loxley fields.

He reined his horse to a halt and stared hard at the men. They were well armed, and there had to be more than a hundred of them—nearly a match for his own force. At the center of the company rode a man he recognized, from the wood in France, and from the dock in London.

As he watched them, the riders spotted him and his soldiers. A great cry went up from the approaching company, and the lead rider pointed directly at him, his finger like an arrow aimed at Godfrey's heart. An instant later, the full company was thundering their way.

Instinctively, Godfrey raised a hand to his scar. Then, with a shout to his men, he spurred his mount to a gallop and made for the road leading away from

Nottingham. He could hear that the riders were gaining on them. Moments later, arrows began to rain down on his men. One of his riders fell, and then another, and a third.

Just a few minutes before he had been ready to count Nottingham as another victory in his march across England. Now, suddenly, he was riding for his life.

EVEN WITH SO many soldiers trapped in the church and beset by bees, Friar Tuck could see that the situation in the village was deteriorating quickly. Cries of outrage and despair, screams of panic and pain—they came from every direction. Children bawled in the lanes, clinging to their mothers and fathers, or desperate to find them. Livestock ran wild through the streets, only to be slaughtered at random by the soldiers. The sounds of shattering glass and rending wood filled the air. Houses were being ransacked; people were losing what little earthly property they had. An old man trying to get off the lanes was ridden down by a soldier—nay, a thug—on a horse.

Tuck had seen quite enough. He still carried his stave, and now he hefted it like a club and waded into the middle of the chaos, swinging it at the ruffians with all the might the Good Lord had given him. He knocked one man unconscious and unhorsed another. He might have been a man of the cloth, but he wasn't above fighting for the lambs he had been sent here to shepherd. He lifted his stave again and started toward two more tax soldiers who were harassing some poor woman. The men backed away at the sight of him. Tuck grinned fiercely and advanced on them, laying them out with two might swipes of his weapon.

He heard horsemen approaching, and turned to face them, prepared for the worst. Instead, he beheld what could only be termed a miracle. Robin Longstride was pounding toward him on his white charger, slashing at the enemy with his sword. And he was followed by Will Scarlet, Allan A'Dayle, and Little John. Perhaps the tide was turning.

BELVEDERE HAD JAMMED the door to the barn shut and despite struggling for some time to free herself, Marion couldn't lift the bar.

Just as she was about to give up, however, she heard a scrabbling sound on the roof of the barn. A moment later, someone punched a hole in the thatch. Marion hurried over to look through, and to her great surprise saw a familiar, youthful face gazing down at her: Loop.

Seeing Belvedere's sword near her on the floor of the barn, Loop pointed to it, telling Marion to pass it up to him. She did, and he used the sword to cut through the roof and make the hole big enough for her to pass through.

Meanwhile, Marion managed to find a barrel on which to stand so that she could reach the opening. With Loop's help, she was soon on the roof, lying flat with Loop and several of his boys, watching the French soldiers. She saw Friar Tuck, who was helping villagers get away and knocking soldiers to the ground with his stave.

But Tuck was only one man, and the soldiers and ruffians continued to attack the villagers, wounding and killing indiscriminately.

Moments later a small group of riders—also men of the king's force—burst into the road, riding at full speed, arrows raining down on them from unseen pursuers.

The lead rider was bald, as Belvedere had been, but his face was clean-shaven. His eyes were deep-set and dark, and even though he was clearly in flight, there was no fear in them, only calculation. He wore a black cloak, clasped at the neck with an ornate silver chain, and beneath it a full shining coat of chain mail and a black tabard bearing a brightly colored insignia.

He reined in his mount and started barking orders to the men, telling them to hold their positions and prepare to face the enemy. Marion motioned for the boys to follow her. "Quickly!" she said, and led them off the roof.

THAT HAD BEEN close. Too close. Godfrey wanted his revenge, but he wasn't willing to die for it.

So, even as he led his men toward the edge of town, where Adhemar's legionnaires would make their stand, he was already plotting his escape.

He could hear people shouting from within the nearby tithe barn. They pleaded for help and pounded on the walls with their fists. The exterior of the building had been soaked with naphtha. The wood shone with it; Godfrey could smell it from forty feet away. Let the poor fools inside shout and pound all they liked. By the time Loxley reached them they would be nothing but smoke and ash.

He rode toward one of Adhemar's captains, and shouted to him, "Defend the position!"

The legionnaire looked surprised. A moment later, though, he seemed to realize that he and his fellow soldiers were about to be attacked. The man barked orders in French, and Adhemar's warriors began to marshal themselves into formation.

As they did, Godfrey took a small group of soldiers and quietly slipped away toward the far end of town. The last he saw, the legionnaires had taken a torch to the barn.

When Godfrey and his guard turned a corner and could no longer be seen by the men they had left behind, they spurred their horses on once more and galloped out of the village. Adhemar's force might be lost, but Godfrey had larger concerns.

MARION AND THE other villagers were still being harried by the tax force, and a large cluster of soldiers waited for them near the tithe barn, which was now starting to burn. She could hear people crying out from within, and she saw dark smoke rising into the sky.

She was desperate to reach them, but trapped between two contingents of armed men.

But then, at last, she saw the company of riders that had been chasing the bald man and his soldiers. And miraculously, Robin and his friends rode at the fore.

A moment later, they swept over the French soldiers, like a wave crashing down upon a sandy beach. Robin fought as a man possessed, dancing his horse like a festival performer, his sword rising and falling until it was stained crimson. All the while he appeared to be searching for something. He turned this way and that, looking frantic.

It took Marion a moment to realize that he was looking for her.

An instant later, he saw her. Their eyes met and a smile crossed his face ever so briefly. Then he was fighting again. Marion still held Belvedere's sword, and she waded into the battle as well. A moment later, Tuck was beside her, wielding his stave with more strength and skill than she would have expected from a friar. The forest boys were with her as well, and together they fought their way to the tithe barn.

Smoke from the building had begun to fill the lanes of the town, and Marion could hear screams coming from within. Flames licked at the walls and the thatch roof had started to burn. It wouldn't be long until the barn was fully engulfed and the people within lost.

Marion and Tuck tried to pull the barn doors open, only to discover that wooden planks had been nailed across them. Using her sword, she began to pry the planks free, all the while fearing that they would be too late. The flames were spreading, the cries within growing more panicked and desperate by the moment. Tuck helped her yank off the planks she had loosened, and they were able to remove the last of them.

Together they managed to unbar the doors which were now ablaze. Black smoke billowed from the opening and within the barn flaming beams and boards of wood began to fall. Many of those inside had nearly been overcome with smoke. But the trapped villagers poured out into the lane, coughing, their faces smeared with soot. Some needed to be supported, or even carried, but all of them made it out.

SEEING THAT MARION was safe, Robin turned his attention back to the battle. Arrows whistled all around him, swords clashed, men shouted.

Robin could see Will and Allan fighting up ahead. They were back-to-back, surrounded by six French swordsmen who were pressing them hard. They needed help, and he was too far away. He looked for Little John, or another Englishman who might lend them aid, but he saw no one.

Will managed to kill one of his foes, and Allan did the same, but they were in trouble. The Frenchmen's swords were bright blurs in the sun and Will and Allan's parries looked more desperate with every passing moment. Robin didn't know how they would manage to fight their way free. That is, until three of the Frenchmen suddenly fell, arrows jutting from their chests and necks. Will killed the last man and then looked up in time to salute Loop and two of his archers, who had fired down on the French soldiers from a nearby roof. The boys returned the salute, then nocked their bows again and searched for their next targets.

Robin continued forward, with several of the barons' men now with him, and together they waded into battle against a large group of French soldiers. They were skilled fighters, these French. Disciplined, strong, agile. Robin parried blows from all sides and lashed out with his blade. His arms and back burned with fatigue, but still he fought on. Every time he dispatched one of the enemy, another was there to take the previous man's place. Robin ducked under swung blades, parried thrusts aimed at his heart, blocked strokes that would have sliced into his side. One deflected blow opened a cut on his brow, but he wiped the blood from his eyes and killed the man who had wounded him.

On the far side of the French force, which was dwindling quickly, Robin saw Little John fighting his way toward him. The big man had his stave in hand, and Robin would have liked to stop fighting, just so he could admire his friend's work. The stave seemed to come alive in John's hands. It whirled and whistled and cracked bones with every strike. For all his brawn and bulk, John moved as nimbly as the forest boys. He spun away from sword strokes, sidestepped mounted soldiers, knocked the riders from their saddles, and then leaped forward to finish them. Robin recalled telling Will that Little John might prove himself useful in a fight. He hadn't known the half of it. The man and his stave were like a storm in the midst of the battle.

With the help of the forest boys and the barons and their men, Robin and his friends soon had the remaining French soldiers surrounded in the town center. Seeing that they were outnumbered and defeated, the French laid down their weapons and surrendered.

Robin dismounted and stood before the captured men. "Who is your commanding officer?" he demanded in a loud voice.

None of the French replied.

"Where will Philip's fleet land?"

Again none of the captured men said a word. Robin glanced at Little John, who shrugged.

Robin grabbed one of the French by the scruff of the neck and roughly led him over to a nearby building, one of the few that still stood unscathed.

"Rope!" he called.

It took a moment, but Will found him a piece of rope that Robin then used to lash the man to the door. Stepping back a few paces, Robin pulled out his bow, nocked an arrow to it, and fired it at the man. Or not exactly at him. *Thwap!* The arrow struck the door less than an inch from the French soldier's cheek. The man flinched, his eyes wide with terror.

Robin pulled out a second arrow, nocked it, and fired again, aiming lower this time. *Thwap!* This one struck the door in between the man's leg's, just below his crotch. The soldier began to whimper.

Robin nocked a third arrow and drew back his bow, the tip of the arrow leveled at the man's heart.

"Attendez!" the soldier cried. Wait! *"Je vous dirai!"* I will tell you!

Robin lowered his bow.

The man closed his eyes for a moment and swallowed. Opening his eyes again, he took a breath and said. *"Le roi attaquera a Dungeness en deux jours."* The king will attack at Dungeness in two days.

Robin turned to the barons. "We ride for Dungeness. May the Good Lord grant us speed."

Even as Robin spoke of riding to Dungeness, he spotted from the corner of his eye a figure leading a cart into the village center from the direction of Peper Harrow.

Robin recognized Gaffer Tom immediately. It took him a few seconds, though, to understand what the man carried. When at last the realization hit him, Robin staggered as if struck by an arrow. He looked quickly to Marion and saw that she had frozen where she stood, her eyes fixed on Tom, her cheeks ashen.

Tom's face, ruddy as always, was streaked with tears, and he carried Sir Walter's sword cradled in his arms, as though it was the most precious thing in the world.

The body of the old knight lay in the cart, as still and pale as a stone effigy on a tomb.

Tom stopped in front of Marion, sobbing, his eyes downcast. And even as she took the sword out of his hands he wouldn't look at her. Robin moved to her side and put his arm around her. She leaned against him, her head resting on his shoulder, her legs buckling. If he hadn't been holding her, she might have fallen.

No one in the village center spoke, although a few of the townspeople began to weep.

Robin's grief was nearly too much to bear. He had known the old man only briefly, but in the few days they had shared, their friendship had grown quickly. He could have learned so much more from Walter, if only he'd had the chance. Not just about himself and his father, but about England, about being a knight, about the land on which he now stood.

Slowly, Robin led Marion back up toward Peper Harrow. Tom followed, leading the cart once more, for the last journey of Sir Walter Loxley to his beloved manor.

A PYRE HAD been built at the ruined gate of the Loxley manor, to Marion's precise instructions. Walter's hair had been combed, he had been dressed in unbloodied clothes, and then he had been placed in an open coffin of woven osiers. With help from Will, Allan, and Little John, Robin carried the old man to the pyre and set him upon it. Children had picked flowers for the occasion, and these were spread around Walter's body. And Marion, who until this time had not relinquished the old man's sword, now stuck it in the ground in front of the pyre.

As the sun went down, Tuck offered a brief prayer. When the priest had finished, Robin and the others brought torches forward and thrust them into the great pile of wood. Marion stepped forward and placed a flower within the coffin, before stepping back and watching the fire grow. Wisps of smoke curled upward, the wood began to crackle, and soon the fire was burning brightly, illuminating the faces of those who had gathered to say farewell to the man. Loop and his boys were there. Tuck stood with Marion and Robin. Will, Allan, and Little John stood a short distance off, their heads bowed.

There was little sound, save for the snapping of the flames and the gentle rustle of a light wind that carried smoke out across the fields of Peper Harrow. Robin sensed that the people around him were mourning more than just one man, great though he had been. Too many had died this day, and Godfrey still lived. More would fall before this was over.

THE FOLLOWING MORNING, Robin put on his leather breeches and his riding cloak, strapped Loxley's sword to the side of his belt and his old dagger to the back of it, and went down to the courtyard to saddle his mount. Marion had risen early and was already in the yard, waiting for him. She watched him wordlessly as he cinched his pack, and then walked with him out onto the road, where Will, Allan, and Little John were waiting for him, already sitting their horses.

Robin turned to Marion, not quite knowing what he ought to say. She was wearing a simple green dress and, on her wrist, a pearl bracelet he had given her the night before. Her hair was tied back loosely, and the morning sun shone gently on her face. He had never seen her look more lovely.

"Once before, I said good-bye to a man going to war," she said, gazing at the bracelet. "He never came back."

Robin looked at her, a sad smile on his lips. "Ask me nicely."

Marion came to him. Taking her in his arms, he kissed her. She clung to him, returning the kiss passionately. But then she stepped back and smiled, letting him go. Robin gazed at her for another moment before swinging onto his horse.

"I love you, Marion," he said.

And wheeling his horse, he led the others away at a gallop, in the same direction the barons' army had gone a short while before.

CHAPTER

❦

TWENTY-EIGHT

Godfrey and his small entourage rode south from Nottingham as if pursued by the devil himself. After fleeing the hamlet, they didn't stop until well after nightfall, and even then, they rested only briefly before continuing on toward Dover Beach. Early in the afternoon of the following day, as they neared London, Godfrey ordered his eight men into a small farming village. There they traded their horses for nine fresh ones. Then they rode on, pushing their new mounts as hard as they had the old ones.

Still, they had miles to go, and Godfrey begrudged every wasted minute. Loxley and the barons would be coming for them, rousing the countryside and alerting every noble they could to the threat of a French invasion. The timing was everything. If Godfrey could signal King Philip early enough so that he and his army could make landfall unmolested and establish a position at Dover, they had a chance. If Loxley caught up with him too soon, all would be lost.

So he drove his men and their animals without mercy. If the beasts died before they reached the Channel, so be it. He wouldn't ruin everything by coddling a bunch of farm animals.

By the time night fell, they still hadn't reached the coast, though by now he could smell brine in the air. They were close. One of the men approached on behalf of the others to ask if they could rest briefly. The soldier looked scared out of his wits, and with good reason. Godfrey came within a hair's breadth of running him through just for making the request. He restrained himself, though, and merely roared a *"Non!"* They rode on.

An hour later, when at last he heard the distant dull pounding of breakers on sand, Godfrey knew a moment of profound relief. He was saddle-weary and sore, but they had made it, with time to spare, he hoped.

More soldiers were waiting for him on the beach. As instructed, the men had built a series of wooden pyramids along the tideline more than a dozen of them evenly spaced along the shore, each tall enough to be seen at a great distance, each soaked with naphtha, so that the beach stank of it.

Godfrey gazed out across the water, peering through the pale mist that hung over the channel. After several moments, he spotted the dull glow of a lantern as it was uncovered and then masked, uncovered a second time, and masked once more. The signal. From Philip's ship, no doubt.

"Allumez-les!" Godfrey shouted as he and his men rode up. Light them!

Responding to the order with alacrity, men hurried forward with torches and thrust them into the nearest of the wood piles. *Whoosh! Whoosh! Whoosh!* Flames burst forth, burning brilliantly in the darkness. Down the beach, soldiers saw that the first signal fires had been lit and rushed to light the others, so that the blazes spread down the coastline one after the other, the firelight reflected in the coastal waters.

HE WAS PHILIP AUGUSTUS, leader of the mightiest army on earth, known for his ruthlessness and keen intelligence, and also for the grace of his court and his own elegance. After today he would be known as well as the Conqueror. He would be remembered in the same breath as William, who had sailed across the channel a hundred and thirty years before to defeat the English.

He didn't like having to rely on a man like Godfrey; he would have preferred to rely less on subterfuge and more on the might of his military. But Godfrey thought his plan would work, and Philip had chosen to believe him. Woe to the man if events proved him wrong.

He heard footsteps behind him, and turning saw that the captain was approaching him, navigating the deck with ease, his steps sure and confident, despite the motion of the vessel.

"Votre Majèste," he said, pointing toward the English shore. *"Les voîlà les feux."* Your Majesty, the signal fires.

Staring across the churning black waters toward the English coast, Philip saw the fires burning along the distant beach like a string of diamonds gleaming in candlelight, their glow illuminating the pale cliffs beyond with a faint golden hue. Land at last, and the promise of an end to this slow torture on the swells of the Channel.

Philip faced the captain once more. *"Commencez l'embarquement. Des que je pourrai descendre de ce miserable bateau, tu m'en informeras."* Begin landing. Tell me when I may get off this wretched boat.

The king turned away from the man and looked toward the shore once more. The fires gleamed in the night, beckoning to him. At last his invasion could begin. He looked left and right to admire his armada, which was anchored out here in the deep with his own ship. Four hundred vessels strong, some of them war ships bristling with cannons, others landing craft filled with soldiers. Even if John knew of his plans, he could not possibly summon an army to match Philip's. With this invasion, he could finally claim these isles for France. He smiled at the thought.

ROBIN, WILL, ALLAN, and Little John caught up with the barons and their army just after midday of the day they left Nottingham, and they rode the rest of the way southward with Baldwin and Fitzrobert. Robin wanted to go after Godfrey without delay, but the barons had agreed to meet up with King John's army at the White Horse, just west of London.

While traveling with the barons took them out of their way, Baldwin and Fitzrobert drove their men hard and rode through much of the night. They made good time. By midmorning the following day, they had ridden into a steep-walled valley of lush grasses. Robin looked around him, trying to get his bearings. He had seen the White Horse once before and so knew this country, though it had been many years since last he came. The White Horse itself was an immense and ancient chalk image of a horse that had been inscribed on the top of one of these hills, back before even the earliest written histories of England. It proved easy to find.

The image of the horse stood out starkly on the grass-covered hillside above them, the crushed chalk gleaming in the sunlight. Looking up, Robin patted the neck of his white charger, the horse that had carried King Richard's crown the first time Robin encountered Godfrey, the horse he had taken as his own the day Robert Loxley died. Robin had never been one to read omens in such things, but he couldn't help but feel that there was a portent in this, though for good or ill he couldn't say.

From a distance he spotted William Marshal sitting his horse beside the king. He rode toward the men. Before he reached them, Marshal saw him and cantered over to greet him, concern knotting his brow.

"What news of Walter and Nottingham?" he asked.

"Walter is dead, M'Lord," Robin told him. "By Godfrey's hand."

Marshal sagged in his saddle, a pained look in his pale eyes. He looked like he might ask more, but at that moment King John joined them, his face flushed, an exuberant smile on his handsome face.

"Gentlemen!" the king said. "We go to war! It is my first time. I shall lead."

Marshal straightened and faced the king, his grief hidden, at least for the moment. Robin marveled at the change in him from one instant to the next.

John danced his horse for a moment, as if too excited to keep still. Then he was off, calling for them to ride with him.

Robin and Marshal exchanged a look and together they rode after the king.

With captains shouting orders and men scrambling to take their positions, the army marshaled quickly: the cavalry a thousand strong, and five hundred more men on foot. Within the hour they had set out southward toward Dover, where William Marshal's scouts expected the French invasion force to land.

For the rest of the day and all through the night, the riders crossed the English countryside at a steady canter, with King John, Robin, Marshal, and the barons at the fore. The foot soldiers jogged just behind them, silent save for the rhythmic beat of their footsteps and the clanking of their swords and armor. They encountered few people on the road, though they did occasionally see faces peering out at them from the doorway of a farmhouse or lamplit window. A gibbous moon carved through the night sky overhead, and a few clouds scudded past, briefly obscuring the stars.

Robin wasn't yet sure that he trusted this king, but he couldn't deny that John had rallied his army to the task at hand. He hoped they would be enough to hold off the French.

As the first faint glimmerings of dawn began to appear on the eastern horizon, Robin caught the scent of salt water riding the breeze. He looked up into the dawn sky and saw gulls wheeling overhead.

Glancing back at Will, Allan, and Little John, he grinned.

They nodded in return, all of them looking eager to get off their horses and take up their weapons.

PHILIP'S SHIPS WERE still on the water as the eastern sky over Dover began to brighten with the pinks and blues and pale yellows of dawn. Sitting his horse, Godfrey could see the vessels clearly now, and he could not help but be impressed with the size of the French fleet. They were slow, though. Too damned slow. If he thought it would have helped, he would have swam out to the ships and pulled them to shore himself.

The landing craft—ugly, flat-bottomed scows—bristled with oars and battle pikes, like hedgehogs floating on the swells. Crossbowmen stood at the squared bows, looking over the raised wooden ramps toward shore, their weapons ready, lest the English appear. Given how the ships rose and fell and rocked on the swells, though, Godfrey wasn't sure how the bowmen would manage to hit anything if they had to fire. Fortunately, there had not yet been any sign of King John's army.

The boats approached the shore steadily, all of them moving in tandem, the men on sweeps rowing with precision. They hadn't yet been taken by the incoming tide, but they were close to the foaming waters. Once they got that far, the Channel might do the rest.

Some of the craft held horses, and even from this distance Godfrey could see that the animals were struggling against their riders and grooms, no doubt panicked by the motion of the ships. Some of the creatures had started to buck and lunge. If the vessels didn't make land soon, soldiers would be trampled by their own mounts.

French soldiers on the beach near Godfrey called to their fellow soldiers, urging them on. Godfrey thought that their shouts of encouragement were sounding increasingly apprehensive.

And he could see why. With every minute that

passed, Godfrey's initial faith in the French fleet dwindled. They were approaching fast enough, but for all their purported skill on the water, they appeared to be at the mercy of the tide. The first of the landing craft reached the surf break only to be turned to the side by the current. Almost immediately, a wave hit the vessel broadside, nearly overturning it. The craft teetered on its edge; horses skidded across the deck, crushing men against the side, and several armored men fell out of the craft and into the surf. Then the ship fell hard, back onto its flat bottom. Had the water been any deeper, the men thrown from the craft would have been lost, dragged under by their chain mail. As it was, the water was shallow enough that they were able to stand.

The men who had been tossed overboard by the tide straggled ashore, plodding heavily through the surf and sand, water pouring from their chain mail as they emerged from the Channel.

The landing craft finally came to a stop at water's edge, half askew, its hull grinding loudly against the sand. The landing gate flopped open and the war horses—huge, armored, panicked beyond control— lunged toward the opening, lashing out with their hooves, kicking the walls of the ship, each other, and any men in their way. A groom, who had been standing too close to the gate, was trampled as the beasts poured out of the ship and onto land. Cavalry men grabbed at the reins, trying to calm the creatures, or at least hold them back. Some succeeded in doing so; others were dragged onto shore.

In the moments that followed, Godfrey saw several other landing vessels make it onto the beach. Their gates dropped open and men and horses began to disembark. For a short while, it seemed quite orderly. But then more vessels came in, carried by the surf, uncontrolled. A few of these slammed into the ships that had landed ahead of them and were still disgorging soldiers. Men and animals were thrown from both vessels. Some were able to get their feet under them and continue on toward the shore. Others flailed in the water, or cried out in pain. A few didn't move or make a sound.

STANDING AT THE prow of his flagship, King Philip watched, disconcerted, as his men made their way onto Dover Beach. This was not the well-coordinated landing he had envisioned as he and Godfrey planned the invasion.

He wanted to dismiss what he saw as a trifle, a momentary lapse in what would be a glorious battle. But he couldn't help wondering if it was more. If his men couldn't even make landfall without falling out of their ships and being crushed by their horses, how would they fight the English army? Were they on the verge of a disaster?

CHAPTER

TWENTY-NINE

Riding alongside Marshal, Robin could hear the surf pounding. The dawn air was heavy with brine here, and the cries of gulls echoed all around them. They cantered up a rise and, reaching the top, saw in the distance Dover Beach and the waters of the English Channel. A line of bonfires burned on the sand, and dark ships approached the coast.

Reining his mount to a halt, King John stared down at the scene before them. "That's a lot of French," he said. Robin thought he heard a note of doubt in the man's voice. "What's to be done?"

Robin pointed toward the cliffs overlooking the beach. "Archers to the cliffs," he said.

Marshal nodded, adding, "And cavalry to the beach."

Robin spurred his mount forward again, calling for the archers to follow him, and heard Marshal call to the cavalry.

"An excellent plan!" King John called, riding after them.

The wind rushing in his ears, Robin knotted the reins in his fist and checked the hang of his sword with his other hand. For the moment, their grievances with the Throne were forgotten. The French had come to England. They would drive the invaders from their shores or die in the attempt. For now, nothing else mattered.

As the English forces reached the headland, Robin split off from Marshal and the rest, signaling to the army's mounted archers—four hundred men strong— that they should follow him onto the top of the cliff. He dug his spurs into the flanks of his horse, keeping the animal at a full run. And the archers followed, riding along the cliff's edge until they were above the French landing area on the beach.

THE TIDE WAS rising. A wave swept over what was left of the bonfire nearest to Godfrey, sending a plume of vapor into the morning air, and tugging the charred logs, a few of them briefly still aflame, out into the Channel.

The French had finally figured out the current. More landing craft scraped up onto the beach, their gates opening to allow men and horses to file off the vessels and onto the sand. There they immediately began to form up with the same quiet efficiency Godfrey had observed in Adhemar's men during their march through the English countryside. And none too soon. Somehow King John had come, leading an army far larger than anything Godfrey had expected. There was supposed to be civil war. John was supposed to be under attack by his own people. Instead he was here. Godfrey could only assume that Loxley and Marshal were to blame.

PHILIP HAD HOPED that his men would have time to establish a position before being challenged by John's army. Clearly that was not to be. The captain of his flagship stood beside him, pointing toward the English cavalry, which had appeared at the far end of the beach. Its riders were arraying themselves for a charge on the French lines.

But Philip's eye was drawn elsewhere. For at that moment, the golden glow of the rising sun struck the cliffs, as if Midas himself had reached down from heaven and touched the stone. And what that light revealed made the king's stomach heave. Hundreds of riders had steered their mounts onto the top of the promontory, all of them bearing longbows. These men quickly arrayed themselves along the cliff's edge directly over his army, while the cavalry started forward.

It would be a slaughter.

"Mon dieu . . ." The king whispered. My God.

THE ARCHERS LEAPED from their mounts and lined themselves along the edge of the crag, their bows held ready. Robin remained on his horse, where the men could see him. Looking down on the French, he saw that they were aware of him and his men, but utterly helpless to do anything about them.

He raised his hand and the English archers nocked arrows, drew back their bowstrings, and aimed skyward, judging the arc of the shot, the distance to the enemy below. Then he swept his hand down and the men released their arrows as one, the thrumming of their bows making the air around them sing, as if a thousand harps had been plucked at once. Robin rode across the front of his army, watching as the arrows climbed into the pale sky and, reaching their zenith, seemed to pause briefly above the earth, before beginning their steep, deadly plummet toward the French army.

A moment later, screams from below rent the false calm of the morning. Men fell with arrows buried in their chests, their heads, their throats. And already Robin had signaled for his archers to aim and fire again.

The thrum of the bows, the deathly, expectant silence, and then more cries from below. Robin's men shaped a terrible rhythm, a counterpoint to the steady crash of the waves. The song of war.

AT THE BASE of the cliffs, below the archers, all was tumult and carnage. Dead men were sprawled on the beach, their blood staining the sand. Those who yet survived scrambled for cover, holding shields over their heads to protect themselves.

At the same time, the English cavalry at the far end of the strand had started their charge, war cries on their lips, swords held ready.

Godfrey wheeled his horse back and forth, marking the progress of the charge, watching death rain down on the French soldiers, astonished at how quickly all his planning had been undone.

One last volley flew from the archers on the cliff, and then the soldiers there remounted and swept down toward the beach, with Loxley leading them.

The men continued to loose their arrows, until the charging cavalry smashed into the French lines. In moments Loxley's soldiers would join the fight with their compatriots, crushing the French between them. Those of Philip's men who hadn't been killed by the archers would die on the edge of an English sword.

More landing craft continued to wash up onto the beach, but Godfrey didn't think they carried enough soldiers to turn the tide of this battle.

The fight spilled into the surf, men struggling with their footing in the shifting sand as they hacked at one another with swords. Within moments, the tidal sand and the pale foam of the breakers were stained red. Men and horses whirled in confusion and panic, parrying blows, lunging at enemy soldiers, falling at the water's edge with blood blossoming from their wounds.

As waves continued to hammer at the shore, landing craft were tossed forward, crushing men both living and dead. Horses fell, arrows embedded in their necks and flanks. Some men were simply dragged under the water by the weight of their armor, unable to find their footing as the surf surged and retreated.

Seawater mingled with ever more blood. Bodies rolled in the waves and were tossed onto the sand like seashells.

THE TWO HALVES of the English cavalry battered the French army like tidal waves, rolling over the invaders with the sound of summer thunder, leaving death and mayhem in their wake. Before long Robin had fought his way to William Marshal's side. Fitzrobert was there, too, and they were quickly joined by King John. All of their swords were bloodied, but the king watched the center of the battle avidly, clearly itching to plunge in.

Marshal steered his mount in front of the king's and reined it to a halt, forcing King John to do the same.

"Close enough, Sire!" Marshal said.

But John shook his head defiantly, a fierce look in his dark eyes. "No, by God! It was not close enough for Richard!"

Before Marshal could argue, John spurred his horse past the old knight toward the heart of the fighting. Marshal watched him go, concern etched in his face. A moment later he rode after the king, as Robin had known he would. Marshal had been risking his life for the Plantagenet kings for too long to stop now.

PHILIP SAW HIS men fall under a storm of arrows and then watched as the English cavalry crashed through the lines of his army. The army that he had sent to conquer all of England. His force was being wiped out right before his eyes.

He turned to his captain again.

"Ce pays est-il vraiment rongé par la guerre?" he demanded. Is this a country at war with itself?

The captain said nothing. Philip turned back to watch the rest, though he already knew how it would end. Damn Godfrey to hell; he knew.

GODFREY THOUGHT ABOUT fleeing, as he had at Nottingham. But on that day he'd still had this battle to fight. The rout of Adhemar's men had been of little consequence in the larger scheme of things. This was different. Even if he managed to get away, even if Loxley or Marshal didn't chase him down, where would he go? There was nothing left for him in

England. He had betrayed the king, and would hang for it. And if he ran now, he would have no future in France, either. Philip would never forgive this failure.

His only hope was that somehow he and the French could still turn this fight and win the day. Failing that, he was a dead man no matter what he did.

And so Godfrey steered his mount into the maelstrom of blood and flesh and steel, and fought as he never had before. His sword rose and fell, slicing through the English lines like the scythe of death. He and his horse moved as one, dancing away from the blur of a sword or the thrust of a lance, and then leaping forward once more to deal a killing blow.

The men around him might have been fighting for England or for France, but he was fighting for his life. No man could stand before him.

THE FRENCH WERE in disarray, but they weren't yet beaten. Those who had survived the fusillades from Robin's archers and the initial onslaught of the cavalry were trying to regroup. And more were still coming ashore in landing craft and pouring out onto the beach.

Robin fought from atop his mount, his sword flashing in the sun. Allan and Will, also still mounted, had their bows in hand, and their aim was lethal. They fired as quickly as they could, nocking and loosing arrow after arrow, dropping French soldiers as they came ashore.

Little John had dismounted and was wielding his stave to devastating effect. The broken bodies of the enemy lay strewn in the sand around him, and yet still the French continued to attack the man. Robin was surprised to see Friar Tuck fighting near Little John, using a stave of his own and doing a good deal of damage with it.

But he had no time to ask the priest what he was doing here. Men came at him from all sides, trying to unhorse him. He lashed out at the helm of a French soldier with a spurred boot, and hacked at reaching hands with his sword. He wheeled his horse in tight circles, first one way and then the other, fighting, killing, keeping himself alive.

As he turned, glancing up to mark his position and check on his friends, he saw what appeared to be a familiar helmet and coat of mail on a horseman who was riding down toward the beach. In the next instant, he had to give his full attention to a broad-shouldered French soldier with a battle pike, who tried to stab Robin's horse. Robin danced the beast out of reach, then darted back in from the side, hacking at the man's neck. The Frenchman fell, and Robin looked up again.

It took him a moment to locate that soldier he had seen. There, at the fringe of the battle. Yes, that was the armor of Loxley. But it couldn't be, unless . . . The soldier turned revealing an all too familiar face, far too lovely to be here, amidst these horrors.

Marion. And at her back rode the forest boys on their ponies.

Robin's heart rose in his throat. He shouted to her, screaming that she should get away while she could, that she should pull back to the cliffs. She didn't hear, or she ignored him.

He spurred his mount in her direction, trying to fight through to her. But there were too many soldiers between them. With every step his horse took, Robin had to fight off another attacker. But at last he reached her.

Before he could tell her to take the boys and leave, though, she glared at him, as if daring him to speak. "Not for you, Robin!" she called to him, sitting straight in her saddle. "For Sir Walter!"

She didn't wait for him to answer, but spurred her mount and rode away, followed by Loop and his boys. Robin nearly screamed aloud in his frustration. Were they mad?

A French soldier grabbed for him, and Robin raised his blade and brought it down with all the power he could muster, as if killing this man could lessen his fury. It didn't.

He searched for her again, saw her riding toward the thick of the fight, the feral boys wheeling around her on their mounts, like hive bees guarding the queen. Robin had to admit that Marion rode well and swung her blade with the grace and precision of a seasoned warrior. But she had no business being here. When she cried out Walter's name, hacking at a French soldier, he rolled his eyes. And was immediately beset by two men. He kicked out, swung his sword.

But he couldn't stop himself from searching again for Marion.

The English infantry had reached Dover Beach and was marching into the mêlée. Swordsmen, pikemen, spearmen, and additional archers strode across the sand. They chanted as they marched and banged their fists against their shields, creating a formidable din that carried over the sounds of the surf and the cries of battle.

Seeing them come, many of the French began to break ranks and run. They had nowhere to go, though, except back into the sea to their landing craft.

The surf tossed the empty vessels as if they were corks from a flask of wine, bashing them together, so that the oars splintered and fell uselessly into the water. Still, the French waded out to the craft and tried to climb back into them. Some men were crushed between two boats or driven underwater, but others managed to get themselves into the craft, where they could at least take shelter from the fighting, using the boats as floating fortresses.

Soon, though, English archers began to shoot flaming arrows into the boats, setting the vessels ablaze and forcing the French into the open once more.

The battle swirled around Robin. He fought, he tried to keep an eye on Marion, tried as well to mark the progress of the fight. It was easy to be distracted, and he suddenly found himself wheeling his horse hard to block the attack of a French knight on horseback. He tried to raise his sword to protect himself, but wasn't sure he could do so in time.

Thwap!

An arrow took the French knight in the chest. He swayed and fell off his horse. Robin twisted around and saw Will Scarlet reaching for another arrow to nock. They exchanged nods.

Then Robin was looking for Marion again. After a few moments, he spotted her a good distance away, still surrounded by her entourage of forest boys, still riding hard, sword in hand. And now he realized where she was headed. She was riding straight toward Godfrey. Truly she was mad. She charged the man, a cry on her lips, and managed to knock him off his mount. A moment later though, she was unhorsed as well, and Godfrey was advancing on her. Robin spurred his horse to a gallop, desperate to reach her in time. The distance, however, was great.

CHAPTER

THIRTY

An Englishman came at him from the left, hacking at his leg, trying to knock him off his horse. Godfrey blocked the man's blow and slashed him across the neck. Blood fountained and the man fell. Another of King John's soldiers attacked from the other side, but Godfrey pivoted too quickly for the man and swung his blade again, a silver and crimson blur in the morning light. This man died as well.

Blood dripped from his sword, and his arm and shoulder felt leaden. Still, Godfrey could have gone on killing all day long if he thought it would have done him any good. But the battle was lost. Despite his best efforts, King John had managed to rally too many men to the defense of the realm. He still didn't know where he would go next, but he was not foolish enough to believe that there was nobility in dying well. It was time for him to leave Dover Beach.

Not far from where he fought, a landing craft still rested in the sand, waves lapping at its hull. It was intact, seaworthy from the look of it. And a group of French soldiers were massing around it, attempting to shove it off the sand and back into the Channel, so that they might make their escape. Godfrey had every intention of going with them.

Slamming the blade of his sword into one last English soldier, he broke away from the battle and drove his mount through the shallow surf toward the craft.

So intent was he on reaching the vessel before the Frenchmen pushed it out from shore, that he didn't even see the knight riding directly at him until it was too late.

He tried to rein to a halt, tried to raise an arm to shield himself from the collision, but the rider crashed into him at speed, sending him flying from his saddle.

Godfrey landed hard in the shallows. He took a second to clear his head, then tried to stand, but at first his spurred boots couldn't gain purchase in the wet sand. By the time he found his footing and began to stumble toward the craft, the French soldiers had it free of the sand. While some of the men began to row it away from the beach, others raised the gate.

"*Attendez!*" Godfrey bellowed. Wait! "You French dogs! Would you abandon me?"

He could still wade out to it. He started sloshing through the surf, but the knight steered his mount in front of Godfrey, cutting him off.

A wave hit the craft, lifted it, and the oars bit deep into the water. With a sudden surge, the boat pulled away.

Roaring with fury, crazed beyond reason, Godfrey whirled toward the rider, swinging his blade with all his strength. The knight danced his horse around Godfrey, dodging his blade and leveling a savage blow of his own at Godfrey's head.

Godfrey ducked, grabbed hold of the bridle and yanked the rider out of his saddle. The knight fell hard, but quickly righted himself. Heedless of his own safety, Godfrey rushed the man, raising his sword again.

The knight, tall and slender, met the attack, blocking one blow and striking at Godfrey. Godfrey parried easily and slammed his blade at the man's helmet once, twice. The knight staggered, his visor flying open. And . . .

Godfrey stopped, his sword back to strike again. It was a woman. The face staring out at him from within the helmet was that of a woman!

Not that he cared. This woman—this whore!—had kept him from escaping. He would die on this miserable, bloodstained beach because of her. But she would die first.

She was still addled, although she had her sword raised defensively. Godfrey lunged toward her, his sword high for the killing blow, and he struck her hard on the back of her helmet, near the base of her skull.

The woman went down hard into the shallow water of a receding wave, blood from her neck turning the surf crimson.

Godfrey would have run her through to finish her, but he saw that another rider was bearing down on him, battle lust in his eyes.

Loxley.

* * *

ROBIN THREW HIMSELF off his mount, desperate to get to Marion, who lay in the wet sand, her life bleeding away. Godfrey stood over her and Robin charged the man, knocking him down into the surf and grappling with him in the shallow water. After a few moments, they broke away from each other. Robin pulled his sword free and Godfrey did the same. The bald man grinned.

"Archer!" he said. "Let's see how you fare against a swordsman."

Robin swung his sword, smacking the flat into Godfrey's side. Godfrey was staggered, but he swung at Robin, blindly, viciously, his sword blade whistling past Robin's head in a wide, useless arc. Robin stepped in once more and struck again with the flat of his blade, this time catching Godfrey in the side of the head. He would humiliate the man before he killed him, just as Godfrey had done to Robert Loxley.

But Godfrey wheeled hard, swinging his blade again, not at the head or body this time, but at Robin's leg. Robin tried to parry, failed. The blow sliced into his thigh and Robin fell to his knees in the surf, gritting his teeth at the pain and the sting of the salt water.

Robin forced himself up, looking at Marion, growing more frantic by the moment. She floated listlessly in the surf, and with each wave that ran up on the beach, water filled her mouth. Blood still flowed from her neck, but she hadn't moved or made a sound. Was she dead?

He glared at Godfrey, who looked like he might say something. "Save your words for God," Robin warned. "They're your last."

Robin leaped forward, hammering at the man with his sword, and driving him down into the water. Godfrey got to his knees, staring up at Robin, breathing hard. Robin advanced on him again.

"Look to the lady first, or she's drowned!" Godfrey shouted at him, climbing to his feet.

They stood facing each other, both calf deep in the water. Then, at once, they both flew at each other, exchanging blows, both parrying and then falling back a step.

"You are as good with a sword as a bow," Godfrey said, offering a mock salute and a smirk.

Robin could see the man growing more confident with each swing of his sword. Robin was more archer than swordsman; they both knew it.

Another wave broke at the surf line. Water and foam swirled around their legs and up toward Marion, washing over her. Robin glanced anxiously at her.

And Godfrey saw his opening.

"And so you die together!" the man roared.

He bounded forward, hacking at Robin again and again, driving Robin back, forcing him to parry one chopping blow after another. Robin fought for his life, his feet slipping in the sand. But he blocked every strike, and when one of Godfrey's swings glanced away awkwardly, Robin renewed his own assault.

Now it was Godfrey's turn to parry. Robin struck at him from the top, from the left, from the right, and yet the bald man blocked every blow. At one point, Godfrey stumbled into the surf, and Robin leaped forward, intent on finishing him. But Godfrey managed to parry this attack as well, and all Robin got for his efforts was another notch in his blade.

The two men lunged at each other, coming together

in a clash of steel. Godfrey's blade gashed Robin's face; Robin's blade just missed the man's neck. Once more they fell back eyeing one another.

And then charging again. This time Robin drove Godfrey back, keeping him off balance with his sword strokes. Godfrey made one last desperate thrust. Robin side-stepped the attack and swung. Godfrey blocked it, but only barely. He nearly fell again, back-pedaled. Robin stalked him.

As he did Robin noticed that Godfrey was looking past him, to something on the water. Robin turned just in time to see two of the empty French landing craft surging in his direction, driven by the tide toward him and toward each other. He heard Godfrey laugh, and did the only thing he could to keep from being crushed between the boats. He dropped down underwater. The surf was shallow here, and it was all he could do to go low enough to keep the boats from hitting him.

Even under the surf, he heard the vessels pound together again and again, still at the mercy of the tide. His lungs began to burn, but he could see no way to swim clear of the vessels.

At last, though, the boats separated, and Robin rose from the water, a scream of rage and bloodlust on his lips.

But rather than finding Godfrey in front of him, he spotted the man running for the white charger, which stood nearby on the beach. Godfrey jumped onto the horse's back and spurred the animal to a gallop. He rode through a knot of men, nearly trampling several of them, and then headed down the beach. Near the end of the landing area, one last landing craft rested in the sand.

* * *

THE BATTLE WAS lost. Philip could see that. There was nothing to be done. The cost in gold and men was not inconsiderable, but he would live to fight John another day. Before he had the captain turn this ship back to France, though, he wanted to see Godfrey dead.

He thought the man fighting Godfrey would manage it, but then Godfrey found that damned horse and started away from the battle. The French king shook his head. Losing the battle and seeing Godfrey escape? *Non! C'est trop!* That is too much!

"*Godfrey!*" he yelled, though he knew the men on the beach couldn't hear him. "*Qu'il soit maudit! Tue-le, quelqu'un!*" Godfrey, damn him! Kill him, somebody!

ROBIN STRODE OUT of the surf back onto the beach, watching Godfrey ride away and knowing he would have only one chance to stop him.

He grabbed his bow, nocked an arrow, and set his feet in the sand. Taking a long, steadying breath, he drew back the bowstring, aimed, and let the arrow fly. It soared high into the blue, and began its long descent. When it was halfway there, Robin knew that he had aimed true.

The arrow seemed to hone in on the man, as if guided by God's hand. Or perhaps by the hands of the dead: Robert Loxley, Sir Walter, and all the others who had perished by Godfrey's sword. It glided down toward Godfrey with deadly grace and hit him in the back of the neck, burying itself all the way to the fletching.

* * *

"FAITES DEMI-TOUR!" the king ordered. *"Reculez! Nous nous battrons encore un autre jour!"* Turn around! Go back! We'll fight another day!

The ship began to turn, and Philip braced himself for the rock and pitch of the voyage back to France.

ROBIN RAN BACK through the shallow water to where Marion still lay in the surf. Blood oozed from the wound on her neck, and her eyes were still closed. He dropped to his knees beside her and lifted her into his arms, convinced he had lost her forever.

But then—it seemed a miracle—he saw that she was breathing, and that there was a faint blush in her cheeks.

He staggered to his feet still holding her, exhausted, but unwilling to let any other man carry her. She stirred, her eyes fluttering open. He smiled down at her, too relieved to speak. But he kissed her deeply, savoring the warmth of her lips. And then he carried her onto dry land. Around them, English soldiers subdued the last of the French. Robin hardly noticed.

KING JOHN WAS still on his horse, shouting orders to his men, imploring them to fight, seemingly oblivious to the fact that the battle was over and won.

William Marshal rode to the king. "Your Majesty," he called. "The battle has ended. The French have surrendered."

John regarded him, looking incredulous. But then, as he looked around, he appeared to recognize the truth of what Marshal had said.

"To whom?" he asked, clearly offended that the French would surrender to anyone but him.

By way of answer, Marshal nodded toward the archer, Robin Longstride, who was bearing Marion of Loxley from the surf.

"To him," the knight said.

John glowered at Longstride.

CHAPTER

THIRTY-ONE

They gathered in the courtyard of the White Tower in London two days later. Nearly two dozen barons waited for King John to make his appearance. William Marshal had greeted Baldwin, Fitzrobert, and the rest earlier in the day and had noticed that they seemed quite pleased with themselves. The French had been defeated, and this day, they expected, would long be remembered in song and lore. For the first time in the history of the realm, a king would sign a document recognizing the rights of those he ruled.

That was what the barons expected, anyway. Marshal had his doubts.

A table stood in the middle of the courtyard, the charter upon it, along with the royal seal, a large silver ink pot, and a quill.

John had kept the barons waiting for some time. Now, though, he emerged from his chambers and made his way down to the courtyard, where Princess Isabella of Angoulême, looking pale and lovely in a satin gown of sky blue, sat beside an empty throne. Marshal awaited John by the entrance to the courtyard, and as the king swept past, Marshal fell in just behind him.

Two chairs had been set before the table: a throne-like chair for the king, and the simpler one in which the princess sat. Marshal noticed that the king's mother had not accompanied him to this ceremony. He took that as an ill omen. He also noticed that the captain of the king's guard stood nearby, directly in John's line of sight. That didn't bode well, either.

John sat, and Marshal handed him the charter.

For a long time, the king studied it, saying nothing. The barons waited.

"Your Majesty?" Marshal said, hoping to prod him gently.

John ignored him. The barons started to grow restless. Baldwin and Fitzrobert glared at the king, their expressions hardening. It seemed to have dawned on them at last that the king had no intention of signing their document. For his part, John appeared agitated, as if he was gathering himself to say something. The hand gripping the charter had begun to tremble.

At last he spoke, his voice imperious. "I did not make myself king! God did!"

The barons muttered among themselves. Isabella, who seemed to understand the danger in what the king was doing better than John himself, glanced at His Majesty and gave a small shake of her head.

"King by divine right!" John went on, heedless of them all. "And now you come to me with this worthless document which seeks to limit the authority *I received from God!* No!"

Baldwin started to say something.

"Did I command you to speak, sir?" John demanded, his voice like a war hammer.

"My lord . . ." Isabella said softly, as if trying to reason with him.

John held the charter over the flame of the oil lamp that had been placed on the table to melt wax for the royal seal.

He glared at Isabella as the paper in his grasp began to burn. "Or you, madam?" he asked icily.

The princess clamped her mouth shut.

John nodded to the captain of the guard. The captain, in turn, banged the butt end of his pike on the stone of the courtyard three times.

Immediately, at least three hundred guards appeared on the parapets above them, armed with long bows and crossbows. The barons were surrounded, beaten. At a word from John, they would all be dead.

They shouted angrily at the king, all at once— Marshal couldn't make out much of what they said, though he heard the words "betrayal" and "lies" and "tyrant."

"Sire, we looked to you!" Baldwin said, overriding the rest.

"Instead go home and look to your estates," John told him. He smiled thinly, knowing that he had beaten them. "You are fortunate that I am in a merciful mood." The smile vanished, leaving him looking stern, his dark eyes burning. "But as for Robin Longstride, son of that mason; for the crimes of theft and incitement to cause unrest, who pretended to be a knight of the realm—a crime punishable by death—I declare him as of this day forth, to be an outlaw, to be hunted all the days of his life, until his corpse unburied is carrion for foxes and crows."

Marshal winced at the words, as if they were a physical assault.

Baldwin and Fitzrobert glared at the king for another moment. Then, with the rest of the barons in tow, they stormed out of the courtyard past more of John's armed guards.

THE SHERIFF OF Nottingham stood at the gate of Peper Harrow, enjoying the feel of the new clothes he wore, his hand straying to the hilt of his new sword, his eyes fixed on his new home. With Sir Walter and the real Sir Robert dead, the Loxley manor house was his now. He was the king's man here in Nottingham; it only seemed right that he should live in a home befitting that status.

But pleased as he was to claim Peper Harrow for himself, that was not the best part of this day. He read the royal proclamation one last time, rolled it up, grinned with satisfaction, and mounted his horse.

With a phalanx of his men behind him, he rode down the lane into the village. The people there had started to rebuild their homes. Farmers displayed vegetables for sale in the marketplace, though the buildings around them were blackened and in ruin. Men and boys hauled planks of wood toward the site of the old tithe barn, so that they could build a new one.

The sheriff and his men steered their mounts into the village center, the people scattering before them to keep from being run down. He halted and climbed off his horse, and as the villagers watched him, he unrolled the proclamation and looked around for a suitable place to post it: somewhere it would be seen by all, including those who might object to what it said. Especially them. He turned a slow circle and finally saw the perfect spot.

He walked over to the wall of one of the few buildings still standing, his men around him like an honor guard. Reaching the wall, he turned, cleared his throat, and began to read in a loud, ringing voice.

"Hear me! Hear me! By royal decree, Robin Longstride, known as Robin Hood, and all who aid him or shelter him, are declared outlaws of this realm! Their property is forfeit and their lives are to be taken by any Englishman, on sight."

The townspeople stirred at this, looking gratifyingly impressed and intimidated.

The sheriff slapped the decree against the wall with one hand and held out the other, palm open. "A nail, please, and a hammer!"

No one came forward.

The sheriff regarded the townspeople darkly. "A nail!" he said again. "And—"

Thwack!

An arrow whistled past the sheriff's head, grazing his cheek, piercing the royal decree, and burying itself in the wood precisely between the sheriff's forefinger and thumb.

The crowd around him buzzed. The sheriff and his men looked around frantically for the bowman, whoever he was. They saw no one. But the sheriff thought he heard in the distance the fading hoofbeats of a galloping horse.

EPILOGUE

I t is a new life—for me, for Robin, for all of us. We are building it ourselves, with our own hands, taming a small corner of Sherwood Forest, turning the wild into a village, and allowing our village to embrace elements of the wild.

It is strange for me, and wondrous, and also perfectly natural. For so long I have been Lady Marion, Marion of Loxley, the mistress of Peper Harrow. Here I am just Marion, which is as it should be.

I watch as Robin rides into the village, our home. He dismounts, strolls among the people who have followed him here, who have trusted him to guide us as we create this new world. His smile comes easily, his laugh rings through the wood. He greets a group of boys, tossing one into the air and then catching him again and setting him on the ground. He tousles the boy's hair and moves on. This place is remaking him, too, and it pleases me to see it.

Friar Tuck stands near a large cooking fire, tending to his bees and roasting venison for our evening meal. Little John hangs game to cure while speaking with a new man, whose name I have not yet learned. John's woman stands nearby, watching John with an admiring smile, a smile he returns warmly. He goes to her and kisses her.

Allan makes arrows for the morrow's hunt. Will Scarlet teaches a boy how to make arrows of his own.

And others join us every day. Our village is growing.

Sun filters through the leaves and boughs overhead, angling through the pale smoke of the fire, casting dappled patterns upon the forest floor. There will be cold days, rainy days, hard days. But we will face them as we face all things: together, as a village, as a people.

Robin sees me, and we share a smile. He walks toward me and when he reaches me we turn a circle as if dancing, his arm around my waist, mine around his. Then we face each other and he lifts me above him as if I am as light as air. And perhaps I am. He lowers me to the ground again, kisses me, reminding me that there is love in this new world we have created. There is a future for us; for Robin and me, for the friends who surround us, and yes, even for England.

For the realm has good men who will defend those who cannot defend themselves, who will fight for causes that the wealthy and powerful would oppose. Men like William Marshal. Men like Allan A'Dayle and Will Scarlet, Little John and Friar Tuck. Men like Robin Longstride—Robin Hood— who has brought us together in this place to live a better life, but also to make a better world.

I rode out one morning with my man at my side.

The forest gods have heard my vow. Now they make me welcome. The greenwood is the outlaw's friend: no tax, no tithe, nobody rich, nobody poor, fair shares for all at nature's table, and many wrongs to be righted in the country of King John. Watch over us, Sir Walter.

And this is how the legend began. . . .